the
smallest
of
dreams

Deborah Rowland

First published in Great Britain by Deborah Rowland, 2019

Copyright © Deborah Rowland

Deborah Rowland has asserted her right under the Copyright, Design and Patents Act 1988 to be identified as the author of this work.

A CIP catalogue record for this book is available from the British Library

Paper used in this book is FSC Registered White 80gsm Bond

ISBN 978-0-9563139-8-0

Printed and bound by Printondemand-worldwide
Typsetting and cover design by Linda Storey

www.deborahrowlandauthor.com

Ignore errors
1st proof

For John

Hertfordshire
English Non-Metropolitan County

Hitchin

Nightingale
Wood

The
Quarry

Whitecross

Marsham

St Albans

Holt
Insurance

William Sutton
Rescue Centre

Blackstock

Bonetti's Deli & Café / The Alderman

The South Coast of England ... Spring 2001

Hypnotherapist: Look down at your feet. Tell me what you see.

Subject: There is warm sand between my toes. I'm standing by the water's edge, looking at the wreck of a fishing boat.

H: What are you wearing?

S: Dirty, ragged trousers and a collarless shirt. There is a scarf tied around my neck.

H: Where do you live?

S: In a cottage, in a small Cornish fishing village.

H: You are now back in the cottage. What is happening now?

S: (clenches fists) My wife is crying. She wants to have a child, a family. I say we are too poor. We argue. She says I am frightened. She says it's because I lost my family in the storm.

H: What do you do now?

S: (distressed) I walk out the door without looking back.

H: (calms the subject). On the count of three, you are at the end of your life. *Three.* Describe these final moments.

S: I am drowning. There is no struggle; everything around me is fading.

H: Are you in any pain?

S: No. (subject whispers tearfully) I am relieved.

H: You are now in your current incarnation. Recall the face of your wife from your previous life. Who is this person in this life?

Chapter 1

Isabella Burnett rolled up the shutter from the shop door of Bonetti's Deli and Café for the millionth time, her back groaning with the effort. She wanted to get rid of the blasted thing but after the burglary, the police and the insurance company strongly recommended the installation of an aluminium security shutter. It was, they said, another necessary act of prevention against the unstoppable crime wave sweeping the countryside. Isabella however was more optimistic. The Blackstock residents took their neighbourhood watch duties seriously: every second person owned a dog and crime was relatively low in the town.

In this case, the burglars were apprehended. The *imbecilli* thought they could uninstall six grand's worth of sleek racing-red *Gaggia Deco* espresso machine without a) setting off the alarm, or b) disturbing Betty, the next-door-neighbour's Alsatian. Her lunatic howl along with the ear-splitting alarm had the comic duo legging it sharpish until the lanky one tripped ungracefully over a pothole, spraining his ankle in the process.

That was five years ago. This morning, under a bleached blue January sky, the smart Regency town square was coming to life. Opinion was divided as to its true status: you can't call it a town with no town council, some said; but we have a regular market and annual fair, said others. It made no difference to Isabella, nor most of the other shop owners who had a long-standing arrangement to supply each other's needs wherever possible. Faulkner's Bakery produced a fine selection of artisan cobnut, olive and pistachio loaves which kept Bonetti's Deli and Café lunchtime trade content, while they in turn supplied the bakery with traditional, bona fide ingredients to make said mouth-watering breads and cakes, and so it went.

The deli wasn't due to open for another hour, but there was always so much to do, even though her cherished nephew would have already prepared the refrigerated meats and mixes and put the croissants in the oven. That left just a couple of tasks Isabella felt she alone had to carry out. Try as she might, it was hard to let go of them.

Daylight flooded the shop as Isabella walked in, returning the keys to her bag. The doorbell's distinct tinkle was as much a part of the atmosphere as the interior itself, suffused as it was with the aroma of *Lavazza* coffee and warm pastries. The former wool shop's mahogany panelled wall opposite the counter had been divided into squares. Each one showcased a raft of Italy's finest produce: packets of multi-coloured-shaped pastas; slender and squat olive oil bottles; jars of anchovies, peppers, capers, preserved apricots and lemons soaking and floating in aromatic oils and juices.

Bottles of excellent regional wines and liqueurs were laid down in metallic rows, waiting for their new owners to claim them. The four dark brown leather bar stools which stood against a slender countertop in front of the main window overlooking the square provided the perfect place for a quick espresso and a flick through the newspaper.

At the back of the shop, several circular café tables and chairs were laid out randomly. Sprigs of rosemary, parsley and thyme in recycled aluminium tins sat on the tabletops, releasing their herby scent into the snug atmosphere. The ancient walnut bookcase, whose arthritic legs were supported by four densely folded coasters, housed a bulging collection of cookery books, magazines and an old box of dominos.

Postcards, photographs, flags and memorabilia covered every gap on the main wall, all of which belonged to Isabella's beloved late father, Francis Burnett, who had a wide range of acquaintances: Boxers, actors, cyclists and persons of importance, each one captured forever in a warm embrace. In pride of place hung a *Giro d'Italia* pink jersey alongside an old black and white framed photograph of Francis and the famous cyclist Gino Bartali, who won the Milan-San Remo classic sprinter's race in 1950. It was a dream-come-true handshake for the teenage Francis. Those were the days.

Isabella paused to breathe in the familiar scents and smells. Ghostly whispers of thousands of conversations, gossip and laughter echoed around her. She loved the early hours in the shop as in those moments, she had little idea of what lay ahead, or which new face would present itself at her counter. She was just a few years off her sixth decade and preparing the way to pass such nostalgia into her nephew's capable hands. At the end of today's trading, they'd sit down together for a talk about the future.

Her reverie was broken by a crash coming from the back room. '*Buongiorno*, Luca. Everything alright back there?'

Isabella's nephew appeared from the back of the shop wearing a half-embarrassed grin. He brushed his navy and white striped apron down whilst bounding towards his aunt to greet her in their traditional way of a kiss on both cheeks, a daily gesture that filled Isabella with pleasure. It was extremely fortunate that the oldest son of her oldest sister, Donna, had worked happily alongside her these last ten years, and he seemed to have no wish to be frying fish elsewhere.

She'd had her eye on him to assist her in the shop from way back. The opportunity came when Luca was eighteen and floundering, at odds with his parents and angry at the world. With great reluctance, Donna and Vincent Santini shelved their scholastic ambitions for Luca and released him into Isabella's loving care. She was the only one in the family able to bring the best out of their frustrated son. Time had proved everyone right.

Tradition was everything. It meant a lot to her that Luca had chosen to follow in the family footsteps, especially as Isabella had no children. Luca was popular with the customers and being fair of face as only a Monday child could be, blushed at the slightest hint of attention which was endearing. His looks were not a blessing.

'I thought I'd have a go at rejigging the shelves when one of them gave way. There's some wood out back. I'll fix them up tomorrow if that's okay with you.'

'But that's Sunday, Luca. Won't Greta have other ideas?'

His girlfriend always had other ideas, but Luca didn't always fancy them. He tactfully changed the subject. 'Coffee's ready. Have you had breakfast yet?'

Isabella smiled at her nephew's attentiveness. 'Let's have a cappuccino and toasted panettone with quince marmalade. Saturday mornings fly by, and we know there won't be much chance for lunch. What time is Greta coming?'

'Six o'clock. We're supposed to meet Nathan and his latest flame at the new wine bar in Marsham, but you never know with Greta. She can't stand wine bars and isn't that enamoured of my cousin, come to think of it, but I promised we'd be there.'

Luca's face turned pink. Isabella wondered why he felt the need to provide moral support for his cocky cousin, especially as the evening was certain to be a strain. She suspected it was the end of the road for Luca and Greta as they'd let it go on way past its sell-by date, but that was Luca all over. He didn't possess Nathan's 'gift of the gab': if anything, Luca's plain, economical way of speaking often sounded harsher than he intended. Consequently, he said little, or nothing at all. 'If you've got time later, I'd like to chat to you about something important. Don't worry, *tesoro*, all is well. It won't take long.'

Luca's stomach turned over. His first thought was to wonder if he'd done anything wrong, but quickly batted that off as Isabella was not one for bottling things up. Maybe she was ill? No, she was as strong as an ox, just like his grandfather. Whatever it was, Isabella didn't look unhappy, but time was creeping on and they hadn't yet prepared the olives. Luca was a stickler for timekeeping.

Chapter 2

It had been a busy day, despite the freezing January easterlies. The extreme cold had done little to deter the locals or several courageous tourists staying at either The Alderman Pub in Laundry Lane, or the boutique B&B just off Blackstock Square. These two establishments were both, of late, serving midmorning coffee to non-residents, along with the three other cafés in the town. The British café culture never ceased to amaze Isabella, as she remembered a time when tea shops were the preserve of quaint seaside resorts, and her father's shop was closed half day Mondays and Wednesdays. Who cared whether it came from the Continent or not? It was here to stay.

Her father had been on to something. Francis had joined forces with his brothers in London in the early seventies, building a business in the restaurant trade. After years of hard work and some success, brother Gino left Soho for Whitecross, a fast-growing Hertfordshire village-cum-suburb in which to raise his family and set up his own restaurant. Francis declined his offer of a partnership as he was ready to strike out on his own.

The food industry was rapidly changing. With the likes of *The Galloping Gourmet*, Keith Floyd and Delia

Smith, people wanted more than a Berni Inn meal and spam fritters. When Francis and Maria Bonetti visited Blackstock for the first time, the only establishments open for business that afternoon were the small supermarket, The Alderman pub (for the lunch period only), and an ice-cream van sitting adjacent to the pond. A queue of freckle-faced children waited impatiently for a *99* or a *Red Arrow*, neither of them a patch on Bonetti's ice-cream, even if the locals weren't yet aware of it. The couple were thrilled to see such a variety of businesses and cottages which blended tastefully around the smart Georgian square, everything from butcher and baker to a post office, estate agent and bank, and one very nice restaurant. They counted twelve shops in the main square, and a further eight situated in the cobbled lanes around it.

A quick look in the estate agent's window revealed the exciting news that the empty wool shop with a two bedroomed flat above was within their means. Francis was a man on a mission: offers were accepted, and contracts signed. The couple rented Weaver's Cottage, a knocked through workers cottage and the largest in a row of three, just a few minutes' walk from the shop.

It took a while, but Francis' hunch about Blackstock paid off. The Bonetti family had connections: there were restaurants and hotels to supply as well as the locals themselves, once they discovered the delights that Italian produce had to offer. The joke was that Francis needn't have bothered to change the family name to 'Burnett' in a bid to fit in, as everyone called them 'Mr and Mrs Bonetti' anyway. His prediction that people would travel for his flavoursome *ciabatta* and *rigatoni* was vindicated. Francis soon had the Blackstock ladies eating *panettone* crumbs from his charming hands.

In the summer months, there were queues for Bonetti's *gelato*, made from freshly picked soft fruits and Blackstock Manor's organic milk and cream. It was impossible for the locals to resist such a patriotic gesture from the gregarious anglophile whose good food was becoming as important to their culinary heritage as beer, pork scratchings and a Sunday roast.

To Maria's eternal delight, the family were sought out by the titled incumbents of Blackstock Manor who hosted the annual Spring Fayre, a tradition that stretched back for centuries. On Mayday bank holiday, the couple proudly presented their authentic food and wines alongside other local food producers and artisans in the splendid manor grounds.

It was lovely to savour the remembrance of things past and release them safely back into memory. In this present moment, however, two flutes of arctic, bubbling Prosecco waited to be sipped. Isabella wondered what her father would think of her plans to pass the reigns to Luca. She once read that if you kept a space filled, nothing new could get into it. It was time to let go.

Isabella studied her nephew's face. A lock of thick, black hair had fallen across his forehead and his cheeks were rosy from the morning's exertion. Thankfully Luca's nose had been spared from his early boxing days, and the scars acquired from such combats had almost faded from view. She smiled, recalling the day Luca was born. Isabella knew they were going to share a lifelong connection and she was right. All her nieces and nephews were adored, but Luca was the child closest to her heart. 'Okay, this is what I want to say. I've decided to reduce my week to two days, and by the end of the year, I will finish completely. Your grandfather would agree with my decision to offer you the business, to run as you please, as he wanted to keep it in our family.'

Luca stared at his aunt. He had not seen this coming. When it came to the business, Isabella always treated it seriously, and right now, she did not look as if she was joking. Luca had, on the odd occasion dreamed of what it might be like to run the deli and café: an extension into the garden for alfresco dining on Saturdays; a modern, bright interior; remove the old photos and repaint the walls. Luca had even deliberated about his grandfather's cycling shirt (maybe he'd frame it?) Oh yes, he had dreams, but he never imagined they'd come true.

The rather large gulp of cold wine sent bubbles jiggling up Luca's nose, conveniently masking his watery eyes. Isabella laughed at her precious nephew as she passed him a napkin. His crisp white shirtsleeves were customarily rolled up to reveal muscular forearms dusted with fine dark hair. He had taken her advice to keep his hands nicely manicured. Even at work, he turned himself out well.

'This has obviously come as a shock, so while you digest the news, I'll fill in the gaps. I will sign the deeds of the flat over to you. No more rent. You've earned it after everything you've done for me over the years. I will still own the freehold unless you can raise the funds to buy it. If not, it will be kept in my name until it is either sold, or

I die, and the proceeds will be divided between you and your cousins.'

Isabella paused as she waited for Luca to absorb this information. His eyes shone like lighthouse beacons, which endeared him to her more. It was the right decision. 'You'll have complete control of the business and can pay me a fixed wage for my two days after which I expect to receive a nominal rent, as your landlady. I will, of course, be here to advise you for as long as you need it, but you know everything there is to know about the business, and I have every confidence in you, my darling.'

Luca was so moved by his aunt's generosity and faith in him he was at a loss for words. He *knew* he could do it. At twenty-eight, he was ready to stand on his own feet. Exhilaration filled his chest, a glimpse at a tremendous future. Luca wiped his eyes, feeling steady again. 'What did Mum and Dad say? I guess you've talked to them.'

'As a matter of fact, Luca, I have not. It's none of their business. The shop, flat and cottages are mine. I gave my sisters their share years ago. It's up to you.'

Luca's smile was so wide it could have joined the planets together. He jumped up to hug his aunt. 'Please may I say yes to your generous offer? Thank you so much for believing in me, Bella. I won't let you down.'

Chapter 3

Luca had just got out of the shower when his phone pinged. Greta's train wasn't due in yet, so he had plenty of time to get to the station. Perhaps she was early? He checked his phone.

Sorry Luca. Something's come up. Call you later. Greta

Drying himself off, he tucked the thick navy towel around his waist and sat down. Greta was often late, but she hadn't cancelled before. Maybe she wanted to call it a day? That would be a result. Much better if she broke it off, as right now, there were other things on his mind. They'd been seeing each other for six months but seemed to be running out of steam. Luca recalled their first encounter. Hartburn were playing their monthly gig at The Alderman, thanks to landlady Nancy Beck's patronage and the fact that her offspring were in the band. Years of hard work had established Hartburn as a tight, energetic act with a loyal following. The regular blend of Blackstock locals and suburban hipsters enjoyed an interesting cover version and were scarcely disappointed.

Greta Munroe was not, however, a local. Her *Mia Wallace* hair style and lime-green racerback top shone out like a night fire amongst the throng, and Luca was more interested in why she was uninterested in the band that night. During the interval, Luca stood chatting while he waited for the band's drinks. The mystery girl had her back to him, her black bob nodding in animated conversation. In the next moment, she spun around, and asked him if the band would play *Sunshine on Leith?* Maybe it was her unexpectedly soft Scottish accent, or the way her impossibly bright eyes challenged his, he'd never been able to work it out, but she had somehow disarmed him. Luca found himself mumbling that the only Proclaimers song they knew was *Five Hundred Miles*, but if she came back next month, he'd make sure it was on the play list. When the band packed up later that night, Nancy slipped him a note with Greta's phone number on it.

To begin with, Greta's anarchic attitude was refreshing. Luca was proud to announce she was a politics graduate and his first steady partner after a long period alone. He didn't mind Greta's lack of cash. She spent a vast amount of her free time volunteering at various events and rallies which was admirable, even if Luca had little clue who she was fighting for or against. Greta said she was certain the right job would come along soon and wasn't prepared to compromise. Her cultural criticisms were relentless, however, and she was spectacularly untidy. Although she stayed just one night a week, the thought of Greta lazing in bed until early afternoon was pushing his buttons.

What a day it had been though! Isabella had said he should take some time to think about her offer, as he had to be sure it was what he wanted. He could call her with questions, or simply pop over for a chat anytime. The only thing she asked was to keep it to himself until she had talked to her sisters. Luca had learned to be discreet, unlike Nathan and his equally slack-jawed sister Juliet who was just like her mother when it came to gossip. Maybe he'd score a hat-trick tonight and Juliet would finally leave the band? She was generally unreliable but had got so much worse since getting involved with a flash, small-time drug pusher who had caught her eye. Thankfully he'd been barred from most of the pubs in the area, but he was proving to be more than a nuisance. Luca would talk to Nathan later at the wine bar: he'd know what to do.

Hunger pangs had replaced the morning's euphoria. Luca busied himself in the kitchen preparing a snack. Greta may have been lazy, but she'd eat anything he cooked for her. The stir fry could wait as there was a good-sized bowl of minestrone left over from the morning's trade which he'd have with bread and cheese. Isabella had taught him how to make the soup. It was a winter favourite and almost always sold out. The café menu was deliberately limited as the shop's kitchen was on the small side. Luca thought about the menu: anti-pasti or cheese board, soup and bread, pastries and a few tarts. He understood why Isabella kept the menu restricted as there were five other places to eat in Blackstock, not including the Co-op's sandwiches. Bonetti's offered authentic Italian cuisine, albeit limited, and it was popular, so why change it?

As the soup bubbled on the stove, Luca's mind ricocheted. He tore a few pages from the back of the order book and began scribbling down ideas. Between mouthfuls of cobnut bread and hot soup, a list of anything and everything was captured on the page until finally there was space in his chaotic mind. Luca slid off the bar stool, cleared away the tea things, fastidiously wiping the counter tops and the hob as he moved about.

Luca loved his flat, probably a little too much for Greta's liking, but he couldn't change the way he felt. When Isabella vacated the flat for Weaver's Cottage, Luca saved determinedly for two years in order to renovate it to his taste. It helped to have builders like Ben and Uncle Neil in the family. The stainless steel open-plan kitchen with black marble worktop and integrated appliances gleamed under the spotlights. Luca loved the clean white walls, polished cherrywood floor and integrated glossy white storage unit that housed his wide screen television, DVD and music collection. One fawn-coloured faux-leather chair and two-seater sofa completed the picture of masculine, minimal living space. There wasn't a candle, cushion or rug in sight.

Bella once said that Luca's compulsion for clean and tidy spaces was probably the result of the clutter at home. His parents were too busy to be tidy, or that's what his mother used to say when he complained he couldn't find anything. On the rare occasion Donna and Vincent went out, Luca and his younger sister would clean the entire house, taking care not to disturb the piles of school paperwork, but restacking, filing and dusting the newly revealed gaps. Rosa loved it as she got to hang out with her big brother who played Black Eyed Peas records at full volume whilst waiting for the illicit takeaway to arrive.

Rosa was under pressure, of that there was no doubt. Luca felt sorry for his musically gifted sister as it was clear their parents' hothousing was in danger of backfiring. Everyone, including Rosa, had a breaking point. Luca had fought with his mother to allow her to play in the band, insisting she needed an outlet, a bit of fun with her cousins. Vincent had played in several bands back in the day and could scarcely deny his daughter the right to follow in his footsteps, especially being a music teacher. And so, Rosa became integral to Hartburn's success. In addition to playing piano and violin, her harmonies brought something special to their sound which set them apart.

Luca took his notebook to the sofa. A huge black and white Jimi Hendrix 'Montagu Place' print hung in the centre of the main living room wall, opposite which were suspended the holy trinity of guitars: a Gibson *Les Paul*, a Fender *Stratocaster* and a Taylor 800 series acoustic. He'd never be anywhere near as good as Hendrix, but at least he played lead guitar in a band, and if you were going to aspire to greatness, who else was there? Luca was lucky. Plenty of his friends didn't have what he had, but he'd kept his head down, worked hard, and now he was on the up.

Before setting off for the wine bar, Luca decided to brave the weather and get some air. Wrapping a thick cashmere scarf around the collar of his woollen jacket, he headed out into the freezing January night. He knew Blackstock like the back of his hand. Adjusting his step to the dark, Luca stood for a moment by the huge oak on the green, bracing himself against the cold. He couldn't understand what was so wrong with street lighting until his uncle Tom took him and his cousins to the Lake District. The boys were mesmerised by millions of silvery glints piercing the dark Northern skies above Scarfell Pike. Tom said that if they lived on Jupiter, there were no stars to look at. The experience was a baptism of fire, and one that had marked his young soul forever. When the town voted to keep the streetlights to a minimum, Luca was relieved.

He pulled the scarf up to cover his nose. There were few people about, just the odd, brave dog-walker hurrying to get back to a cosy fire. Something swished past his ear, making him jump. It was probably a Barbastelle bat, out on the prowl, disturbing its hibernation. Blackstock was one of the few areas to attract the endangered creatures and the local bat protection league had taken to holding their animated meetings in the café every second month. It was surprising how much Luca had learned about the tiny creatures just by serving coffee. He glanced towards a row of Edwardian villas whose lights split the dark night screen. Rita would be tucked up in the flat with her mother and her little brother Finn, no doubt enjoying a quiet evening.

Rita Redwing. She'd worked at the deli for almost two years. Isabella took her on when the family moved to the area as she had been desperate for work. Rita had said very little about her family's relocation to Blackstock that day, only that her mother hadn't been very well. They were a Sunrise Trust refuge family, which guaranteed them local work and good health care. Even though Isabella didn't need extra help, Rita and her young brother, Finn, looked a sorry sight that day and he guessed rightly that his aunt would take her on. The drenched siblings sat shivering while drinking mugs of hot chocolate and Rita had tried her best not to look embarrassed. Two years on and he still knew so little about her, partly as he was too polite to ask. According to Bella, life with the Redwings pre-Blackstock had been a rollercoaster ride.

Looking back, he had to admit it was a good decision. It suddenly occurred to Luca he'd have to hire another member of staff to replace his aunt. How stupid of him. It should have been his first thought, rather than steaming ahead with ideas for fancy menus and lush interiors. Luca laughed to himself as he walked back to pick up his car. That was something else to add to his list.

Chapter 4

Joe Faulkner loved Saturday nights at home. He rarely went to the pub other than to attend the monthly retailers' association meetings, after which they'd play Scrabble which was usually a rambunctious affair. It was surprising how competitive they were, especially when he and Isabella were pitted against Jenny and Terry Cox who knew every sodding two-letter word in the dictionary. Saturday nights were about feet up, a couple of bottles of real ale, a takeaway curry with all the extras, and his wonderful wife Nell's company.

The bakery had never been so busy. Joe's tasty artisan breads were popular, although he promised the regulars he'd always sell white split tins and custard tarts for as long as they wanted them. Nell put their success down to the hundreds of cookery programmes on the television. Whatever it was, Joe was grateful as it had given him a new lease of life. He loved the early mornings alone, just him and the dawn chorus as he mixed together combinations of herbs, spices, fruits and cheeses, and often surprised himself at how well they tasted.

Demand may have been outstripping supply, but he and Nell had no wish to expand. If anything, at fifty-five,

Joe wanted to take his foot off the gas a little, perhaps take an extra day off in the week to take his wife to those lovely National Trust places she talked about. His only hobby was the allotment, and there was little going on in the winter, so apart from the odd puzzle and walking his faithful dog Dora over the quarry, baking was his passion. Joe was proud to be the latest in a long line of Marsham bakers. They dated right back to the eighteenth century, when horses and carts rolled along the cobbled streets, and blacksmiths, wheelwrights and saddlers brought a bustle to the villages. Who could claim that heritage these days?

It was a real shame he was the last in the line, as there was no one in the family who was interested in taking over the business. His daughters were settled in London, only occasionally returning to Blackstock for 'home comfort' visits. Joe had worried how Nell was going to cope without Chloe and Cherry. It took a little adjustment, but the couple had come to enjoy the peaceful evenings alone, and the flame of their love-life didn't require rekindling since Nell had sailed through the Change. They shared an intimacy that was the envy of many. Joe smiled. Thinking about his passionate nights under the covers with Nell wasn't going to answer the question of his successor. Perhaps young Leon Pereira might want an apprenticeship? He was as keen as mustard, and it would please his mother no end.

Joe's thought about Isabella. She was lucky to have Luca as it was obvious her nephew would relish the opportunity to take over, if asked. She'd also benefitted from a constant stream of helping hands from her nieces and nephews, some of whom had assisted him in the bakery from time to time. The Bonetti family were industrious, Isabella especially. At the last meeting, she had dropped a hint about slowing down, but he'd heard that before.

With steady hands, Joe lifted out the various boxes from his specially adapted takeaway bag as Nell laid out cutlery, napkins and warm plates. 'Good choice of music, Nell. We haven't listened to *Acoustic Moods* for a while. It reminds me of our holiday last year in Kerry. Where shall we go this year, love?'

'My sister has invited us to Portsmouth again. If we don't go soon, she'll stop asking. The business is doing well, so we can afford to book a nice hotel nearby rather than stay at her house. In fact, if we did it that way, we'll have an escape route. What about that for a nifty idea, husband?'

Joe licked sticky jalfrezi sauce expertly from his fingers as he mulled over Nell's suggestion. Dora's customary dinner-time whine required attention. He shushed the disgruntled dog out of the kitchen, slipping her a biscuit as consolation before guiltily closing the door. *Peace at last.* Joe got on well with Nell's sister, but it was that idiot of a husband he couldn't stand, bossing everyone around as if he was still in the Navy. He was just about to answer when the phone rang. Who on earth was calling on a Saturday night? Nell had dashed into the hallway to pick it up before the answerphone cut in. 'It's the nursing home. They want to speak to you.'

Bad news carries its own weight and Joe's stomach dropped like a stone. He *knew* his mother had passed away. She'd been poorly, pneumonia, they said, so please don't visit as many of the residents had gone down with chest infections. He had taken their advice and stayed away. He should have gone. An overwhelming nausea engulfed him as he took the telephone from Nell's hand.

Joe sat in his favourite armchair; his heavy eyes lost in the butterscotch flames that danced in the small open fire. Marion Faulkner had been a wonderful mother and had lived a happy life, despite losing her darling Walter to cancer years before. Eighty-eight was a good innings, even though towards the end she hardly recognised her oldest son by sight.

There was nothing wrong with her mind, though. Joe and his mother did the crossword every Wednesday afternoon over a cup of tea and a slice of his special fruit cake. She loved the bits of orange peel in it. He could scarcely believe she was no longer there, that he'd never see her again, after so many years together. The pain in his heart was intense.

Nell brought him a glass of brandy, interrupting his remembrances. 'Joe love, you must contact Rik. He'll need time to get back for the funeral.'

Blast it. He'd forgotten about his brother. They hadn't been in touch for years. In fact, Joe couldn't be sure where Rik was living now. Marion always maintained her youngest son was born with ants in his pants and wasn't in the least surprised when he left home. Rik's globe was his constant companion: he read every heroic story and adventure of the great, bygone explorers he could lay his hands on. When he wasn't reading, Rik would be drawing treasure island maps and make-believe lands with such intensity, Marion had to drag him away to have dinner. By the age of thirty, he'd already travelled across much of the planet, working as a cartographer for a conservation institute whose name Joe couldn't recall.

Rik had apparently given it up to become a crofter on some remote Scottish island. It was his destiny, Marion had said. She'd received cards and letters from her youngest son for as many years as he'd been away, but like a petulant child, Joe never asked what they were about. Marion only ever said that 'Rik sends you and the girls his love.' God bless her though, his mother never complained, although Joe knew how much Rik's absence made her heart even fonder.

As far as he was concerned, Rik may as well have disappeared from the face of the earth. His brother had an inability to live amongst people. 'I'm not like you, Joe. I can't be boxed in', were his parting words. Rik was selfish and aloof. He'd chosen the right life, alright, and too much water had passed under the bridge. Joe took the glass of brandy from his wife. 'To tell you the truth, Nell, I'm shattered. I'll look up Rik's details tomorrow. Right now, all I want is a cuddle.'

He pulled his wife to him and cried.

Chapter 5

'Rita, where's Mum? She promised to make me eggy bread.' Finn sat at the kitchen table, his eight-year-old legs dangling as he balanced the *Horrid Henry* book on its spine.

Rita walked towards the kitchen and laid down a basket of wet washing. She looked at her little brother's eager face. 'If you wait a minute, she'll be in to make it.' To distract Finn from his rumbling tummy, Rita put her two closed fists out in front of him, both concealing a chocolate frog. He tapped on her right hand which revealed the treasure. Squealing with delight, Finn expertly unwrapped the chocolate bar and shoved it into his mouth in case it was snatched away from his greedy fingers.

Rita laughed. 'That'll do you for a little while.' She put the other chocolate bar back in the cupboard and gathered together a frying pan, a small Pyrex bowl and a couple of eggs in preparation for her mother to take over.

These last couple of years had been good for the Redwings. Finn never asked for much as he was mostly content to draw or read. He'd made a few friends at his beloved forest school, and constantly talked about Mr Sullivan who taught the children how to feed the chickens and guinea pigs and showed him the best way to stroke the donkeys as one of them was temperamental. In Finn's opinion, this was the next best thing to having a dog as he'd asked repeatedly for one even though they were expressly forbidden at Larkspur House. That was another good thing about Blackstock - there were loads of dogs around and most of the owners were only too pleased to let you pet them.

The most awesome thing of all, though, was his bike. On his seventh birthday, Luca brought around a surprise. The bright blue six-gear Muddyfox was even better than Jay Nelson's old grey one, *and* his feet touched the ground. Luca said the cycling club members were always swapping bikes so when he got taller, they'd exchange it. One day, Luca said, he'd be big enough to enter the *Tour de Yorkshire*, as it was good to have a goal. Finn couldn't understand why his mum and sister cried that day, as what was there to be sad about? They were always saying how good it was to play outside, and as soon as the weather got better, he'd be back out with his friends over the park.

Later that morning Finn was off to Jay's birthday party. Rita knew only too well what exclusion felt like, so she was tremendously relieved to see her brother become part of a little gang of nice country boys who cycled and played football without causing too much bother. Finn loved it when Luca called him *Huck*, as Rita had read him the Mark Twain classic which was one of his favourites. The irony hadn't escaped Rita that her brother's life shared a few uncomfortable parallels with the book's hero. She wondered if Luca was aware of that.

Rita had saved almost enough money to pay for a little holiday for Finn's birthday. It was out of necessity she had kept it secret from her mother, as it wouldn't have been the first time her wages had disappeared down the neck of a bottle. Rita kept her savings account book hidden at the bottom of her satchel which she carried everywhere. Now, however, her mother would never take anything from it. During the last year, Alison Redwing had turned a corner. She even cooked the tea every day and insisted on taking less housekeeping now she was earning a regular income from sewing and clothes repairs. The best thing was the time her mother spent with Finn as it gave Rita a little freedom.

With her brother safely deposited at the party, Rita and her best friend and neighbour Libby began their journey to the William Sutton Rescue Centre. It was a joy to join the other volunteers who walked the various inmates around the two-acre site near Marsham's cricket ground. Libby Spires was a total animal nut and would give anything to have one of her own. She had initiated Rita into the wonderful world of dogs after the Redwings arrival at Larkspur House, insisting the fresh air and the walking would build Rita up.

Rita loved Libby. She had lived at the house for almost three years and knew everything and everybody, so she showed the family the ropes. The young women became essential ingredients in each other's lives. Libby was solid: nothing rocked her boat. She described her extra bit of padding as Anglo-Saxon armour, and bound her ropes of long flaxen hair so tightly, as if their appearance might reveal a secret. The duo often wondered if their grim history might interest Mike Leigh or, indeed Spike Lee, but after half an hour of attempting yet another screenplay, the depressing results were abandoned in favour of an old black and white classic film, a mug of tea and a couple of cherry flapjacks.

When the young women weren't at William Sutton's, they went to the cinema in Marsham or Hitchin, as the eleven o'clock Sunday morning show was half price. It was generally quiet, although during *Poor Cow*, the last in the *Kitchen Sink* film season, Libby had to ask the ladies in row Q twice to 'please stop rustlin' your pear drops', in her not-so-quiet south London posh accent. After that, the Sunday morning show was never quite the same.

Whenever Rita felt sorry for herself, she immediately thought of Libby who was the bravest young woman she'd ever met. She couldn't imagine growing up in care as her friend had. 'I'm sorry to moan, Lib. At least we've got a mother.'

'Yeah, in theory. But neglect is almost as bad as having your head bashed in. It's another form of abuse, Reet. They just do it in an invisible way. There should be a law to prevent children from raising their parents. Don't you think it's bizarre that no qualifications at all are required for the two most important jobs ever: pet ownership and parenthood?'

Rita couldn't argue with Libby, except that as statistics went, there were many thousands of children parenting their parents. Alison Redwing may have fallen off the wagon a few too many times, but at least she had kept her children with her and was well enough to work. Since arriving in Blackstock, the ancient black Singer sewing machine had been dusted off to take up the hems and sleeves for the town's residents. Alison also recently started making clothes which revealed a talent that took the family by surprise. The rehabilitation programme was working and so far, she had stayed sober.

It was the longest the Redwings had lived anywhere. Their silver lining, however, had its own very dark cloud in the form of Finn's father who was nearing the end of a three-year prison term, and due for parole. This disquieting fact alerted Rita to the possibility he may soon try to contact her mother. 'Not-so-clever-Trevor,' as Libby called him, was not Rita's father and she was old enough to look after herself. She loved her brother, but what could she do if her mother forgave Trevor Jenkins his sins and took him back? The thought of it made Rita's skin creep, so she pushed it away.

Together, their fortunes were changing. Libby worked at Summerfield Health and Wholefoods four days a week, and behind the bar at The Alderman for two evenings. She also helped in the bakery when they were short. Nell gave Libby unsold bread, pasties and cakes, which she shared with Rita's family. Isabella insisted Rita take home *prosciutto*, fish trimmings, cheese and unsold soup, which made her cringe with embarrassment in front of Luca, even though he couldn't see what the fuss was about. 'It only goes for compost, so we may as well have it between us', he'd say. With all of that combined, along with fruit and veg from the health shop, they no longer needed the food bank. The friends decided not to discuss Trevor's return as, fingers crossed, it might never happen.

Out of breath from their scramble to flag down the 262 to Marsham, Rita followed Libby to an empty seat at the back of the bus where they flopped down laughing. There was only one return bus on Sundays, so they couldn't afford to miss it. Soon they'd be out with the dogs. Although incredibly cold, it was dry and brightening up with every hour. Stubborn white clouds were moved on by an insistent breeze, revealing a sky that stopped you in your tracks, if you cared to notice.

The friends chatted about the new dogs that may have arrived during the last week, and whether Felix the lurcher was still there, but suspected he'd have found a new owner, being such a beauty. Rita's fear was that one day, Libby might smuggle a rescue dog into her flat and it was certain to get her evicted. The Sunrise Housing Trust may have been a lifeline for vulnerable women, but that did not include the four-legged variety. Libby wondered out loud if the centre's most popular vet, Hamish Bell would be around and quickly batted off Rita's rib-tickling that there was such a thing as a 'good man' after all.

The conversation, as inevitable as the Solstice moon, turned to the band. Hartburn had more than its fair share of talent, Nathan Westleigh especially, despite his profile being partially obscured behind a rather large drumkit. 'He's got a soft spot for you, Reet. In fact, Nate was asking after you at the pub on Friday.'

'Pull the other one, Lib. He's got a new girlfriend. Luca and Greta were meeting them in the wine bar last night, apparently.'

'So, Luca's still with bob-a-job then? I'm surprised she didn't dump him when he told her off for coming down to the shop in her pyjamas.'

Rita laughed. 'Poor Luca. I've never seen him so embarrassed. Anyway, why would she dump him, Lib? Surely, she's the lucky one. Greta may be a graduate, but she *still* hasn't found a job. I don't know how she manages to survive, unless she sponges off her mates as well as Luca.'

Libby looked at her friend. It was hard not to be protective of someone so unbelievably lovely, especially as Rita had no idea of it. She reminded Libby of a wren: petite, super-soft caramel eyes, and such a powerful singing voice for one so small. Libby knew everything she needed to know about men, and Rita's torch for Luca broke her heart. He was a nice bloke, you couldn't argue with that, and he had taken little Finn under his wing, not like Nate who just acted nice but was shallow.

For men like Luca who, as far as Libby could see, never had a day's struggle, who had inherited money, had good family, and the face of an angel, well, it was obvious Rita was never going to be on his radar. 'Look, Reet, Greta is far too intelligent to stick around for the likes of Luca no matter how tasty his minestrone is. She probably just got caught up with his fine figure, and those lovely pastries. I can't imagine Luca being interested in the Suffragette Movement or the failings of a long-term Conservative government.'

Rita laughed out loud, prompting the eight other heads on the bus to turn towards this extraordinarily joyful sound. Libby's perception and intellect never ceased to amaze her. She always had her nose in a book or was taking a course or two in the little spare time available. It was so sad, as in different circumstances, Libby could be a prime minister, a film director or anything she wanted. Rita couldn't remember the last time Libby went out on a date, let alone had a boyfriend, so together, foot-loose though not quite fancy-free, the young women enjoyed their films, and the unconditional love from the awesome William Sutton canine companions. If they didn't reflect too much on the hand they'd been dealt, you could almost say life was good.

The driver called out their stop. The friends grabbed their bags and headed for the exit. They jumped off the bus, thanking the driver as he pulled away, waving back at them.

Chapter 6

Isabella stayed in bed for as long as her lumber spine allowed. Just once, she'd have loved to spend a Sunday morning under her goose-feathered duvet with her body's permission. Hattie was coming for lunch and was bringing the pudding which meant there was little to prepare. Her dear friend's request of a roasted squash risotto with *Cavallo Nero* and winter cabbage made her smile. Hattie Summerfield's direct manner often upset newcomers to the health shop. Hattie had said on more than one occasion that a post-menopausal woman was in no mood to mess around being polite, a statement Isabella mostly agreed with.

She too had discovered an inner confidence and serenity after a few stormy hormonal years. Isabella had hugely benefitted from Hattie's recommendations of natural remedies and various treatments, along with a diet chock-full of phytoestrogens. Gemma had been suffering too, but as her spikey younger sister rarely took anyone's advice, Isabella stopped giving it. At least the sisters still met for a delicious lunch every month, courtesy of their octogenarian mother whose energy and verve seemed to increase with age. She was the only one who had the means to put Gemma firmly in her place.

Luca had arranged to pop over for a chat mid-morning. As it was still early, Isabella decided to run a bath. A long, hot soak was what she needed, especially with her father's favourite Puccini opera singing out through the speakers. She watched distractedly as the powerful stream of steaming water cascaded into the bottom of the copper freestanding bath, dissolving the handful of mineral salts sprinkled on the bottom.

The bathroom was Isabella's favourite room. It was partially panelled and painted a saturated turquoise, the latest shade of blue, according to Ben Westleigh, his master craftsman's tongue firmly in cheek as he had expertly popped open another tin of paint. The colour contrasted well with the cherrywood floor and the other accoutrements which included a copper inlaid wash bowl on an antique Edwardian washstand, stacked with white Egyptian cotton towels. Several bottles of exquisite oils, bath lotions and creams lined up behind the doors of an art deco glass cabinet. To complete the luxurious tableau, a delicate maidenhair fern sat regally in an old terracotta pot and was itself currently bathed in reflected light from the weak morning sun.

Isabella's bedroom had received similar attention. It was unlikely anyone was ever going to see it, apart from Ben, whose eyes twinkled when asked to wallpaper the entire wall behind the gilded iron bedstead with a mural depicting Botticelli's *Primavera*. The duvet was covered with a scarlet and burnt orange satin throw, while two ash wood antique wardrobes and a dressing table stood next to an elegant Zoffany chaise. Isabella had come to love reclining on the chaise by the sash window with a book in one hand and a glass of red wine in the other, laughing at her airs and graces.

Lowering herself into the tub, Isabella sighed, feeling the heat instantly ease her aching tailbone. At long last, the updated cottage interior mirrored her status as an independent, mature woman. She had made-do for many years, but as her nieces and nephews had long since grown out of sleeping over, it was time to enjoy the fruits of her labour without guilt or embarrassment. Apart from the occasional weekend visitor and Hattie's company, Isabella spent much of her time in the comfort of Weavers Cottage happily alone. Her circle of friends was small but adequate. She and Donna occasionally went to the theatre and on the odd occasion when she needed to buy clothes, Gemma was only too happy to accompany her drab older sister.

The long working days, months and years had finally caught up. Isabella was forever grateful there was no commute, as within minutes of leaving the shop, she'd kick off her shoes, shower or bathe depending on the state of her back, whip up a light supper and either watch a documentary or drama, or listen to the radio. She kept much of her reading for bed as the electric blanket took the edge off the cool sheets. A threadbare teddy kept her company on the other pillow. With these new part-time hours, Isabella would have time to reflect on her life and take stock.

The exquisite sound of *Un bel di vedremo* filled her ears. It reminded Isabella of her sixteenth birthday gift from

Francis and Maria, who took her to see *Madame Butterfly* at La Scala. Since that day, Isabella's love for opera had grown, along with other classical composers. Donna said that dinner at Isabella's was a toss-up between sobbing to Cecilia Bartoli's rendition of *Casta Diva* or if you were unlucky enough to get Leonard Cohen, searching for a rope to hang yourself with.

As a birthday celebration, Isabella's sisters surprised her with a ticket to a Take That concert and were stunned to hear her sing every word to *Could This Be Magic?* That was the last time she and Amanda went out together. Knowing she would never again see her baby sister's lovely face tore her heart. Ten years on, and the family still struggled with her shocking exit from this world. At least Tom was, at long last, moving on.

Her brother-in-law had been so embarrassed to ask if he might bring his new 'friend' to the café. Isabella was looking forward to meeting the woman who had caught Tom's attention. Donna and Gemma were sworn to secrecy, at least until they knew if Karen Shaw was to be a serious contender for his heart before breaking the news to their mother. The sisters agreed that Tom Lockhart was too good a man to be without a love in his life, and in their opinion, he had waited long enough.

The water had cooled. Isabella hauled herself up and wrapped an old towelling bathrobe around her as she stepped gingerly onto the mat. The robe was a gift from her musician ex-partner, but for some inexplicable reason, she was reluctant to put it aside. It wasn't as if she missed him. Daniel Overton's peripatetic lifestyle meant they never got beyond the occasional evening meal and frenetic night under the covers. Initially, this laid-back relationship suited Isabella, but their sporadic encounters eventually became something to endure. When Daniel confessed to having met someone else, Isabella was relieved. He never alluded to her loss of libido as the reason for moving on, but not long after they parted, she heard he'd become a father.

Throughout their long relationship, Daniel insisted he wasn't the paternal type and she neither questioned nor challenged it. Even though her attention was taken up with the shop and her family, the news had shocked her. It released a deep, emotional longing for a baby that frightened Isabella. She began to have dreams which painted various scenes of motherhood: breathing in the smell of her baby's skin; rocking her to sleep; reading to her (the baby was always a 'she'). The dreams only ever featured Isabella and the baby. There was never a man in the picture.

This misery went on for weeks, compounded by the mistaken feeling that every other woman Isabella met pushed a pram. A deep sense of sadness hung around her like a shroud, provoking cascades of tears most evenings. It was painful to accept that falling pregnant was no longer possible even though it had never been consciously on her agenda. Eventually Isabella confessed all to her trusted friend Hattie who suggested the appropriate therapy. The counselling sessions helped to move Isabella into a space of self-care which, in time, allowed her to accept the new reality. Gradually, she readjusted to a life without a companion, sensing the creeping inevitability of a solo future.

Daniel's legacy was Hartburn. He inspired the cousins to form a band. It was his suggestion to merge the family names of Lockhart and Burnett which had annoyed Nathan and Juliet who tried but failed to make their surname 'Westleigh' fit. Daniel had been on hand to advise the group on musical arrangements and gave extra tuition. If their aim was to sustain regular gigs and gain a good reputation, he helped them cultivate an attitude of flexibility and professionalism. Isabella had no objections to Luca's continued contact with Daniel as she had long-since moved on.

Before dressing, Isabella took a long, hard look at her body in the mirror. There was no doubt her shape had morphed into Aunt Carmelita's, but there was still a waist. Years of standing had resulted in a few ugly, painful veins here and there, but these could be removed. It was something to address in the coming months. Her skin was good, helped no doubt by a tendency to plumpness and her meticulous care of it. Isabella's previously ink-black curls were now streaked with gunmetal, but she liked them.

Her body was never a source of anxiety in the way that Gemma's was. Isabella had never dieted and avoided much of the image-driven pap that seemed to make so many women miserable, although things were finally changing. Well-made clothes were a must, though, and despite having a small collection, miniscule compared to Gemma's, it contained several classic, versatile pieces with the occasional new addition as demand dictated. Isabella put the final touches to a casual Sunday outfit of navy jersey pants and a cream lace shirt and wandered barefoot downstairs to make coffee.

Chapter 7

Luca sat in front of the stove, warming his hands. He liked this room, even though it wasn't his taste. The Shetland Tweed sofa and armchairs were the colour of pheasant, or so Isabella described it, and so nicely upholstered as to be extremely comfortable. The vanilla walls displayed two oil paintings: a still life of a peach and an old brown jug sitting on a rustic table, and a landscape, probably Venetian, judging by the buildings. They were bound to be originals, knowing Isabella.

The warm Herringbone floor was covered by a couple of large antiquarian red and gold rugs, one in front of the wood-burner, and the other underneath the large rosewood dining table. Isabella's ceiling-to-floor oak bookcase contents could keep him busy for years, such was the selection of European films, books and art memorabilia. Luca read little these days, much to his English teacher mother's disdain. It was on his mind to start again, though. Perhaps he'd ask Isabella to lend him a book? She'd be delighted to introduce him into her cultured world.

Luca had got quite cold while working in the back of the shop fixing the shelves. The job took longer than anticipated, leaving little time for more than a quick wash and brush up which annoyed him. He remembered to bring his notes and scribbled a reminder to ask Isabella's opinion about Juliet. Nathan didn't seem too bothered about his sister's obsession with the drug dealer, but then again, his attention was fixed on Claudia Huxtable. Nathan was punching above his weight there, but his persistence had won out. Claudia knew what she was letting herself in for.

There was talk of Gemma accompanying Juliet to Milan. A family friend had opened a new women's clothes shop and needed an assistant who could model some of the outfits. It was right up Juliet's street, especially as Maria Burnett insisted the family kept up with their mother tongue. That would mean a change in the band's line-up. Isabella interrupted his train of thought.

'Would you like scrambled eggs, Luca?'

'No thanks, Bella. I had a bowl of porridge earlier. I'd love a coffee, though. Can I help?'

'It's ready. I've warmed a couple of almond croissants, just in case.'

Isabella's strong maternal streak was never overbearing. Luca often wondered why she didn't have children of her own but hadn't the courage to ask and she never brought the subject up. Luca was shocked to find out about Daniel's baby, as he and Isabella had scarcely parted company. Luca took the tray from her and set it down on the coffee table. Isabella looked so relaxed; he hadn't realised until that moment how much she may need this break. After all, when had his aunt taken serious time off?

'You look ten years younger, Bella. Is it because you've made the decision to retire?'

Luca wasn't a flatterer, so Isabella accepted his compliment.

She smiled at the word 'retire', wishing there was an alternative. 'Thank you. It certainly feels as if a weight's been lifted. I didn't realise just how tired I was. I slept very well last night. How was your evening?'

Luca wiped almond crumbs from his mouth with the linen napkin. Isabella's advice was often sought-after by the family although her honesty could be bruising. He rarely consulted his parents. In any case, they were supporting Rosa through her final year at the music college which meant a tense household. He wondered what the reaction would be when they heard the news about the shop? His mother had never got over the fact that her first-born hadn't gone to university, as much as she tried to hide it.

That had been a bad time in his life which he chose not to recall. Thank God he and Rosa weren't forced to attend the secondary school where their parents taught. It was worth the long bus ride to Marsham County High to be away from their influence however respected their teaching skills were. Thankfully the siblings' musical talents were free to grow independently.

Of late, the band were experiencing a bit of a lull. Maybe at the next meeting they'd look at the playlist and audition for a new singer as from what Nathan said, it was likely Juliet was going to leave. They may have to look outside the family but in many ways, it was a good thing, as new energy could give them the boost they needed. The sound of a spoon tinkling against the china cup broke off Luca's mental meanderings.

'Sorry, Bella, I was just thinking about the band. My evening was a bit of a non-starter as Greta didn't show, and Nate's new girlfriend was stuck to him like glue, so I left early. And before you ask: yes, Greta has broken up with me.'

'You don't look upset.'

'You know me too well. I think the novelty wore off for both of us, but at least she can say she finished with me. The timing is good, though, don't you think?'

They laughed in agreement. 'Yes, you may be a little busy for a while. I see you've made a few notes. Shall we go through them together?'

Aunt and nephew spent the next thirty minutes running through timings, legalities and staffing issues. Part-time assistant Kit was saving like mad to get to New Zealand and was sure to want extra work while there were plenty of cousins eager to cover holidays. Isabella waited for him to mention Rita, but so far, her name hadn't come up. 'You'll need a number two. I assume you'll want a holiday and I may not be able, or willing to cover. Have you thought about Rita? She'll take on more hours. You could train her as your assistant.'

Luca was staggered. Rita? It hadn't crossed his mind to even think about increasing her hours, let alone train her, but now Isabella said it, of course, it was the perfect solution. There wasn't much Rita didn't already know. She was reliable and hardworking. He'd never seen anyone move so efficiently and still have time to chat or greet the dogs. Rita got on well with the suppliers too.

Come to think of it, Rita was the one who had suggested the winter porridge pots, fresh local fruit and yoghurt for summer, and the vegan lunch platter, all of which increased breakfast and lunch trade. She was always cheerful, humming a nice little tune to herself, the name of which he almost remembered. 'That's such a great idea, Bella. I don't know why I didn't think of it. I'll talk to her on Monday. How about if you came in on market day and Friday as they are the busiest. We can cover the rest.'

Isabella smiled. Luca already sounded as if he was in charge. This would be the making of him. 'Okay, that's the staffing issues sorted. Now, what else?'

Luca coloured a little. 'Look, Bella, I know it's early days, but I've got an idea to extend the café out into the garden, perhaps have Saturday evening suppers? Ben will cost it out, and I can help with labour and brickwork. I still have Grandpa's money plus a bit more I've saved.'

It was Isabella's turn to be astonished. Her nephew moved fast. The idea was fabulous, and it wouldn't cost the earth. That was the way it was going: everyone wanted to eat quality, local food and there were only a couple of good restaurants in Blackstock. With the population slowly increasing, she was sure there would be a demand as it was a bit of a schlepp to Marsham and sometimes it was nice not to drive. 'Luca, I love it. Get your quotes, make your plans. It's still wintry, so you won't want to start the build for a little while, and you need time to adjust to being boss, as that will take all of forty-eight hours.'

They laughed companionly. 'What are your plans, Bella? You won't know what to do with yourself.'

'I promise not to do what my father did and haunt you every week over an *espresso*. Once I've finished, that will be it. Hattie and I have talked about travelling although I'm not sure her idea of travel matches mine. There are a few things I'd like to do outside of Blackstock. I'd also like to spend time out back. Your grandma has been nagging at me to revive her beautiful garden. By the way, I'll phone your mum later to tell her the news. Gemma can wait as she's got her hands full. She messaged me earlier. Apparently, Juliet has agreed to go to Milan, which may not be good for the band, but it will be good for her to get away.'

Luca grinned. 'You're wrong, Bella. It will be *great* for the band.' They laughed as everyone had experienced the pain of Juliet.

Coffee and chat successfully concluded, Luca stood up, aware that Hattie was due any time soon. He gave his aunt a huge hug and wrapped himself snuggly in his coat and scarf before leaving her to the warmth of the fire.

Chapter 8

Hattie clattered through the utility door into the kitchen. She was fully loaded with large jute bags containing upside-down fruit pudding, a bottle of organic Pinot Noir, pots of red, white and purple cyclamen and a couple of new books. Heavenly aromas assaulted her red nostrils and steamed up her specs as she closed out the bitterly cold afternoon air.

Isabella had learned not to protest at Hattie's renowned generosity, and to simply accept the gifts with a 'thank you'. Hattie shucked off the enormous, hairy purple coat they affectionately called 'the beast' and unpacked her bags. 'My, oh, my, it's blowing a gale out there! Have you stocked up your log supply? Looks like we're in for another huge dump of the white stuff.'

Isabella laughed at her stripy tangerine and mint green toe socks.

'Present from my lovely daughter. Hand-woven lama wool, courtesy of the ladies from Patagonia, Syd's latest expedition.' Hattie slipped on a pair of thick-soled slippers. Painful experience had taught her just how cold the flagstone tiles were.

'It's so nice to see her back home again. That's a lovely

blouse, Hattie. I'll bet it's one of Alison Redwing's creations.'

'Ten out of ten for observation. She made this from the fabric Syd brought back from the trip-before-last. I have a job trying to get Alison to take good money for her work. She's got a waiting list now, can you believe?'

'It's great news for the family. Come and get warm by the stove, Hattie. Tea's nearly ready. We had a delivery of that lovely loose-leaf *Chun Mee* tea this week, so I've made you up a packet to take back. Lunch in an hour?'

'Perfect. Syd's got her friends over this afternoon, so I have an excuse to stay out of the way. The flat gets a little cosy with a crowd.'

For over a quarter of a century, Hattie's main residence had been the large two-bedroomed flat above the shop, previously owned by her parents, Beatrice and Gilbert Summerfield. The zealous environmentalists rejected conventional life in favour of a west country commune where they helped found an ethical wholefood collective. Years later, the couple moved to rural Hertfordshire and set up the health shop.

Although extremely bright, Hattie had shown little interest in formal education and at sixteen, took off for the streets of London. Such a hands-off parenting style had the opposite effect than one might have imagined as, after many wild and wonderful years, Hattie was only too happy to re-join her parents in Blackstock, finally releasing them into a retirement of sorts.

At first glance, several Blackstock Retailers Association members thought the aliens had landed. Hattie's spiky vermillion hair, blue lipstick and kaleidoscopic smocks took a bit of getting used to, but 'Mad Hattie' as she was henceforth to be known, along with her delightful young daughter, won over minds and hearts. In addition to various community initiatives, she set up a programme of talks and events under the umbrella name of 'Off Centre' whose speakers' expertise ranged from ancient healing methods to the history and practise of traditional crafts. The most popular evenings were the clairvoyants and esoteric practitioners who drew people in from neighbouring counties. They were exciting days.

The flat provided ample room in which the two women could live comfortably, despite the paraphernalia generated by the shop. Sydney's overseas work for the VSO was coming to an end and she agreed to take over the business. Hattie's plan was initially to spend time by the coast. She had inherited a tiny holiday cottage in Norfolk by way of a distant uncle, which provided her circle of waifs and strays a much-needed retreat from whatever disaster befell them.

It was clear to Isabella that her friend was once again getting itchy feet. Today there was much to discuss. She put the tea tray on the table, along with two hazelnut *crostini.*

'Luca was here this morning. He accepted my offer and was gob smacked when I gave him the flat. He's a funny boy. When I mentioned Rita's name as a possible assistant, he looked startled. After I pointed out that she is perfectly capable to take on more responsibility and needs the extra money, Luca agreed to ask her.'

'Rita Redwing is a real asset. Luca will wake up to that very soon. On that note, I am going to ask Libby if she'd like to manage my shop. Syd thinks it's a good idea and I am ready to set sail. What do you think, Bella?'

Isabella laughed. It was, indeed, all change. 'Rita and Libby are extraordinary young women. When you consider their backgrounds, they deserve every opportunity.'

Hattie sighed as she sipped her tea. Yet another chapter was about to close and a new one open. Summerfield Health and Whole Foods had given her a good life, but she'd taken it as far as it could go. The shop had retained a loyal clientele which had spiked in number with the new treatment rooms and small studio for group work, yoga and T'ai Chi. She was grateful her only child was willing to take over, and would be even happier if Libby agreed to her proposal.

Isabella interrupted her thoughts. 'You realise the Trust could end Libby's tenancy as her extension to remain is almost up. The local authority is due to step in, but where might she go then?'

The Sunrise Trust's rehabilitation programme had a time-limit and its rules had remained the same since its inception. The wealthy founder and women's rights campaigner, Virginia Knight-Bell, had purchased several countrywide properties to be used as refuges for vulnerable women and their children. The Trust enlisted the assistance of sponsors to help in whatever way possible. There was a raft of initiatives available, such as counselling, nutritional advice, self-empowerment classes, gardening, and many local businesses provided jobs.

The Trust had strict rules in its houses: no male visitors, no drugs; no pets; no rent arrears and a maximum three-year stay with rare exceptions. They enjoyed a terrific success rate as many women left with improved well-being and good references, which boosted job prospects. There was a long waiting list.

'I'm surprised Libby has stayed so long at Larkspur House, as the tenants generally move on after an average of two years, don't they?'

'Yes, but Libby has settled well in Blackstock and wants to stay. I'm sure we'll find a solution, Bella.'

'Hattie my dear, I have a solution. Mrs Abbott in Spinner's Cottage has just given notice. I'd like to offer it to Libby for the same rent. I'm sure she will ask Rita to share, as there are two bedrooms.'

Hattie marvelled at Isabella's splendid plan. Everyone would benefit, and it may influence Libby's decision to stay on and manage the health shop. 'Why don't we speak to her tomorrow with our joint offer? I'm sure she'd be prepared to share with Rita, if needs be.'

'Mrs Abbott has offered to leave the furniture for a small sum which, if suitable, I will pay for. If Libby agrees to our proposals, she can get the dog she's always wanted. Would you allow it in the shop?'

'Of course Bella. The customers loved Myrtle, poor old girl. I'd get another but don't want to be tied up right now, so this is the next best thing.'

Isabella smiled in relief. Mrs Abbott had been an excellent tenant for the last decade, and the thought of finding a replacement didn't exactly fill her with anxiety, but it was one less item on her long list of issues to resolve. With the renovation of Needlepoint Cottage almost complete, there was plenty of time to think about letting it out, and Isabella already had someone in mind.

'Your dad's dream of his daughters living in Weavers Cottages was never going to happen, was it, Bella?'

'Can you imagine Gemma and Donna living next door to each other? I think Dad was pleased he saved the cottages from demolition though, don't you? He must have known that one day, Blackstock property prices would rocket.'

Hattie could not agree more. Seventeenth century Hitchin's prosperous and burgeoning wool industry had spread out to the surrounding villages and towns such as Blackstock. Workers cottages such as those in Weaver's Row provided clean, reasonably priced housing for the hundreds of incomers to the area. Spinners, Needlepoint and Weavers' cottages were three of only a handful that remained of such dwellings in the town and were subsequently sought after.

Crunching her way through the delicious pastry, Hattie's heart swelled with admiration for Isabella. Apart from her long list of philanthropic deeds, she had the knack of making any visit a treat. The pantry was better stocked than the health shop, stuffed with a multitude of goodies which Isabella transformed into mouth-watering meals. Why she remained single was a mystery to Hattie. Living alone was liberating, but everyone needed at least a little physical contact and it had been years since she and Daniel had parted company. Hattie felt Isabella's eyes resting on her.

'I've decided to step down as chair of the retailer's association. I will announce it at this Tuesday's meeting where I'll formally introduce Luca as my successor. Four years at the helm is long enough. It's time for someone else to take over.'

Hattie was expecting this and had already considered Isabella's replacement. 'Jenny Cox will do it. She's got tremendous energy and has been looking for another outlet since her girl left for college. The chemist is well-served with staff, and I hear they have taken on a new pharmacist.'

'I'd like to see a new generation shake up the town. We've done our bit, haven't we Hat? I won't feel so guilty knowing we've got someone like Jenny to take the association forward.'

Thanks to Hattie and Isabella's infectious activism, the association continued to keep Blackstock on the map. Parking fees remained reasonable, the 'Britain in Bloom' green-fingered maintenance team kept the town looking spick and span, and a few rather tasty articles published in the county glossies had showcased Blackstock's progressive attitude. It was one of the first small towns to introduce 'Fair Trade' products; to ban plastics; to buy and sell local produce; to welcome dogs and cyclists into several shops and cafes and to actively support each other's businesses. The black and white Blackstock reusable hemp bag was carried with pride.

'It's an exciting time, Hattie. You've taught me well. I'm finally releasing my grip and allowing others to step in. As you say, if not now, then when? Now, stay nice and warm while I make the risotto. Why don't you open that rather splendid bottle of wine you brought?'

Chapter 9

Rita didn't sleep well at all. Luca's text earlier that afternoon was playing on her mind. He scarcely ever sent texts as there was little to say. The uncomfortable sofa bed didn't help, either. She could use the holiday money to buy a new mattress but quickly swiped that idea. Rita was so looking forward to renting Hattie's Norfolk cottage. The family had never been on a week-long holiday before. Even when there was a bit of cash, her mother and Trevor had soon swallowed it down. Rita's wages paid the rent. Without a roof, the slope was all too slippery.

She dreaded to think how much their drinking habits had cost financially. Physically, the alcohol's effects on her mother's small frame were shocking. There was nothing to her anyway, but she looked twenty years older than her forty with dark-circled eyes, thin hair and patchy skin. In the few family photographs Rita possessed, Alison had been a true beauty in bud. Her mother's attempts to disguise her wasting body under baggy clothes fooled no one. On the rare occasion they had a cuddle, Rita would almost recoil at the feeling of skin on bone.

Lately though, the family were seeing the benefits from the various treatments and support provided through the

Trust. Rita hadn't fainted in a long time, even though occasionally when she felt light-headed, she managed to cover it up. Everyone was keeping an eye on Finn, especially at school. Alison regularly attended the women's group as well as undergoing her own individual therapy sessions although now they were less frequent. The changes were so incremental Rita could scarcely believe it until she looked back. The Redwings were mending.

Rita's concerns for her mother's welfare were, little by little, being superseded by admiration and pride. The family were learning to accept Blackstock's beneficence. They'd never eaten so well, and her mother's sewing brought in regular money. The flat was dry and just about warm, the community were in the main, a caring bunch, and, of course, she had Libby who suggested they make a pact to take care of each other, no matter what.

Why, then, did she feel so anxious? What could Luca want to talk to her about at eight o'clock on Monday morning? Had she done something wrong? Maybe they wanted to cut her hours? No, it couldn't be that as the shop was so busy, and often needed extra help. Rita rubbed the back of her neck. Her decision to sleep in the living room was not just for her brother's privacy. It was worth the inconvenience to have time alone, to be quiet, and as she was generally the last one to bed, it worked well. The old mattress was, however, taking its toll.

Rita pulled back the curtain. The silent ink-black sky was occasionally broken by a slight breeze rippling over a thick white crust covering the lawn. The birds must have stayed in their nests that morning. Finn had taken to keeping the feeder topped up using his pocket money. He often nudged his sister to look through his tiny binoculars when the naughty magpies chased away the single, persistent squirrel. Rita's heart swelled as she reflected on her brother's fascination with the birds, and how he could now name every species of visitor to the feeding station.

The hot water bottle had long since lost its heat, and Rita could almost see her breath in the cool living room air. She'd never get back to sleep feeling this cold. It was six o'clock. Perhaps a cup of tea would help? The thick sheep's wool cardigan swamped her diminutive frame, its huge hood practically obliterating any hope of seeing a yard from under her nose. The electric heater warmed up quickly, taking the worst of the winter's chill from the room, and a reheated water bottle was certain to help. Rita had no worry of waking her mother or brother. Finn could sleep through a thunderstorm, while her mother's sleeping patterns had improved considerably without the need for her previous cocktail of sleeping tablets and alcohol.

The boiling kettle spluttered droplets of scalding water over the worktop. Rita carefully filled her mug and placed the hot water bottle back under the duvet. Camomile tea would sooth her nerves, or so Hattie told Libby, who told her. She'd only ever drunk cheap tea, so these last years were a revelation. Rita thought about Bonetti's, and that fateful day when, rain-soaked and losing hope of finding work, Isabella had said, *yes, you've come just at the right time*, and without asking for a reference, hired her to start the following week. Gradually, Rita's one day became three and a half, with pro-rata holiday pay. She loved every minute in the shop: preparing the flavoursome dishes; the orchestral sounds of the coffee machine; seeing the regulars and meeting new customers; clearing tables; closing the noisy, stiff shutters; Luca.

Just saying his name sent her insides into spasms. She thought that after two years such feelings would have worn off. He may not have been aware of her presence, but she sure was aware of his. Luca was always so nicely groomed and wore a subtle, aromatic fragrance that sent her taste buds into overdrive. A tiny bit of dark chest hair escaped out of the top of his crisp white shirts, bearing witness to some hidden secret underneath. He reminded her of a panther: strong but light, powerful but gentle.

Rita felt so sorry for those unfortunate customers who stood opposite such a handsome face and struggled to get their words out. He was just as embarrassed, and did his best to make jokes, to talk about the weather, or generally redirect their attention.

There was such a warm atmosphere in the shop, a continuity, a security Rita had rarely experienced. Most of Luca's cousins and friends had worked in the deli at one time or another and they were always popping in, or she'd see them play at The Alderman. From that very first day, Luca had been particularly attentive to Finn. When her brother asked him why there was a pink jumper pinned up on the wall, Luca patiently explained the history of the famous cycle races, and how his grandfather was a keen cyclist, as were many of the Burnett family to this day. Rita would never forget seeing her brother's eyes widen in awe as Luca conjured up the magic of Gino Baldini passing the winning tape, his arms in the air, the crowd hollering and screaming in delight at their hero.

Luca encouraged Finn to sign up for the under-elevens football squad of which he and Ben were coaches on Sunday mornings, as well as cricket during the summer. He also offered the family a *Freesat* box that had been knocking around, and which he patiently set up, talking the family through the channels. Rita had been so embarrassed that day as their impoverished lifestyle was hard to conceal. Luca, however, had been upbeat. He accepted a cup of tea and a biscuit from Alison as if it were a daily event, and if he noticed the folded-up duvet and pillow in the corner, nothing was mentioned. Luca admired the bright rooms and the view of the garden and had asked Alison how her business was going - *her business.* Rita's mum nearly fainted to hear her sewing described that way. How could you not love a man like that, she'd said to Libby later that day.

Changes were afoot. From sheer necessity, Rita had developed a heightened sensitivity to the slightest atmospheric flutter and had detected a shift in Isabella. During the last year, her boss had taken a little more time off than usual, leaving Luca, Rita and Kit to carry on in her absence. Isabella was still young, so surely it wasn't time to retire. Maybe she wanted to sell the shop? What if she was unwell? Oh my God, please don't let it be anything serious. Rita's thoughts were running riot now. Hattie said that in times of stress, remember to soften, soften, soften, and breathe. Now was the time to try it. Rita put her mug down, tucked herself under the duvet with the water bottle nestling next to her belly. Her breath moved in and out, becoming steadier and before too long, she fell into a deep sleep.

'Whaa…whassthat…?' Rita sat bolt upright, brushing her brother's insistent hand from her shoulder as if it were a tarantula.

'It's half past seven, Rita. If you don't hurry up, I'll be late for early morning club. Mum's still fast asleep. I've had a bowl of cornflakes…'

Rita scrambled out of bed, dazed and confused. The remnants of the nightmare jangled her nerve endings as she squirted toothpaste on the brush. Thankfully Finn had school dinners, so all she had to do was splash her face, get dressed, and get going. In under ten minutes, sister and brother scrambled to their neighbour's house, Finn trying to hold on to his rucksack while Rita pulled him along by his wrist. With her grumpy brother safely deposited, she arrived at the shop with two minutes to spare.

Luca was watching her. 'Steady on, Rita, where's the fire? Has something happened to Huck?'

Rita stood in front of the counter, half-bent over, catching her breath. She took off her coat as by now, even though it was minus one degree outside, she was sweating under her woolly cardigan. 'So sorry…I woke up late and panicked. Everything's fine, really.'

'Don't suppose you've had time for breakfast, then. Cup of coffee? Grab a croissant, they're just out of the oven. I'll bring the drinks over.'

Rita took a warm croissant from the basket and carried it towards one of the café chairs. Luca put two large cups of milky coffee on the table and passed her a plate. They sat down, a sudden awkwardness between them. There had been plenty of times when it was just the two of them in the shop, but this felt strange.

Luca gave Rita time to eat her breakfast, making small talk as he knew she was embarrassed to eat in front of him. He talked about Nathan's new girlfriend and how he'd give it a month before the next one came along. He mentioned that Greta had broken off their relationship, prompting a stupendous coughing fit which took Rita a full two minutes to regain composure before being able to finish her coffee. Luca wasn't good at beating around the bush.

'I asked you in early because I want to talk to you about the shop. From this week, Isabella will be working just Thursdays and Fridays, and will retire by the end of the year, if not sooner. She's asked me to take over.'

Luca's face flushed a brilliant crimson as it was the first time he'd said it out loud, and he felt like a prat. He sensed Rita's stare, probably shocked to see him blush, as it was usually her that flared up. 'Isabella and me had a long chat about extra help. Kit's working the lunchtime sessions, apart from Saturdays, but we can cover that through the family. We - I'd like to train you properly to be my number two. It means an increase in salary, of course, and the business will pay for any extra training. It may be a while before I go on holiday as then you'd have to cover, you know, be in charge. What do you think?'

Rita's long silence threw Luca. He didn't know what to expect, but some small reaction would help. Perhaps it was a shock? 'Look, Rita, you don't have to decide right away. It's just that Isabella is keen to get the ball rolling, and we agreed it was best to sort the staffing situation first. Nothing else will change initially, although I do have plans. It's taken me by surprise too, as Isabella only asked me on Saturday.'

While Luca was speaking, Rita attempted to digest the startling news. It felt as if she was still in the dream state, but this wasn't her recurring nightmare, where the door to the flat opened to reveal that her loved ones had disappeared. This felt amazing. This was real. Luca was asking her to be his assistant. She wanted to jump up and wrap her arms around his neck, to shout at the top of her voice 'Yes, yes, yes!', but instead, her eyes welled up in the most terrible way before she could prevent him from witnessing it.

Luca passed her a napkin, smiling. 'I take it that's a yes?'

Chapter 10

Later that night, Rita and Libby sat across the kitchen table with a bottle of the Co-op's finest Cava standing proudly between them. Libby's flat was uber cosy. The tenants were permitted to paint the walls provided they repainted them white before they moved on, but it hardly ever happened. The kitchen walls could only be described as puce but luckily, the south-facing room absorbed sunlight like a thirsty marathon runner. Libby had pinned up posters of the film greats, from Garbo to Munroe to Binoche, and several old green bottles filled with candle stubs listed on the wonky windowsills, their weak light giving the room a Toulouse Lautrec glow.

Libby was constantly amazed by her charity shop finds: a bright satsuma and banana-coloured fruit bowl; floor length apricot voile curtains; scarlet cushions and a deep purple sofa throw, somehow, taken together, made for a bohemian shabby-chic paradise. Libby had painted the cheap MDF bookcase the darkest shade of green to house her myriad books, DVDs and CDs. The Verve's *Lucky Man* strained admirably through the speakers of a tiny music centre. Libby filled the amber embossed vintage glasses.

'Okay, you first, Reet. What are we drinking to?'

'Here goes… Isabella is retiring, and Luca has asked me to be his official assistant, that's the first thing. And Greta broke up with Luca.'

Libby put her glass down. Her jaw dropped open, and closed, and opened again but no words came out. This was a first.

Rita burst out laughing. 'I'm not joking, Lib. At eight o'clock this morning, a miracle occurred. I didn't get a chance to say yes as, shame on me, I cried. Luca was so good about it. We shook hands on the deal, and he's getting a contract written up to reflect my change of status and wages, just to be formal. As from today, I am now assistant manager at Bonetti's Deli and Café with four weeks paid holiday, and Luca is a free agent, whatever that means.'

Libby took a gulp of wine. 'That is fan-tas-teeq! Good on ya, girl! But I can top that. Hattie called me into the office today to offer almost the exact same thing. She wants me to take on the role of trainee manager, if I decide to stay in Blackstock, that is. But there's more. Isabella was there, too. She said that her tenant in Spinners Cottage, you know, Mrs Abbott, is about to leave, and she's offered me the cottage at the same rent as I'm paying now. It's got two good-sized bedrooms, Reet, so you can share with me.'

It was Rita's turn to be struck dumb. She jumped up and put her thin arms around her adorable friend. This was the best thing ever to happen to them, especially Libby, who deserved more than a turn of good luck.

'You know what that means, don't you Lib?'

Libby looked blank.

'You can get a dog.'

Libby's stool crashed to the ground as she danced

around the tiny kitchen, waving her arms in the air. 'Oh my God, I hadn't thought of that! A dog - a beautiful, friendly, happy, hairy wet-nosed beauty who will love me forever. Reet, who the hell needs a man?'

Chapter 11

Joe was relieved to be rolling dough. He felt worse than when his father had been buried. At least back then his mother had taken charge and it was all mapped out beforehand. This time, the arrangements were down to him, alone. Nell, bless her, offered to help with the wake, but it was his responsibility to go to the registrar, the solicitor and to see the funeral director. Joe was glad to see his dear old mother laid out though, to say a final goodbye. Marion looked so peaceful, and she had been dressed in her favourite pink and lilac frock. The staff were ever so kind. Mrs Faulkner had been popular, they said, and was going to be missed.

The night before, his brother had finally called him back. It had taken almost the entire morning to locate Rik's details, but even then, Joe couldn't get through. The Highlands and Islands were undergoing the worst storms since records began, so it was no wonder Rik's reply was delayed. Joe may as well have been talking to the gas man for all the brotherly love he heard down the phone line: Yes, he was sorry to hear about their mother; no, he didn't know she was so unwell, a fact Joe already knew but couldn't stop himself asking anyway; and yes, he would like to come to say a final goodbye. Rik hadn't managed to get back for his own father's funeral as he was in Bhutan, or Bengal, or somewhere in the Himalayas, another detail Joe found hard to forget, so he ought to feel grateful this time around.

As there was business to attend to in London, Rik said he'd take the opportunity to sort it out during his visit. He had arranged to stay at Blackstock Manor with Rupert Huntley, his Cambridge pal, so as not to inconvenience his brother. This had really annoyed Joe, as it seemed to him there was no attempt on Rik's part to be friendly. Nell was going to be upset at his refusal to stay with them. His brother had been as cold as ice back then and Joe could detect no hint of a thaw.

Joe finished off the last of the loaves, washed his floury hands and reached for the phone. He had planned to call Isabella but there was so much to do, it had to wait until this morning. Joe was a little surprised to hear she was at home, but she insisted there was nothing wrong, and said to come over after lunch. Isabella had been very fond of Marion and had visited her regularly in the nursing home. He wanted to tell Isabella in person before the Blackstock brigade got going.

Joe eased off his brogues and left them next to the piles of outdoor shoes in the cold utility room and walked directly into the warm kitchen. He called out to Isabella.

'Joe, lovely to see you. Have you time for a coffee?'

Isabella made to kiss his cheeks as was her custom, but this time he moved into her arms, hiding his face in the warmth of her neck.

'Joe, darling, whatever's wrong? Come and sit by the fire.' She led him into the living room, already warmed by a few hours of heat. The faint smell of burnt pine enveloped them as they sat side-by-side on the sofa. Isabella took Joe's hand in hers and looked directly at him as he wiped his eyes. 'It's Marion, isn't it? She's passed away. I am so sorry, Joe.'

They hugged for a while, both awash with emotion for this marvellous woman who had been so important in their lives. When Marion and Walter Faulkner moved from Marsham to Blackstock after their retirement, they threw themselves into active community service. Everyone liked them, especially Walter as he helped the town regain the 'Crown Bowls' trophy from their arch-rivals. Such events live long in the memory of a small town.

Isabella released her friend to make a pot of strong tea. By the time she returned, Joe had composed himself to the point where he was able to update her and to ask if she'd help with the tea at the village hall. It was to be a proper afternoon tea with scones and sandwiches, the send-off his mother had expressly asked for.

'But of course, I can help, Joe.' She passed him a large mug of dark tea and waited a moment for her old friend to take a sip before sharing her news about the shop, and her decision to step down as chair of the association. Joe was momentarily gobsmacked. Isabella was an integral part of the Blackstock community, she was as respected as her father had been, and as well-loved. A few of the older shopkeepers had talked wistfully about retiring, but the reality of it felt like another blow. It seemed that for years, nothing happened, then everything changed at once. He was finding it hard to cope. 'Are you ill, Bella?'

'No, no, there's nothing wrong, I promise you. It's just that I'm tired Joe, and I'd like to do something new, or at least different. Almost forty years working in the deli is a lifetime. You've been in the bakery for almost as long, so you know what I mean. It is not easy to let go is it, but it'll be good for me. Luca is the perfect age to take the business forward, and Rita has agreed to step up, so I know they'll be fine. He already has plans to extend the café. Luca will be at the meeting tomorrow night. Will you make your announcement about Marion there?'

'Yes, although you know how news travels, so I probably won't have to bother. My brother is coming back for the funeral.'

Isabella looked quizzically at Joe. Did she know he had a brother? Yes, of course she did. Her memory wasn't what it used to be. Joe saw her confused look and filled her in. 'Rik is my younger brother. He hasn't been in England for years. In fact, I worked it out and it seems we haven't spent any time together for almost twenty years. He lives on a croft in Scotland, the isle of Coille, to be precise. I'm not even sure he'll be able to get off as the weather is so bad. In any case, he's arranged to stay at the manor with his old college buddy Rupert, for at least a week.'

Isabella scrutinised Joe's face. She detected more than a hint of bitterness which surprised her as Joe had always been even-tempered and generally upbeat. They had shared so much together over the years, becoming part of each other's family. 'Will you be pleased to see him?'

Joe smiled. Isabella missed nothing. He could always rely on her to be forthright. 'I don't know, is the answer. Rik's always been a funny so-and-so, that's why I don't talk about him. He was a cartographer, took off after his degree to travel around the world, mapping out remote regions and suchlike. We were never close, well, that's not strictly true as we got on well enough until he got sick at the age of eleven, I think. Nell tells me off when I call him 'the ice-man''

They laughed. If Nell couldn't melt the coldest heart, no one could. The old friends spent the next hour chatting, after which Isabella sat and pondered on the nature of Joe's relationship with his estranged brother. It was hard to imagine ever cutting off from her family, even if they occasionally got on each other's nerves. Her family were her life. Isabella knew a little about crofting but struggled to imagine what everyday life was like. The romantic in her pictured empty, wind-swept lochs and beaches, rugged hills, songs around the fire during long, cold winters but the reality proved to be much harder.

Isabella suddenly recalled a tiny snow globe, a present from her father, containing a miniature model of the earth. How she was fascinated with it, spending hours imagining where she might travel to one day when she was a grown-up, who she might meet along the way. Soon after, her mother said they were leaving the country, moving to England, and the eight-year-old Isabella felt her secure, unshakeable world fragment, fall in splinters around her and she was never be the same again. In a fit of anger Isabella had thrown the globe into the river, believing that if the smallest of dreams did come true, it was far better not to dream at all.

The memory of that time sent a chill through her. Isabella got up to put more logs on the stove. These early events mark us forever, but they don't have to define us, she thought ruefully, knowing she had been deeply affected by it. Years of self-reflective work with Hattie and her groups had revealed the sore spots. It was possible to let go but it took courage.

Looking at her collection of books, she pulled out a copy of Gavin Maxwell's *Ring of Bright Water*. Isabella recalled Maxwell's determination to set up his otter sanctuary on Glenelg, and the huge challenges he faced which ultimately overcame him. Not much remained when she and Hattie visited years ago, just a large boulder that marked the spot of Camusfearna, the original cottage. Isabella's abiding memory of the sad visit had been framed forever by the loch's blue-steel water shimmering under that fresh, spring sky.

Not so long ago, Hattie had talked about taking a year off to live remotely and asked Isabella to join her. While flattered to be invited, Isabella could think of nothing worse. She was embarrassed to let her friend down and would never forget Hattie's reply: 'My dear Bella, armchair Sagittarians are content to travel to distant lands from the comfort of their living rooms. If that makes you happy, then does it really matter?'

Isabella frequently reflected upon this observation. It wasn't so much the material aspect even though Isabella enjoyed her copper bath and cosy bedroom. She didn't really believe these things were essential for inner contentment, but maybe she was kidding herself? Hattie reminded her that we are products of our culture and conditioning. The Italian culture had instilled a love of close family life, and authentic food was integral to that life. It was one of the reasons it was used by the marketing people as an ideal. Life in England, too, had left an imprint. It may have made Isabella who she was, but that wasn't the whole picture.

Was she happy? Isabella had travelled across Italy and to other parts of Europe, mostly to look at art, or to meander through ancient streets, marvelling at the architecture. The rural family small holding near Parma continued to delight her, and she returned almost every year for some weeks as it gave the entire Bonetti family the opportunity to reconnect. It was wonderful to recall how she and her young cousins roamed around the countryside until sunset, either on foot or on bicycles. She adored the huge, noisy family meals extending long into starlit evenings, particularly when they coincided with the professional cycle races. This happened rarely in England as everyone was busy, but when they went 'home', there was continuity, tradition.

At Weaver's, Isabella invited the family around her table as often as possible. She could not imagine a time when she wouldn't be closely involved with them, even less what the daily grind of an existence on an isolated, inhospitable part of the British Isles was like. An endurance, probably, she concluded, thinking once again of that snow globe disappearing under the fast-flowing water. Isabella shivered again. She lit a candle for Marion, pulled her long cashmere cardigan tightly around her and put another log on the fire.

Chapter 12

'*Grazie tesoro*. How lovely. I have just the right spot when the weather improves. They can sit in the greenhouse for now.' Maria Burnett put the large pot of slate-grey hellebores on the worktop and kissed her daughter. Isabella always brought her a gift, no matter how often they saw each other. Maria generally looked forward to the monthly lunch with her three daughters, but today was going to be a trial. She never regretted her girls for a single moment, but sometimes wondered if sons would have been less worrisome. Her sister Carmelita often said it didn't make a difference what they were as the lives of her three boys kept her awake at night even though they were themselves parents. 'It's a mother's job to worry', she had said on more than one occasion.

After Francis' death, Maria's decision to move from Weavers Cottage to live with Donna and Vincent had been a good one. 'Siskins' was an extremely smart 1930's double bay-fronted detached property situated on the western side of Hitchin. It was within walking distance of the town which provided regular exercise. Maria had paid for the one-bedroom annexe conversion as it kept the finances neat and tidy; she helped upkeep the house and maintained the garden beautifully; a few close friends provided stimulation and company.

Maria left her daughter and son-in-law to themselves, although invitations to dinner were forthcoming. What Maria loved most were the grandchildren's visits which may not have been as regular as she'd have liked but they too had busy lives, and who was she to complain?

Maria occasionally wondered if the family had stayed in Italy, whether Amanda would still be alive. But that was stupid. The Bonetti family had been very happy in England. It was Maria's English teacher who had introduced the class to the Romantic writings of Wordsworth and Coleridge, inspiring the adolescent students to daydream of green pastures and rural idylls from bygone days. Such musings left an indelible mark on the impressionable Maria. Her dream was to one day live in a quintessentially English village or town: and so, it came to pass.

During the hot 1970's summers, Maria and Francis spent their Sundays travelling around the south eastern countryside with four boisterous girls, a frisky cocker spaniel called Bunty and a large wicker picnic basket, all stuffed into the back of a groaning Morris Minor. It was on one such Sunday they came across Blackstock and were delighted by it: geese and ducks wandered around the green like bouncers outside a nightclub while the St Mark's church bell ringers' ecclesiastical clanging filled the town's airwaves.

She loved the road and house names: *Sugar Loaf Lane, Bluebell Wood, Candytuft Meadow*. The ancient trees delighted her, particularly the aged behemoth, the great oak, rooted majestically in the centre of the green. The fine Elizabethan manor house, an imposing maypole, several panting but enthusiastic Morris dancers and thousands of daisies and buttercups stippling the common entranced the family.

With London a long-distant memory, Blackstock continued to exceed Maria's expectations. She encouraged Francis' wish to strike out on his own, but she had been worried about his suggestion to set up a delicatessen, as who would even know what that was, out in the English sticks? It was the right time, however, for her daughters. Donna had already begun a teaching degree; Isabella had finished her O Levels and was set to follow her father in the business and Amanda was due to start at Marsham County High. This left Gemma, halfway through secondary school, and furious to leave her friends behind, but too young to stay in London alone. Maria and Francis calculated that three out of four children's happiness at the move were good odds.

Maria sighed. The tenth anniversary of Amanda's death was fast approaching and had somehow grown in importance as time passed. She had no wish to recover from it, to move on, as had been suggested. Hers was a profound grief kept hidden from view, although now and again she sought out Isabella's wise counsel.

Maria looked at her now, thinking how little her daughter had changed. Back then, Isabella had been just as much a hit with the customers as the ice-cream: a fresh-faced, cheerful tomboy in dungarees, so vivacious and eager to please. She had badgered her father to work in the shop, spending every spare moment making herself indispensable. Francis allowed Isabella to serve the customers even if on occasion she cut too much cheese or put too few olives in the pots. The book-keeping course was a masterstroke as once qualified, there was no way her father could refuse her assistance.

When Francis' heart was too weak to continue, Isabella came into her own. The café had been her inspired idea. Every Wednesday morning until he was unable to leave the cottage, Francis joined his daughter and grandson for an espresso and a catch up with the customers. Maria was deeply saddened that Isabella seemed to have chosen the business over having her own family. She would have been a fabulous mother. *I hope Isabella has no regrets.* Maria sighed again. It was almost time to serve lunch.

Donna was noisily laying the table, muttering not quite to herself how typical it was of Gemma to be late. Maria hoped Donna was going to welcome retirement, but as the date approached, she was more short-tempered than ever. Thankfully, Vincent had made his own plans. Apart from teaching the occasional piano lesson, a new woodworking hobby making garden furniture for the Wildlife Trust kept him out of the house. After discharging his duties, Vincent spent as much time as was decent either at the Trust or whittling away happily in his shed, listening either to his precious vinyl collection or to test match cricket, and wisely keeping a low profile.

Maria took the long view. Perhaps a lifetime of tension had become hard-wired in her daughter and was going to take time to release. What Donna needed was to get her hands in the soil as that was certain to calm the nerves. She needed to nurture, so why not nurse a few seedlings instead? It was Gemma who worried her the most, though.

Maria often spent sleepless nights wondering how much longer her saint of a son-in-law Neil could hang on to the marriage, especially as Juliet's behaviour had created shockwaves throughout the family, rippling all the way to Italy's shores.

Vincent came in to greet his sister-in-law. She reminded him of a steady drumbeat, a metronome, the person who fused the familial fault lines. '*Ciao*, Bella. So good to see you. I know I'm banished, but I wanted to greet you before …'

'*Ciao*, Vincent. Don't tell me, you're off to your woodwork class. It sounds like fun. Perhaps you'll sell me some new garden furniture for the cottages? I've got new tenants coming in soon.'

'That's so generous of you, my darling. The Wildlife Trust are doing wonders with the proceeds.'

'Good for you for doing your bit. Clearly there are benefits to be had away from home.' They smiled knowingly at each other. The men in the family deserved medals for taking on the Burnett girls. 'Luca is looking forward to the St Valentine's party. He said to tell you there's a surprise in store, whatever that means. Hopefully not a Neil Young song.'

'That's the trouble with you, Bella, no musical taste.'

They laughed as he made a swift exit, keen to avoid Gemma as they always rubbed each other up the wrong way.

'What does Donna think of Vincent's new hobby, Mum?'

Maria made a face. 'As long as he isn't spending too much money, she's simply glad he is out of the house. You know I don't poke my nose in, but they have been arguing more since he retired. Thank God I have my own apartment. They think I'm deaf as the television is up loud, but it's the only way to drown out the noise.'

The women laughed. The absence of Santini marital bliss was well known even though they tried to kid everyone to the contrary. Gemma and Neil did the opposite, often airing their dirty linen in public. Maria couldn't make up her mind what was worse.

Chapter 13

The four women sat around the large pine kitchen table with steaming bowls of polenta and asparagus while cold Pinot Grigio frosted the wine glasses. Maria watched Gemma help herself to a portion so small, it would scarcely have filled a sparrow. 'So, Gemma, has Juliet decided to take the job offer?'

Donna and Isabella looked up. Their mother clearly was in the mood for answers. Juliet's fascination with the drug dealer had stirred the family to boiling point, particularly Gemma. For some reason, she believed her children were hard done-by and it was deeply unfair to have to temporarily banish her precious Juliet even though it was the best solution.

'You'll be pleased to know I've booked our flights to Milan. Juliet can't wait to go as she's sick of everyone sitting in judgement. I can't blame her, as even the band have turned against her. Nathan's so busy with Claudia, he hasn't even tried to help his sister. As for Neil, well, what a useless, waste…'

'Hold it right there, Gemma. Let's not get into this again, blaming everyone else but Juliet.' Donna's patience with the situation was running out the closer it came to her departure from a school she had loyally served for decades. She was in no mood to listen to Gemma's constant lament about what she and hers didn't get.

Maria watched Donna fly off the handle yet again, wondering why she did little to soften such a harsh appearance. Those awful rimmed spectacles were either suspended from that old chain around her neck, or perched on the end of an unfortunate nose, peering down at everyone. The image didn't exactly promote warmth. On the rare occasion the family was graced with a smile, Donna's eyes would crinkle like tissue paper, and the tiny gap between her front teeth gave her a childlike air.

Before Gemma had a chance to reply, Isabella cut in. 'It can't be easy to part with Juliet, but under the circumstances, you are doing the right thing.' She paused, feeling her breath flutter a little in her chest. As she told the family of her plan, Isabella saw Gemma's cats' eyes narrow, a familiar warning of imminent attack. 'Before you say anything, Gemma, don't forget I gave Nathan and Juliet the opportunity to come in with me and they weren't interested. Neither were Amanda's boys. Luca was the only willing family member to step in. He has accepted my proposal, so that's that.'

Donna jumped in quickly. 'That's great news, Bella. It's time you had a break. I know how years of work can wear you down. The responsibility will be good for Luca. I'm sure he appreciates your confidence in him, doesn't he Ma?'

'*Wear you down?* Don't make me laugh, Donna. What about those ridiculously long school holidays you have? And you would say that about Luca as he's your son.'

'That's enough Gemma. I know you're upset about Juliet, but please don't take it out on your sisters. Remember how difficult it was for Donna and Vincent when Luca was ill. No parent wants to see a child in distress, do they? Isabella has helped so many of us, especially after Amanda…' Maria's tears had a sobering effect on her daughters. The anniversary year was affecting each of them in their own way.

Gemma wished for once Donna would ditch the 'older-sister-knows-best' routine. She may well be a good teacher, but when it came to her own kids, there seemed to be little in the way of affection. It was always about the grades. 'Sorry, Mum. I miss her, too. Amanda would be shocked to see how frumpy her older sisters have got, wouldn't she?'

Despite themselves, the women laughed in agreement.

'Once Juliet has gone, I'll be fine. There will be more time to fill. Maybe I'll invite Tom and his new…ouch! What was that for?'

Donna and Isabella exchanged worried glances, but it was too late as Maria's wily eyes noticed everything. 'Tom's got a new partner, has he? Well, that's a relief.'

'You're not upset, Mum? We thought…'

'Bella, it's been ten years. Every man needs a woman to love, especially Tom. Silly boy. Why couldn't he tell me himself? When you see him, Bella, please give him my love and ask him to come over soon.'

'I'm sure Tom will be relieved. He was so embarrassed to tell me about Karen. I plan to invite them to dinner Sunday week. Gemma, as you'll be away, should I invite Neil?'

'Do what you like, Bella. Neil's always up for a roast. Anyway, I've got to go as there's such a lot to organise. I'll call you when we get to Aunt Carmelita's, okay, Mum?' Gemma kissed her mother and allowed her sisters a brief hug before banging the door on the way out. The collective sigh said it all.

'I think we got off lightly, don't you? At least now Gemma knows my decision, not that she can influence it, but perhaps in time she'll accept it.'

Donna got up to clear the dishes. She was on the attack. 'Gemma will never accept anything at face value, Bella. She is spiteful and sadly her children have followed her lead. I have had enough of it. I'd have given anything to have her flair for languages, wouldn't you? What a waste, to be a bloody travel rep when she could have gone to university. Poor Juliet never had a chance.'

'What do you mean, Donna?'

'Juliet has the same affinity for languages as her mother and should have gone to college. I'm not saying there's anything wrong with the performing arts, of course not. Gemma pressured her to change direction, telling her she had so much talent, but Juliet wasn't up to it. That's why she ended up on the cruise ships. This business with the drug dealer is attention seeking, pure and simple.'

'Maybe you're right. I don't have children, so what do I know? There aren't many kids who get to follow their dreams without some parental or educational steering, though. You must admit how extremely disappointed you were when Luca chose a brick-laying apprenticeship over university.'

Silence. As Donna's bony shoulders rose in defence, Isabella stood in front of her big sister and rested her quiet hands on them, feeling them drop. 'Donna, I'm not judging you. We all want things from and for others without realising it. Let it go.'

Donna huffed in resignation. Isabella was right, as usual. 'Anyway, I wouldn't be surprised if Neil bails out. If you weren't here Mama, I wouldn't give Gemma the time of day, sister or not.'

It was Maria's turn to sigh. Gemma had become so bitter since her sister's death. She had taken on the entire family's grief just for herself. Donna's tolerance was at an all-time low. Thank God for Isabella's calm attitude, and of course, the sanctuary of her own little apartment.

Chapter 14

The first week of the new regime had gone better than Luca had hoped. The silent transition from loyal nephew to head honcho percolated quickly. He and Rita had got into a nice rhythm, beginning their morning, now a regular eight o'clock start (she insisted on this earlier time, which pleased him immensely) over flat whites and a pastry during which time they discussed the day: what orders to prepare; what stock to replenish; planning the new season's produce. Rita seemed to anticipate his thoughts, working in tandem, with little to disturb the flow.

Her mood board suggestion had baffled him at first, until she explained it was a great way of collecting ideas for the new café. Rita got him started with a few clippings taken from several of the shop's magazines, and they hung the board up in the kitchen as a reminder.

'I'm getting the hang of this now, Rita. What do you think of this picture of a roof lantern? Bella took me to the British Museum a couple of years ago. The café roof there is fabulous. It got me thinking about a miniature version here.'

Rita was surprised to hear he'd been to the museum as Luca didn't strike her as particularly cultured, although Greta had dragged him out and about. A child born to teachers must be bright or at least have exposure to books and learning, though. She remembered when Alison used to take her to the library where on Saturdays, a group of earnest, bright-eyed children sat cross-legged in a circle while Mr Gribble delighted them with his magic storytelling. That was probably the last time she felt carefree.

Luca had been so much more relaxed with her these last few days, sharing the odd vignette from his past which Rita found intriguing. It was as if he was beginning to see her as a three dimensional being whose point of view he valued, even if there were no enquiries made into her former life. In turn, Rita became emboldened, venturing opinions and ideas for discussion. It was thrilling. 'Can you show me the roof online? I've never been to London.'

'You've never been, Rita? Well, we must do something about that. Look, why don't you have the iPad for research?'

'Oh no, Luca, I couldn't possibly accept it.'

'You'd be doing me a favour. The mood board was your brilliant suggestion, and there will be loads more once you get going. It will also help Finn with his homework. I've got the laptop haven't I, so between us we can pool our resources. It's good business practise.'

His grin, so utterly beguiling, took her breath away. Luca wasn't going to take no for an answer. The nearest library was in Marsham and there was talk of it closing. Rita's mind summersaulted at the benefits the iPad would bring to her and Finn, and her mum too, as they could look at past and present design. She became aware of Luca's eyes watching her expression. He did that quite a lot now. Rita smiled. 'On behalf of the Redwing family, I accept. Thank you.'

Later that night Rita sat up in her sofa bed, notebook and pencil on one side and a mug of tea going cold on the other. A glance at the time told her she really must get some sleep. After all, the iPad was theirs now. Her head swam with pictures, drawings and designs for the extension. Images of sparkling, pared back interiors whooshed, mixed and melded in her exhilarated mind. Rita had stumbled upon one website whose designers were responsible for the well-known restaurant, *Piccante*, whose interior looked fabulous. She couldn't wait to share her discoveries with Luca. He'd be so pleased to see the fruits his generous gift had brought already.

Rita placed her cardigan on top of the duvet as she slid underneath. The hot water bottle would have to stay cool, and in any case, sleep was beginning to claim her. She switched off the lamp, curled up tightly and whispered a 'thank you' to the universe before falling asleep.

Chapter 15

'Yo, Luca! A couple of filter coffees for me and the old man, if you please. It's cold enough to freeze the nuts off a brass monkey.'

Luca took the two recycled cups from his cousin, making sure to thoroughly rinse them out before refilling them. The rewiring job was nearly finished with just two weeks before the new barber's shop opened its doors to the men and boys' heads of Blackstock. Luca couldn't wait. His cousin's regular visits were getting on his nerves, and the reason why was just beginning to dawn on him. Nathan always paid for his food and drink and he was generally cheerful - too chirpy sometimes, but tolerable. He'd taken to 'popping' in, sometimes twice a day, and Luca suspected it had something to do with Rita.

She had come up trumps since he gave her the iPad. That very next day before the shop opened its doors, Rita showed him pages of notes, scribbles, miniature design doodles which made him laugh out loud. He was amazed at her perpetual energy and enthusiasm. They needed time to talk through what they had discovered so far, but he was reluctant to ask Rita to give up her Sunday. *Pay her overtime, you idiot. It's your business*. Luca smiled. The fact that he was the boss hit him once again. The weather had been too cold for football training, so maybe Rita would spare him a couple of hours on Sunday?

As promised, Tom Lockhart had stopped by to introduce his new partner. Luca was chuffed for his uncle, especially to see him colour up at the word, 'partner'. It must have taken a lot of courage to commit to someone else after losing Amanda, even if it was ten years ago. *Time doesn't erase pain: it just buries itself deeper in your heart.*

Over cappuccinos and Portuguese custard tarts, the quartet chatted comfortably. Luca and Isabella took to Karen immediately as Rita quietly refilled their cups, politely declining their invitation to join them. Karen was quiet but not shy, and she laughed a lot, particularly with Tom. He was proud to announce how Karen's daughter had spent a fun evening with Ethan and Louis, and as St Valentine's week fell during half-term, his sons had invited her along to Hartburn's forthcoming gig at The Alderman.

Luca was delighted for them. The entire clan were gathering to listen to the new auditions. Karen Shaw's introduction to the family would be that much easier in such a relaxed environment. Tables were booked for an early supper, and everyone was keen to stay on to watch the band. He was even looking forward to seeing his dad who was much more laid back these days.

Later, after the shop's 'closed' sign' was up, Luca shared with Rita the terrible circumstances of his aunt's death. Amanda had been driving back from a birthday celebration on a foggy night when a lorry driver unknowingly edged her car over a bank, killing her instantly. Luca painfully described how the family dealt with the devastation and subsequent aftermath.

He'd never told anyone this before and Rita had listened attentively, with tears in her eyes. He was beginning to see a side to her previously hidden. Isabella had been right about her, which was no real surprise knowing his aunt. She and Hattie had organised a celebratory meal the day after the gig. It was also to be a pick-me-up for Joe as the funeral would be over by then and Isabella seized the opportunity to offer her good friend a little respite.

Joe's mysterious brother Rik was coming back and had also been invited. No one had met him, and Luca was fascinated to see if he was like his baker brother. Uncle Neil was also invited which was a first. He scarcely went anywhere without Gemma who never let him get a word in. He wondered how Neil felt about Juliet's departure. It was certain to pile pressure on Nathan as his mother's attention would fall on him alone.

Luca was really looking forward to sitting at Bella's table alongside a few new faces. The only other time he'd been remotely in Rita's company was when she watched her brother play football or cricket. She was such a good listener, asking the odd question which had the effect of retrieving stored memories, some of which were uncomfortable. She never pushed, though. Rita seemed to sense what his limits were.

He'd never had a female friend, apart from Isabella, who sort of doubled up. His aunt had been his go-to person, but it looked as if she was making her own plans and wasn't going to be around as much. If Luca was nervous about undertaking sole responsibility for Bonetti's, he felt better knowing Rita was going to be there to help in her own quiet way.

The only fly in this soothing ointment was Nathan. Once again, he'd buzzed into the shop, spouting the same old spiel while poor Rita, the kind person that she was, laughed politely at his jokes. Nathan was clearly delighted to have a new audience. He was immune to the fact that his cousin had heard his wise-cracks a thousand times before. Luca couldn't wait for the job to finish and Nathan pissed off back to Marsham. He loved his cousin, but you could see too much of someone.

'How do, *Reet-petite*. I hear congrats are in order. Looks like you and Lucky are going up in the world.'

Luca looked at Rita and then at his cousin. He hated it when Nate called him 'Lucky', as if he wasn't a lucky git himself, with his new BMW *Roadster* and flash new drum kit. Isabella said she'd tell the family about the shop, so the news had to get out at some point. Exactly how much Nathan knew was hard to tell. He continued making the coffee.

Rita, meanwhile, unaware of Luca's familial torment, assumed as normal a voice as possible.

'Oh, thanks Nate. It's good news all round, especially for Isabella.'

'How about we celebrate at The Alderman, tonight? I'll buy the drinks. Say, eight o'clock?'

Without even looking, Luca knew Rita was blushing. 'Sorry, Nate, I'm busy tonight.'

'That's a shame, mate. What about you, Rita?'

In her confusion, Rita muttered a weak reply. 'Okay. Yes. Thank you. Um, see you there?'

A grinning Nathan bounded out the ringing door, leaving a five-pound note to flutter on the counter. Luca could not believe it. There he was again, his cocky cousin, breaking and entering into his life. Greta had batted off Nathan's attempts at flattery like an annoying wasp which was one of the reasons he had liked her. It was always the same with his cousin: *anything you can do; I can do better* was the routine.

This time though, Luca's irritation was infused with an unpleasant aroma. He felt inexplicably annoyed at Rita. Why the hell did she say yes? She knew how self-centred Nathan was. *But it was a generous gesture. Why be annoyed at that?* The stupid thing was, Luca had nothing to do tonight, so why did he lie? Maybe he'd pop his head around the door anyway and say his plans had changed.

Kit interrupted his anguished mental chatter. 'Luca, the B&B are asking if we can spare any olive bread. Joe's sold out.'

Luca took the phone from Kit, grateful not to have to think about this disturbing turn of events.

Rita, meanwhile, had resumed her job of making a filter coffee for Deidre Lowe who had rushed over in between putting together a birthday posy and completing Joe's order of white lilies for his mother's funeral. 'Best wrap a couple of pastries to keep us going, Rita. It'll be a late night for me and Evie. She's so nervous about the audition this Saturday, I've had to keep her away from making the bouquets.'

Rita smiled absent-mindedly as she put the money in the till. She swiftly excused herself, desperate for a quiet moment out the back to think about what had just happened.

It had been a strange afternoon. Luca wasn't generally moody, but he'd hardly spoken to her. Things had been going so well. Just that morning, he'd asked if she was free on Sunday to discuss the café extension, as overtime of course. He seemed surprised to hear about her dog walking commitment at the rescue centre and said not to worry as it wasn't urgent. It was clear that neither of them wanted to let the opportunity pass, so they agreed to get together when she returned from William Sutton's.

Rita had no idea what she'd done, if indeed anything to annoy or upset him. She resolved to pop in and see Libby before tea to ask her advice. Thankfully the weather was so cold, it wouldn't matter too much what she wore to the pub that night, perhaps a pair of jeans and a roll-neck sweater. She didn't want Nathan to think she was making a big effort. He was just being polite, after all. Rita was so relieved that Luca wasn't joining them, as to sit between the fractious cousins was too much.

Libby opened the front door with a wholegrain rice cake slathered with cashew-nut butter in her left hand which was about to blast her taste-buds. Rita grinned. It wasn't so long ago when chips and burgers were the staples. Hattie had converted many of the Larkspur House families to good nutrition and they were her latest disciples. Rita sat at the kitchen table while Libby made a pot of tea. 'You look cheerful, Lib. Have you had a good day?'

'Yes, oh yes! Hamish came in to pick up his homeopathic remedies. He spent an hour in deep conversation with Hattie in the office, and I must say he looked better when he came out. Poor sod. Don't know how he's coping without his wife although Hattie said they'd had problems for a long while. Anyway, he asked when we'll be at the centre next as there's a lovely new inmate to meet, a wirehaired fox terrier called Tilda whose owner has gone into a nursing home.'

'No, no, no, Libby, Hamish didn't mean for you to *have* her, so don't go getting ideas just yet. He was just being nice, like he is to everyone. Do you want to hear my news?'

Libby laughed. There was no way she would risk ruining her good tenancy record for a dog as you never know, one day, she might have to come back. But it was nice of Hamish to think of her. Rita's news, however, had the jump-cut effect of moving the scene rapidly into one of shock. 'Nate's asked you for a drink! Tonight? At the Alderman? Has he got a brain tumour?'

Rita laughed out loud. She wasn't the least bit offended by her friend's comment. Neither of them could have predicted this in a hundred years. 'He may well have, but I said I'd go.'

'So, this drink is to congratulate you on the promotion. It's a good excuse to ask you out, I suppose. Did he invite Luca?'

'I'm not sure. I think so as he didn't say explicitly his name or mine at first. In any case, Luca is busy. When Nathan left, Luca was a bit offhand. I think it's because Nathan gets on his nerves, don't you?'

Libby looked at her best friend and said nothing.

'Lib, what do I talk about? I feel so stupid.'

The friends spent the next half an hour working on a strategy. They decided Rita should take the invitation at face value, stay for a drink, buy him one back, and make a swift exit. Rita scrubbed up well, and Nathan was sure to notice, so it was best not to risk him making a clumsy pass, as she'd be eternally embarrassed. Libby reminded her she'd be working at the pub later. 'I'll keep my eagle eye on you, Reet, don't you worry, just try to enjoy yourself. I'll call the cops if he gets out of hand.'

Rita smiled to herself as she walked down the stairs back to her own flat, eternally grateful to have a friend like Libby.

Chapter 16

R ita entered the pub, dead on eight o'clock. Nathan waved her over to the bar where he was chatting to Seth and Jodie Beck about the band's forthcoming gig. Without giving Rita time to talk to the siblings, he organised half a sweet cider, a pint of Hertfordshire's finest, and a seat next to the large, cast iron wood burner. Seth and Jodie exchanged glances. They knew Nathan's track record better than anyone. It had become a bit of a thing in the band to bet how many offers came up at each gig, and Nathan was regularly top of the league.

Right now, he was seeing Claudia Huxtable, someone he had wanted to reel in for ages. Why then was he making a fuss of Rita? Jodie decided to have a chat with Libby who had popped out back. Rita Redwing was nice. She hoped Nate wasn't up to his tricks.

Rita unbuttoned her coat, surprised when Nathan took it from her shoulders and hung it on a hook nearby. She wondered if Libby saw this chivalric act but didn't dare turn around to look. Well, she was here now. Best get it over with. Rita took a sip of the cool, sweet cider and looked at Nathan, waiting for him to begin the conversation.

Nathan, meanwhile, scanned Rita's face, trying to work out what was different. Maybe it was the eyeliner, or her curly hair, as she usually tied it back. He was disconcerted. Rita's usual nervousness seemed to have disappeared, and he felt momentarily awkward at the silence between them. He raised his glass to her. 'Here's to your promotion, Rita. Shame Luca can't join us, but let's drink to the continued success of Bonetti's Deli. How long have you been there now?'

They made small talk, discussing work, a bit about his interests. Nathan noticed how Rita asked him the questions so that he was doing all the talking. She certainly was a change to false lashes and skinny jeans. After he downed his pint, Rita insisted she'd buy him another. This dismayed him a little, knowing the family were hard up, but he was pleased to see her return with a refill of her own glass. He couldn't have been that bad company after all.

For all the bluff and swagger, Nathan knew his shortcomings. At twenty-seven, he was getting a bit tired of the same old, same old. He really liked Claudia, but conversation about what was on trend and *American Idol* was already getting a bit samey. Rita was good company. Her face, her expression was open, untroubled somehow. There it was again, that unfamiliar spasm. He gulped a mouthful of tonic water, almost choking himself in the process. Recovered now, Nathan asked about her family.

Rita looked intently at him. 'My mum had me when she was young and was forced to leave home. I don't know who my father is. When my grandfather died, we moved back in with my gran until she died. And then my mum met Trevor, Finn's dad. That's when it went pear-shaped.

We moved around a lot, they drank a lot, so I looked after my little brother in-between working. Trevor went to prison and we ended up here.'

This time Nathan properly spluttered on his drink. Jesus, what a story! Surely Rita wasn't making it up? He didn't dare ask anything else as he was having trouble imagining what her life must have been like. It was in stark contrast to his own spoilt upbringing, that's for sure. Rita thankfully spared him the details, probably as it would have shocked him even more. But as she spoke about it, he was moved by the absence of tears, or 'woe is me.' Rita was no drama queen. He changed tack as best he could. 'You seem to have settled in Blackstock. Finn's doing well at footie, I hear. Ben said he's got talent. Does he play any instruments?'

'The school children sing, and he plays the recorder. He loves to read which is a relief, and of course, he has his cricket, football and the bike. It doesn't leave much time to learn an instrument.'

'How about you, Rita, what are your talents? We're auditioning this Saturday in front of the tribe and it's gonna be a hell of a night. Tickets sold out weeks ago. It's the only way to try out as if you can't perform in front of us lot, you've got no chance on a gig. Do you sing or play anything?'

Rita looked at Nathan, wondering how much to say. She and Libby had got tickets for the St Valentine's gig ages ago. They'd seen Hartburn play so many times that by now, Rita knew the lyrics and harmonies to every song. She was no stranger to music as it had been the one constant throughout her life. She had a little transistor that kept her company and didn't take up too much space. That radio had been her lifeline. Rita's grandmother had shown her how to play the piano when she was well enough. Mrs Redwing wasn't an old lady, but years of living under Mr Redwing's bullying fist had made her nerves bad.

Although Alison and her mother clashed, Rita's presence brought a mote of serenity to the angry women. As a teenager searching for an outlet, she bought a child sized guitar and some music books from the charity shop. Teaching herself the basics had been relatively easy.

Rita occasionally played in front of Finn, becoming ever more proficient during the long, lonely hours, waiting for her mother to return home from whatever binge she'd been on. She also played a little harmonica as that, too, was cheap, and easy to store. Where her voice came from, well, she never questioned it. 'Um, I can sing a little.'

'Why don't you audition for us? You've heard the band and you know everyone. Without Juliet, we'll need another female voice as soon as.' Nathan was feeling a bit puffed up. This was the least he could do for her even though he predicted she'd refuse.

Rita said she'd think about it and thanked him for the invitation. Everyone knew by now about Juliet's departure, and that the band were on the look-out for another singer, although Rita wasn't sure why. Jodie had a lovely voice and Rosa sang wonderful harmonies. No wonder she'd got a music scholarship. It must help to have a musical father. She wondered if it were her own father who gave her the gift. Rita realised she'd gone off on a tangent and wondered if it was time to go home. Libby nodded in her direction. It was almost half past nine. Where had the evening gone?

Nathan noticed Rita look at the clock above the bar. She hadn't asked for his number, or if they might see each other again. What did he expect? It was a friendly drink, after all, but some other force seemed to be working on him. Before he could stop the words from tumbling out, he asked if it was okay to call her.

'Oh, um, yes, alright then. Hang on, my phone's in my coat. I can never remember the number.'

It suddenly occurred to Nathan that Rita hadn't got her mobile padlocked to her hand, like most of his friends. In fact, he hadn't checked his own for almost two hours which was a startling discovery. Rita came back and sat down holding a tiny Nokia phone. As she looked expectantly at him, Nathan just about managed to stop himself asking where the hell she'd got that old thing from. She really was skint. Thank God he hadn't embarrassed her, or himself for that matter.

He tapped in her number, mumbling something about calling later in the week. Rita thanked him so warmly for such a lovely evening, Nathan wasn't quite sure if she was genuine but decided she didn't have it in her to be sarcastic. He held out her coat and walked to the door, pulling it open. She politely declined his offer to walk her home, and so he kissed her soft, pale cheek in farewell. Nathan watched intently as Rita wrapped her scarf carefully around her neck and adjusted her satchel before heading out into the frosty night air.

Libby had witnessed the entire encounter. It had been a quiet evening, so there had been time to keep watch over her precious friend. Something unexpected had happened. She saw it in the way Nathan's eyes followed Rita as she walked away. Instantly, he took out his phone and began sending a message. There was nothing to brag about there, Libby was certain of that.

The phone pinged.

Mate, just had a Bonny Tyler moment. R U in bed?

It was nine-thirty exactly. Luca turned off his phone and switched off the bedside light. Nathan could stick his total eclipse up his arse.

Chapter 17

Joe and Nell waited nervously for the doorbell to ring. Rik had telephoned earlier that day to say he had arrived at Blackstock Manor and asked if it was convenient to call round. Marion's funeral had been arranged for Friday and today was Wednesday. Rik wasn't here long enough to help, but at least he had arrived in one piece.

They were lucky not to have to wait to bury their mother. Father Martin was due to travel overseas and someone had pulled strings. Marion Faulkner had not only been a regular member of the congregation, but she and Walter had donated substantial funds to various church appeals over the years which were gratefully acknowledged.

There was little left to do but wait. Joe had decided he would close the shop for the day, as had quite a few other traders as a mark of respect for a beloved community member. The solicitor was due to formally disclose the contents of Marion's will at the meeting the next day, although Joe already knew what was coming. His mother had left a large legacy for her sons, and had made generous provision for her granddaughters, even after the nursing home costs were met and the solicitor had discharged his duties. There was also Marion's jewellery which had been closeted in the bank's vault for most of its life. That was left to Nell, to do whatever she pleased with it.

Whatever opinion Joe had of his brother, money was not a motivator. After their father's death, Marion sent Rik his share of the considerable proceeds of an endowment. Apparently, he was surprised by the sum and had insisted his mother keep it to meet her own needs. Only after Rik had been appraised of the true nature of the Faulkner's substantial finances, and there were more than enough funds to keep Marion safe and well, Rik accepted the bequest. Joe was interested to see Rik's reaction to the will as clearly, he wouldn't be expecting much.

As for personal effects, Joe had to wait and see if his brother wanted a keepsake, although now he wasn't so sure. When clearing out his mother's room, he'd been knocked for six to find the box of letters and postcards that Rik had sent to her over the years. He was aware they corresponded, but for some reason was shocked to find them. They had been carefully tied and placed within the confines of a fine burr ash box inlaid with exquisite marquetry, which depicted a farmer carrying a bundle of wheatsheaves on his shoulder. Joe recalled the box, a golden wedding anniversary gift from his father. At any rate, he was too emotionally raw to read the contents, but the discovery had shaken him.

Joe was about to look out of the window once again when Dora's bark, seconds before the doorbell rang, made him jump. He hadn't been this nervous since he gave Cherry's graduation party speech. *It's only your brother, silly bugger. Get a grip.* Joe unclenched his jaw but before there was time to breathe out, Rik stood inside the hall, his rangy body buttoned right to the top in a navy sailor's coat, and a chunky woollen hat covering who knew what was pulled down to his eyebrows.

The brothers shook hands. Joe's warm baker's fingers were enclosed in a startlingly glacial, bony grip. He'd forgotten how tall his brother was, almost half a head higher than his five-feet-ten. Nell greeted the stranger like an old friend. In under two minutes, she had taken his coat, hat, boots and any feeling of estrangement away and replaced it with a strong cup of tea, a warm buttered scone and a seat by the fire, with Dora sitting proprietorially by his side.

Unsure as to whether she should leave the brothers to talk, Nell sensed from Joe's awkward demeanour it best to stay. They made small talk for a while until a sort of equilibrium restored itself. Rik accepted Nell's invitation to dinner with a quiet gratitude, which went a long way to breaking the ice. He was quite unlike anyone she'd ever met before. When he asked if her daughters would be joining them for the evening, it shocked her. Nell had no idea Rik knew very much about Chloe and Cherry, let alone want to meet them, although Marion must have mentioned her granddaughters to him in her letters. She couldn't wait for the girls to arrive from London as they too were fascinated to meet their mysterious uncle.

Joe looked at the face of this stranger who was biologically connected to him but bore no other resemblance. Years of nomadic travelling and extreme weather had marked him. If it weren't for the shock of thick red-blond hair and piercing eyes, you could add another ten years to his forty-nine, if not more. In contrast to Joe's strong but protracting body shape, Rik had not an ounce of scrap about him. His long legs bent awkwardly in the low armchair, but he looked strangely at home. It must be the fire, thought Joe.

'Rik, how long are you staying in Blackstock?'

Good old Nell. Just like Isabella, she got straight to the point.

'Apart from a short visit to London and Cambridge, and weather permitting, perhaps ten days. I'd like to spend a little time with you and the family, if it's not inconvenient.'

Joe and Nell looked at each other, momentarily lost for words. They did not expect Rik to be quite so direct. Nell, however, was delighted, as she hoped Joe and his brother might reconcile. With an ever-shrinking family, she was always in tears at those family reunion programmes on the television.

'We generally have late afternoons and evenings free, as I can get my bread and cakes prepared early. There's some paperwork for us to sign at the solicitor's office tomorrow, but apart from that, your time's your own. I wondered if you'd like to say anything at the funeral?'

Rik was silent for what seemed like a lifetime. Joe was soon to discover this was part and parcel of how his brother communicated. Rik reminded him of a mountain: imposing and still. He was clearly on a different time scale.

'I'd like to read a poem, Joe, but only if you are happy with it. I'm aware my long absence must have caused anguish, especially for Mum. There's nothing I can do about that, but I am here now.'

The evening passed off remarkably well, despite Joe's misgivings. His brother was a fabulous teller of tales, much

104

like their mother had been, captivating the family with stories of his exotic travels, and of island life. Cherry and Chloe had joined them in time for dinner and could barely contain their excitement at the newcomer. Over several glasses of wine and tumblers of brandy, the Faulkner family shared what Nell was later to describe to Isabella as the most wonderful evening she'd ever had, despite their collective sadness at Marion's death.

Joe invited his brother to the St Valentine's gig and to Isabella's Sunday lunch the following day, which Rik accepted as naturally as if he'd lived in Blackstock his entire life. In farewell, the nieces hugged their new-found uncle with such tenderness, Joe struggled to swallow the surge of emotion which threatened to choke him. It was almost midnight before Rik made a move back to Blackstock Manor.

Before leaving, Rik had taken four parcels from a large, drawstring bag. For his nieces, two small pieces of maple on which he had exquisitely carved a waterfall for Cherry and a pastoral scene for Chloe, symbols of their zodiac signs. He must have known their birth dates from Marion. Maybe she had put Rik off from sending birthday cards? It was bewildering. For Nell, a sumptuous Fair Isle scarf knitted by an island friend. She was delighted and hugged this tall, thin man tightly. He didn't seem to mind. Lastly, Rik passed a small package wrapped in brown postage paper to his brother. The three women's eyes honed-in on this beloved man as he stood there, motionless, holding the package almost reluctantly.

'Well, Dad, aren't you going to open it?'

He coughed to hide his embarrassment, 'Erm, yes,

Cherry, of course I'll open it. Very nice of you Rik, quite unnecessary but…'

Joe stopped mid-sentence. The paper revealed a tiny ship in a bottle. It was identical to the one he had as a boy, with a navy-blue hull and a pirate's mask on the flag and had since been broken or mislaid in the sands of time. Marion must have told Rik how much Joe had lamented its loss, as no one else could have known about it. With eyes suddenly brimming over, he turned to place the ship's bottle ever so carefully on the mantlepiece, alongside a photograph of his girls.

Joe did his best to remain calm but inside, emotions swirled like a tornado. Memories flashed through his mind: the little bottle sitting next to his prized shell collection on the bedroom shelf; fragments of conversation with his little brother: *Rik, promise you won't touch it as it might break*; warm Cornish wind on their faces as they ran to the shoreline; the salty smell of summer. Joe felt the rug move ever so slowly from under him.

Rik walked slowly along the oak-lined path to the manor, his collar and woolly hat keeping most of the cold at bay. The moon was almost full, casting her seductive light over the quiet Blackstock fields and lanes. It felt a little like the island, the sound of breeze blowing through the denuded branches, reminding him of the sea's lament. Rik had been unexpectedly moved by the greeting of his estranged family. Chloe and Cherry had enveloped him into the fold so naturally, much like their mother, as if he had never been away. He could see why his brother had married Nell. She was a nest-builder, strong and capable, much like Marion had been.

Joe, however, still carried a reserve. It shocked him to be met with what he might describe as hostility, although Nell's warmth masked it to a certain extent. His brother had been an emotional child, always clamouring for Marion's attention, and not a little spoilt. Rik was overjoyed to have an older brother to emulate. He was by nature a quiet, introverted boy with only a couple of friends, and the five-year age gap between the brothers gave him someone to idolise.

Rik had followed Joe around like a shadow until he became ill, during which time there was scarcely any recollection of his revered brother's company. Marion explained it away, saying how Joe struggled to know how to deal with a sick brother but that he loved him regardless. After that, Joe went into the bakery business and he went off to college.

As time went on, Rik single-mindedly pursued his career and for the most part, managed to prevent human contact from buffeting him about. His small band of university friends kept him in touch with daily life as he voyaged around the globe, becoming increasingly self-reliant and solitary. For many years, family life was not a priority. Rik knew he would be unable to visit Blackstock without unsettling Joe and perhaps himself. But now he had seen his brother, their childhood memories disturbed him. After so many years apart, the yearning to be loved by Joe remained obstinately lodged in his being. Perhaps blood really was thicker than water.

And yet, despite the discomfort, Rik felt as if he was being propelled towards an event or a happening, the impact of which was certain to redirect the course of his life. Whatever it might be, he was pleased to have come to Blackstock. He and his brother were united by the loss of a beloved mother. It might help Joe accept him again.

Chapter 18

It was business as usual in the deli. Market day, whatever the weather, brought in the crowds. The café was already full of the first wave of thirsty customers and a few equally dry dogs, despite the cold. The temperature managed to stay above freezing. It was one of those blindingly crisp blue days that lifted the darkest mood, forcing heads to move away from warm woollen scarves and look skyward.

Luca was relieved to have Isabella in the shop. The crushing headache was probably the result of a terrible night's sleep. He may have been the only person in Blackstock not to have noticed the beautiful morning but was reminded by every customer how fresh and lovely the day was. Two strong pain killers eased the clamp that squeezed his temples, and he stuck to drinking glasses of water until his stomach settled down.

Occupation of any kind was the best tonic for anxiety. It had taken until four o'clock that morning to convince himself that Rita was free to see whoever she wanted, even if it was his cousin. Nathan's character was hardly a secret, so if he messed her around, it was none of Luca's business. So why it bothered him so acutely was baffling. He painfully realised what the often-used phrase meant, to not mix business with pleasure, and henceforth it was going to be his manifesto. After all, it worked in Hartburn. Every band experienced tension, so unless they were Fleetwood Mac, best to leave the shagging to the fan club.

Rita hadn't exactly kept her head down during the day as they were all rushed off their feet, but somehow, Luca sensed she had kept out of his way. Their early morning coffee ritual had been abandoned due to his headache, and he hoped Rita hadn't thought she'd upset him. Isabella made sure he took a short break between elevenses and lunch. Despite the nuisance of it, Luca was enjoying the attention.

It was just after five o'clock and only he and Rita remained in the shop. Luca was keen to maintain the good atmosphere between them, especially as the pain had morphed into a slight throb across the left temple which was bearable. He decided to risk it and ask Rita if she'd like a coffee.

'I'd love one. How's your head?'

'It's much better, thanks. What can I get for you?'

'Let me make it. You sit down, take the weight off your feet.'

Luca smiled at Rita's offer. He hadn't upset her after all. She brought over two large americanos and a couple of slices of warm walnut bread. Luca took a sip of his coffee, feeling an instant surge of energy.

'I can't believe we've been so busy on such a cold day, can you, Rita?'

'No, it's been non-stop. I'm looking forward to a hot bath, and an earlyish night.'

Luca had changed his mind a zillion times throughout

the day as to whether he should ask Rita about the drink, but she thankfully beat him to it.

'I was home by nine-thirty last night, so it wasn't late. Nathan talked about the St Valentine's gig and how everyone is looking forward to it. He asked if I wanted to audition on Saturday, as a replacement for Juliet. I was wondering…'

Luca put his cup down, his mind tail-spinning. If Nathan was here right now, he'd knock his block off. What the hell was he up to? Had he heard Rita sing? As the tsunami of thoughts swirled, Luca realised Rita had stopped talking. She was watching him closely. 'I wish Nathan wouldn't ask his girlfriends to audition.'

A heartbeat. 'I'm not his girlfriend.'

A monumental silence sat between the pair. Luca *had* to pull himself together. *She's not his girlfriend.* 'Sorry, I didn't mean to imply you are his … Look, Rita, the only reason I said that is because we try to keep a bit of harmony in the band, and it makes it tricky if any of the members are going out together. That's why I asked. But anyway, forget about that. Has Nathan heard you sing? I mean, can you sing?'

'It's been said … it doesn't matter, I was never going to do it. Nathan was just being friendly. Libby and me will be there anyway. It'll be a great night.'

Luca felt awful. How did this kind, inoffensive young woman get caught between him and his selfish cousin? It wasn't her fault. He had to sort this out quickly, before it got out of hand. He was supposed to be the boss, for pity's sake. Even if Rita did pass the audition, he'd been planning to step back from the band. There were loads of them to choose from, and he was by no means integral.

Perhaps he should support her wish to audition? What harm could it do? 'Rita, I'm sorry if I overreacted. Nathan is a law unto himself, but I can't see the harm in auditioning if you feel up to it. I'm going to take a back seat where Hartburn is concerned as I want to put my energy here. Let's forget I said anything about it. Now, what do you think of these pictures of a lantern roof?'

Nathan had his feet up on the sofa. It was nice to be back in the warm after a day spent under the barber shop's semi-plastered walls and ceilings. He took the cold bottle of Peroni from Luca. It wasn't unusual to spend time in his cousin's flat as Nathan still lived with his parents, albeit in his own space. Luca had taste, he'd say that for him, even if it were on the austere side. Nathan's mother clearly didn't want him to leave, although his dad had hinted on more than one occasion that it might be a good time to look for a place of his own, for his independence.

In the meantime, the entire top floor of the smart Victorian three-storey house had been converted into a one bedroomed apartment. The only thing missing was a full kitchen, but Nathan wasn't one for cooking, especially after a long day's slog, so he'd often eat with his parents or get a takeaway.

The truth was that Nathan was desperate to move out, but he had spent most of his grandfather's legacy, and as soon as it was wages day, the money seemed to slip through his fingers at an alarming rate. He'd never been able to save. It hadn't helped that his mother liked to see her children with the best clothes, the latest car, a nice watch, so he'd become accustomed to the image. If he was going to move out, the lifestyle had to go, and Nathan wasn't sure if he was ready for that just yet. He could invite whoever he wanted provided they weren't partying 'till the early hours. It was extremely convenient.

Last night, however, Nathan found it hard to sleep. His usual untroubled slumber in the king-sized mango wood bed was disturbed by thoughts and images of Rita Redwing: her soft brown eyes, her slightly northern accent, the way she looked straight at him. He'd never met anyone quite like her but was unable to work out why it made him feel so unsteady. Rita wasn't trendy, she lived in a housing trust flat, her stepfather was dodgy to say the least.

Nathan knew he was being a snob but even he could feel sympathy, despite what his mates said about him. In some small way he wanted to take care of her, whatever that meant. It was the birth of a new, bitter-sweet feeling. How much of this should he confess to Luca? He took a swig of his lager. 'Thanks, fella. I needed that. We've finally finished the barber's shop. They've got a grand opening in a couple of weeks and have offered me and Dad free haircuts.'

'What, you'd risk upsetting Ronan? Do so at your peril. Sorry I couldn't make it last night. Rita said you'd asked her to audition.'

Nathan swung his legs off the sofa and looked at his cousin. Luca was as subtle as an air raid. It was well-known in the family that if you wanted to know if your hat was on straight, ask Luca or Isabella. Maybe he hadn't got the text last night? 'Yeah, well, we need a replacement for Juliet, and I don't think too much of Claudia or Evie's chances, do you? If Rita can't sing, she won't audition.'

'How is Claudia? You two still loved up?'

'To tell you the truth, she's already getting on my wick. For the first time ever, I had to switch my phone off. How about Greta? I guessed something was up when you came to the wine bar on your own.'

'Yeah, she blew me out.'

They sat, sizing each other up like middle-weight boxers before a title fight. Any time now, Luca was going to ask him about the text, so he jumped in first. He had nothing to hide. 'Had a great night with Rita. Did you know she had no idea who her old man is? Can you imagine that in our family? She brought Finn up while her mother and the loser were out boozing. What a crap time she must have had...'

Anger rushed up through Luca's body into his face, burning. Rita had never talked about her past, but then again, he never asked her. Why was she telling Nathan, of all people, as if he was someone worth confiding in?

'...we got along really well. She's a great listener. I've never met anyone quite like her.'

'Nate, what are you playing at? Claudia will be at the pub Saturday night. The entire family is coming, even Lord and Lady Huntley, so whatever your plans are, just make sure you wait until after Saturday.'

'Don't get out of your pram, mate. What are you so steamed up about? It really pisses me off that everyone thinks I'm some kind of operator. There comes a time when you meet someone who...'

'Who what, Nate?'

Silence swamped the room. The cousins' eyes locked in combat. 'I don't know, Luca. I've never felt like this before. She got to me, somehow. Like I said in the text, total eclipse.'

Luca was alarmed. Nathan had never acted this way before. He decided to say his piece, and then, well, whatever was going to happen, what was it to him? 'You know Rita's had a bad time, you just said it yourself. Don't make it worse for her, that's all I'm saying.'

'Why are you so bothered, Luca? You should be happy for me. I've finally found someone I really like.'

Luca could not argue with that. How could he say how he felt when he didn't know? It was so confusing, watching helplessly as his emotions swung wildly, from elation to anger, to despair and back again. It was beginning to affect his sleep, to wear him out. There was only so much cortisol you want pumping around the system. Rita had been emphatic - *she wasn't his girlfriend*. He prayed it would stay that way. Luca put a brave face on it. 'Look, Nate, I am pleased, alright. Does she have any feelings for you?'

'I think so. I hope so. I don't think she's seeing anyone right now. There is definitely chemistry.'

'Just promise me you'll sort the Claudia situation out, one way or the other. If there's one thing I know about Rita, she would never do anything she didn't want to do, however nice she is.'

Chapter 19

The turnout exceeded Joe's expectations. He'd been to several funerals where only the first few pews were inhabited, so it was a relief to see standing room only in Blackstock's beautiful Norman church. Even Rupert and Penelope Huntley came along which was a generous gesture. Hattie had said once that the soul of the deceased may still be around until after the funeral, so if that were true, Marion would be content.

Joe was holding up well. His brother's presence had brought an unexpected tranquillity to the proceedings. Even at the solicitor's office, after Edward Winstanley told the brothers they were to expect over two hundred thousand pounds each, Rik remained quite still. In the pub later that day, after they talked through the final arrangements, Joe felt he had to challenge his brother about such a prolonged absence. Nell said if he didn't get it off his chest, he'd explode with it.

When the moment came, Rik simply said he was sorry. No explanation, no argument. This threw Joe as he was expecting a tussle. What had Rik said? *I'm sorry you feel such anger, Joe. Don't hold on to it. Say what you have to say to me now, and let it go.*

But Joe couldn't say any more. The thought of it held so much more power than the thing itself, which now seemed so trivial. Fermenting, that's what he'd been doing, like his sourdough. Joe realised how his stomach had become swollen with unexpressed anger and frustration, fired by his febrile imagination. Rik's offer to give half of his inheritance to Chloe and Cherry shocked him, but Joe was having none of it. The girls were well-provided for, and after all, Rik was Marion's son too.

After the exchange, the atmosphere between the brothers lightened. As the waitress set down their lunches, Joe smiled to see Rik clutch his knife and fork in the same manner as their father had done. They laughed at how much salt Joe poured onto his pie, another inherited trait but this time there was no Marion to tell them off. Joe found himself easing into his brother's equable company which rekindled memories from way back when they played together. Rik recalled several vivid childhood scenes that Joe had buried, a few of which had the brothers laughing at the madness of it.

Rik's innocent charm could make him do things he ordinarily would not have done, like dress up as a *Python-esque* pirate in Rik's comedy version of *Peter Pan* or skip school to travel to London for a Red Bus Rover which they almost got away with. They raised their glasses to Marion, and drank to her safe passage, both a little emotional at the gesture. Rik had idolised him. Joe realised how much he'd missed it.

Isabella sat a few rows back next to her mother and Vincent. She looked at the long spine of Joe's long-lost brother. There hadn't been time for formal introductions, so apart from his profile, only Rik's crop of sandy hair stood well above everyone else, setting him apart from the other mourners. Joe's daughters gave a heartfelt eulogy for their grandmother and the mourners sang *How Great Thou Are* and *Amazing Grace*. The Blackstock choir's voices soared into the vast space, filling the ancient ceiling above their heads and beyond with a joyous sound that made the angels smile.

It was time for Rik to read his poem. Isabella watched as he walked slowly to the lectern. There was much straining of heads, as few people had met him and were curious to see the face of Joe's enigmatic brother. The little that was known about Rik only ignited interest, especially as Joe scarcely talked about him. Nevertheless, the man had an air about him, a detached manner that set him apart, and he looked nothing like his baker brother, so ears were pricked, and who didn't like a mystery?

Rik stood as straight as a mast, looking at a sheet of paper held aloft in his long fingers as if memorising lines. Seconds later, he folded it in the most deliberate way and tucked it carefully into an inside pocket. He looked like a man from a different era, like those sepia photos you see of Ernest Shackleton or TE Lawrence in far-off places. Rik looked so uncomfortable, his brother's tie standing out against the check-weave shirt like an awkward teenager.

He surveyed the congregation. Suddenly, his gaze transformed into a stare as it settled on Isabella's open face. Their eyes fused in a moment of recognition. Rik blinked rapidly before recovering himself and then, in a steady, resonant voice, began to talk about his mother. For what seemed like a moment in freeze frame, he described in an unexpectedly intimate way how much Marion had loved their family holidays spent mainly in Cornwall, as that was where her ancestors hailed from.

One time, he, Joe and their father had gone so far out on the beach, so engrossed in rock pools and sand snakes, that their mother had to call the lifeguard to find them. He described how Marion used to entrance the boys with stories from *The Arabian Nights, King Solomon's Mines* and *The Narnia Chronicles* which stirred a longing in him for strange, exotic lands. She was a fabulous storyteller.

Rik talked of their long correspondence, and how he greatly anticipated Marion's letters as they painted a picture of Blackstock life so vividly, he felt as if he knew many of them. He wrote to her of landscapes and places, bringing his experiences to her door. They shared poems and poets, writers and books. His mother loved Christina Rosetti and he had chosen a favourite poem of hers to share, entitled *Who Has Seen the Wind?*

Who Has Seen the Wind?
Neither I nor you:
But when the leaves hang trembling,
The wind is passing through.

Who has seen the wind?
Neither you nor I
But when the trees bow down their heads,
The wind is passing by.

At the end of the eulogy, Rik moved so quietly from the lectern to retake his seat, there was a collective jolt when the sound of the organ nudged the mourners from their reverie. He had taken one hundred and fifty or so people on a journey into a chimerical land, such was the power of his chronicles.

The remainder of the service went by without Isabella's attention. She had seen a ghost. There was no doubt in her mind she and Rik knew or had known each other, but she could not recall where or when. Isabella felt so discomforted by his ocean-blue gaze, as deep and mysterious as those springtime Sandaig lochs, she longed to go home and lie down. Hattie's gentle prod brought her back to the cold church, and she edged her way quietly out. It was time to get to the hall in readiness to serve the afternoon tea. As the pair silently tiptoed towards the huge oak doors, somehow, she knew Rik was aware she had taken her leave.

Isabella wrapped her scarf tightly around her head before the arctic wind had the chance to bite. The short, sharp burst of cold brought Isabella somewhat to her senses. Thankfully the village hall was just a few minutes' walk away, but she and Hattie scampered like wild rabbits to get back into the warm. The café ladies had done a fabulous job in laying each table with fresh linen tablecloths, china cake stands and silver cutlery. Every guest was to be served a proper afternoon tea, so Hattie and Isabella, together with four friends, were ready with tea pots and cafetières to greet the guests.

Only Joe and the immediate family remained at the church. They stood shivering by the graveside to see

Marion buried next to her dearest Walter. It was a good plan as many of the guests were elderly and Joe wanted to make sure no one got unnecessarily cold. He was still recovering from Rik's homage to their mother. Once again, Joe found himself swept along on the tide of their shared past, helpless to escape and yet, feeling in no immediate danger. On the contrary, a long-forgotten affection for his little brother was bobbing to the surface.

By the time the Faulkner family arrived, chatter filled the hall. Many reunions and reacquaintances were made that day, with promises to keep in touch as is common at funerals and weddings. Hattie and Isabella steered Joe's family towards a table reserved for them. Once they'd had a warm drink, there would be time to circulate.

Rik was the last to arrive. He smiled at Isabella, revealing a row of small white square teeth set against the curve of his surprisingly sensual mouth. It was astonishing. There it was again, a rush of some strange chemical which, without the safety of a pew underneath, threatened to take her knees away. Isabella poured him a cup of tea as he pulled out a chair next to his brother, and with a sense of relief, she made her way back to refill the empty teacups around the hall.

Two hours later, most of the guests had left. Maria Burnett had exhausted herself catching up with so many people she knew and she waited patiently for Vincent. He and Rik had been engaged in an earnest discussion with much nodding of heads. To an onlooker, you might have thought they were old friends. The hall and kitchen had been washed and cleared, and the small group sat together reflecting on the day. Without his mother-in-law's nudge,

Vincent could easily have stayed to chat to Rik who was a most interesting man.

Isabella looked at Joe, concerned for his shattered expression. It was reassuring to see his daughters fussing around their father, and Nell's watchful eye on her brood. The group made to get up with Hattie leading the way towards the exit. Rik waited for Isabella to button her coat before following on. As they approached the door, Isabella's footsteps slowed to a stop as she turned to face Rik. She did her best to find a steady voice.

'Look after Joe, won't you? He's not as tough as he makes out. I'm sure your visit has helped him.' In the absence of a reply, Isabella bumbled on. 'I believe you are joining us on Saturday evening at the pub. On Sunday, if you can bear more of our company, Hattie and I are hosting a lunch, a traditional Sunday roast, at my cottage…' Isabella heard herself ramble. She was acutely aware of their proximity to each other.

'Thank you, Isabella. I look forward to seeing you again.'

Rik took Isabella's warm hand in his own and held it as tenderly as if cradling an injured bird. His thumb imperceptibly moved across the skin of hers and Isabella's eyes suddenly pricked with tears. It was extraordinary. His scrutiny had stripped her bare. 'Goodbye Rik, for the moment.'

When he released her hand and walked away, Isabella felt such loss, she wished he would hold it forever.

Later that night, Isabella lay soaking in the bath. It had been an exhausting week with a busy weekend still to come. Her warm, comfy bed was calling, and a pair of fresh silk pyjamas already lay in waiting. Joe had held up well. He'd always been a man to show his emotions which was handy living with three women - four, if you counted Dora, their gorgeous rescued hound whose parentage no one could work out. Isabella recalled how she and Joe had almost got together, but her father had suffered his first stroke, and then Nell came bursting into Joe's life never to leave it, so that was that. Isabella had no regrets. Nell was a wonderful partner in all respects, and Joe became the brother she never had. It wasn't meant to be.

Joe had scarcely mentioned his brother. She recalled him saying once there was tension between them, but Isabella wasn't one for prying. Every family had skeletons: it was a shame that these days, the trend was to hang them out in public. As the family bakery had been firmly established in Marsham for almost two centuries, Joe's decision to buy the baker's shop in Blackstock might have upset Walter Faulkner. But he and Marion loved Nell, and when she suggested they move close by to spend time with the grandchildren, it was an offer Marion was never going to refuse. Her granddaughters may have made up for the absence of her youngest son, but neither Joe never mentioned it.

Rik Faulkner: brother, uncle, son. Her body shivered involuntarily under the cooling water. She turned on the hot tap, not yet ready to end the soporific wallow. There was no doubt they had met before, but for the life of her, the memory synapses were not ready to reveal the answer. Isabella could not recall a time when another human being had affected her in this way, perhaps never.

Apart from two short-lived relationships, Daniel Overton was the only man to have played his way into her heart, literally and emotionally. His looks may have been unremarkable, but he had charm, talent and was very funny. When Daniel was away gigging for long periods, Isabella never mourned, or kicked her heels: she was far too busy for that. Even after they parted, it occurred to her that there was no unfinished business.

Ah, *unfinished business*, perhaps that's what it was? Isabella was beginning to recall a fascinating book Hattie had given her a decade ago, describing the belief that souls reunite throughout lifetimes, in order to facilitate learning and growth. It had resonated deeply with Isabella, the notion of re-incarnation without religion, although there were religions who held it to be integral to their beliefs. Tomorrow she'd look out the book and refresh her memory. In any event, whether she and Rik had old or new history, these unsettling feelings were not in the least unpleasant.

Chapter 20

There was a buzz about Blackstock that Saturday, more than the usual upbeat weekend vibe that brought families and visitors into the square. The weather gods must have voted to hold off the snow dump and to maintain temperatures to a few degrees above freezing for a while longer. They sent rain instead, which washed the surrounding fields, roads and lanes clean.

Luca had given Rita a half-day holiday. Whether it was to give his new assistant time to practise for the audition that evening, Rita didn't know, but she was so grateful as that was exactly what she planned to do. There were no nerves or fear of forgetting chords or lyrics, as it was the same as reciting her times table. Music had always been her safety net, the place she retreated to where no one could touch her. Practically the entire Bonetti clan would be there, even her mother and brother, as they were looking forward to an evening out. Luca may have tried to bluff it out, as it was obvious he didn't want her to audition and probably thought she'd change her mind. He was clearly embarrassed. So why was she auditioning?

Rita shared the bizarre turn of events with a wide-mouthed Libby, who was desperate to know what Nathan had said during their drink, and Luca's subsequent outburst.

'Sod 'em, Reet. Do it anyway, for yourself. You may decide not to play in the band later, but I'd just love to see their faces when you get up on that stage. Don't get me wrong, I like the band, especially Rosa and the Lockhart brothers, but I can't see why Luca's knickers are in such a twist.'

'Nathan's been in and out of the shop for a fortnight now, and it's getting to Luca. I thought they were friends as well as cousins, but he sure does get Luca's goat.'

The thought had occurred to Libby that Luca had finally come to his senses. Rita was worth a tear up. There was no point in worrying her friend, so Libby held back her conclusions. Jesus, those cousins were so bloody spoilt. 'Let's leave the spat firmly with them. What you gonna wear? How about that black dress with the white collar? Very Dusty Springfield. Shall I pile your hair up?'

Rita grinned at her friend. If this was what having a sister was like, she'd have had ten of them. 'I've got something to show you, Lib. Close your eyes.' Rita quickly pulled off her working clothes to change into the secret outfit. She slipped on a pair of ankle strap shoes and asked Libby to turn around.

'Holy shit, Reet, you look fan-tas-teeque! Where did you … oh, let me guess, your mum made it.'

Rita twirled around unsteadily with her arms outstretched. The silk-sleeved, ebony jump suit was sprinkled with tiny hand- stitched red roses, perfect for St Valentine's Day. It was stunning. Libby burst into tears.

'Libby, what's wrong?' Rita threw herself at her friend,

astounded to see her like this, especially as she never cried, unless it was anything to do with dogs.

'I've never seen you dressed up like this, Reet. You look beautiful. Let me blow my nose. You won't want snot all over your new jumpsuit.'

The friends laughed, their excitement building for the evening ahead. They agreed she should leave her hair down as it was always tied back, perhaps curl it a bit more, and to wear a little more make up. Libby said she'd come down ten minutes before they leave for a final inspection. 'Blackstock won't know what's hit 'em, Reet. I've got an idea. Keep your coat on until it's your turn to play. At least if your singing's off key, your outfit will blow their socks off.'

Chapter 21

The Alderman Public House had been in existence for at least four hundred years. It's history and former clientele made for exciting reading: there had been at least one royal personage to stay as well as the arrest of an infamous criminal on the run from the law. Its current incarnation consisted of several separate snugs on one side of the bar, while the other comprised of a wide, open space, a low wooden performance platform at the far end with ample dancing space in front of it. Several tables, chairs and benches were dotted around the large wood-burning stove which squatted in the corner.

Loud conversation filled the space as the last gathering was at Christmas and there was always a lot to catch up on. Although the main event wasn't until eight o'clock, an impartial observer may have reported that for the forty strong group, the party was already underway.

Isabella loved a reunion. Chloe and Cherry were catching up with Sydney and the twins from the manor; Tom and Karen stood alongside Ethan, Louis and Hannah, parents and children happily getting along; Finn ran around excitedly with a couple of his school friends under his sister's watchful eye. The equipment had been rigged up and tested, while Nathan made last minute adjustments.

Isabella sat next to Hattie and Donna who were in update mode. It was a shame Gemma couldn't be there, but it was probably for the best. Joe looked better, less tired, and was chatting to Alison Redwing, which was itself an event as Alison never went into a pub. An unusually quiet Libby sat with Rita whose guitar case leant conspicuously beside her. If Isabella didn't know better, she'd say the duo were up to something. Rita was almost unrecognisable, with her sparkly eyes and her hair stylishly curled. Rik and Vincent were once again deep in conversation for which she was grateful. They obviously had a lot in common which made her feel unaccountably happy. She and Rik nodded to each other in greeting but had said no more.

The band members had assembled on the stage with various instruments taken up. The sounds of a trumpet parp, guitar string twangs and a tinkle of keys alerted the crowd to the start of proceedings. Nathan tapped on the mic.

'Evening all. It's great to see the tribe, and of course, all our friends who have braved the weather. It's going to be a cracking night, especially as we've got a full band. For your delectation and delight, three brave young women, obviously with nothing better to do (laughs) are going to sing two songs apiece: first a ballad, followed by something a bit livelier. Our last audition was donkeys years ago, so if you've forgotten, or for those of you who don't know how it works, the loudest applause determines the winner.'

Two of the hopefuls waited nervously by the stage, not quite chatting but united by a sense of impending terror. The first to be announced was Claudia Huxtable who was dressed in the most revealing outfit Blackstock had seen in centuries. She tottered to the stage, ignoring Nathan's nervous smile and launched into an interesting version of Katy Perry's *Immortal Flame* accompanied by the band. It was clear she was used to performing, but sadly it didn't extend to her voice, although Rosa and Jodie's harmonies did much to disguise it.

Isabella thought she acquitted herself well under such scrutiny and as a result had received generous applause. Claudia's confidence increased considerably by the warm response. Her gutsy rendition of Lady Ga Ga's *Judas,* which unusually made Nathan flush scarlet, received a huge cheer. News had got around that he had called off the fledgling romance. Isabella was therefore surprised Claudia had shown up at all. It was hard not to admire the young woman's not-so-subtle dig at her conceited nephew. That may well have prompted the rousing reception rather than any great ability to sing.

Next up was Evie Lowe of whom Isabella was fond. She deserved a medal for working with Deidre as she was infinitely more creative at flower arranging than her domineering mother although she scarcely got the opportunity to show it. When the band struck up, the poor thing had her eyes closed to begin with, such were her nerves, but it soon became obvious that Evie's singing was a notch above Claudia's, especially as her choices were well-known with the audience. Perhaps *I Will Always Love You* was a little ambitious, but Evie raised the bar with

Brown-eyed Girl and had the crowd up dancing. In fact, you might say she almost enjoyed the experience, but it was doubtful Evie would be rushing to repeat it any time soon.

Isabella and Hattie smiled at each other, as much in relief that they weren't putting themselves through such torture. Isabella wondered what Rik made of it, but he seemed quite content to sip his pint of ale while observing the proceedings. She noticed how his foot tapped in time to the music and wondered why it surprised her. Isabella was able to detect a slight resemblance between the brothers. Perhaps it was the way Rik tilted his head? She longed to talk to him, to discover more about his life, to hear his voice, but her attention was pulled back to a hush. Rita had taken to the stage with a guitar held by a strap across her body. The band had left her to it, keen to grab a waiting drink as apparently, Rita didn't require backing.

Hattie nudged Isabella, nodding over in Luca's direction. He looked extremely uncomfortable, shifting from foot to foot while trying to appear normal. Nathan, however, was grinning from ear to ear. As the volume of voices fell away, a silence so large emerged, you could hear the ancient roof timbers creak. Rita looked stunning in her glittering jumpsuit and tiny sandaled feet perched on the stool. Isabella stole a glance at Alison who was clutching a glass of sparkling elderflower tightly by her chest and looked as if at any moment soon would burst into tears, the poor woman.

Without fuss or announcement, Rita began to tune her guitar by ear as naturally as if she did this on stage every day. Strumming quietly for a moment or two, she began to sing, looking out towards the crowd, and at no-one in particular, and yet everyone there could have sworn she was singing just for them. Isabella felt the hairs on the back of her neck stand up as the words to *Moon River* swept her away. Rita's voice was so simple, so natural that the sound waves vibrated inside the chambers of her heart. Isabella's eyes brimmed with tears which was so startling, she brushed them quickly away but noticed she wasn't the only one to do so.

When the song ended, the absence of noise was deafening. The entire crowd had been temporarily transported somewhere other-worldly and the emotion was palpable. As if on cue, wild applause erupted as Rita stood up to take a tiny bow. Nathan ran to the stage, swinging her around like a doll as the rest of the band joined in congratulation. Hartburn had found their new singer.

While the cheering faded into excited chatter, Rita, now surrounded by the rest of the band, asked them to accompany her for the second song. Luca was still shaken by what he had just witnessed. When Rita had got to the 'Huckleberry friend' line, she had looked right at him, as only he could possibly know what she meant, His heart was thumping so hard, Luca was grateful for the furore around him. He didn't even care that Nathan had made a grab for Rita as he wished he'd done the same.

Rita had passed around several music sheets and the band re-took their instruments. The mood was by now so elevated, they couldn't wait to get cracking. Luca was amazed that Rita had chosen the song *Sir Duke*, as not only did he love Stevie Wonder, but the horn section was brilliant. It was a clever choice as it highlighted Louis and

Seth's talent. A moment later, Nathan counted them in, and everyone was on their feet. Rita sang out, tapping her right hip with a tambourine as she danced around the stage, grinning at Louis and Seth on trumpet and saxophone. When the song ended, the room erupted with wild cheers, whistles and applause. Luca could not stop himself from laughing. Rita looked completely at home: she was made for entertaining.

Within half an hour, the happy crowd were tucking into baskets of spicy chicken, falafel, thick-cut, triple cooked chips and dips, talking and laughing. There was no need to ask if Rita wanted to join the band as what was the point in waiting? Rosa ran through the playlist, thrilled that in place of her spoilt cousin, Hartburn had gained a terrific talent and who, by everyone's reckoning, was an extremely nice person.

By the time Luca managed to get to Rita, it was almost time to saddle up again as the pub was by now full and the volume of human voices almost too loud to speak over. Her cheeks were flushed, and her eyes sparkled like the sun on the sea. In that moment, Luca saw how beautiful Rita was, not just because she looked fabulous, but she had chosen her second song for the band. Rita could easily have shown herself and her voice off, but the song was for everyone to share an equal part in it. The *Moon River* song *had* to be for him. It was the same song she'd been humming for two years but he couldn't place it until that very moment. By the end of the evening, Luca was in awe at Rita's musicality, timing and the sound of her truly uplifting voice.

Chapter 22

It was midnight. Hattie had joined Isabella in her kitchen for a mug of barley cup and was soaking her sore feet in a bowl of warm, salty lavender water. Isabella let the cold flagstones cool her aching digits.

'My, oh my, I haven't danced that much in years. What a night! I think it'll go down in Blackstock history, don't you, Bella? Did you see Joe and Nell, waving their arms in the air and swinging each other around?'

Isabella laughed. 'Joe loves to dance but he was really going for it. Don't you think it was a release? It's been an emotional time.'

'You're right. It must have felt good to let go at last. It was lovely to see him dancing with Cherry and Chloe.'

Isabella nodded, blowing at her cup. 'What did you make of Rita?'

'Amazing, and such talent. She's quiet, unassuming even, but not shy. Rita has a gift of seeing people as they are, behind the mask. I'm sure she could sing professionally but I'll bet you it wouldn't be of interest. Singing must have been a constant friend to Rita throughout her life. How else could she know such a variety of music? And she has such passion. It comes straight from the heart.'

'I hadn't thought of it that way, Hattie. She's a little like Rosa, and Luca to a certain extent, innately musical. Nathan's got talent but he's mainly there to show off. I wonder what will happen now?'

'What do you mean, Bella?'

Isabella was quiet for a moment. She had seen the entire drama unfold, a classic Shakespearian play, inevitably to end in heartbreak. But for who? 'Luca and Nathan both want Rita. I was watching Luca earlier. Once he got over his embarrassment, when Rita started singing, I could feel his heart bursting. Maybe it's because I love him so much. But I fear for him. Nathan's had a bee in his bonnet about his cousin ever since they were little, no matter how much Luca tries to play it down.'

'I hope it doesn't end in tragedy, Shakespeare or not. Now, what about Rik?'

Isabella put down her empty cup. 'What do you mean, 'what about Rik?''

'Oh, come on, Bella, don't be coy. Even Father Martin could feel the heat rising. You two have loose ends, that's obvious.'

Isabella felt her cheeks colour. It had been so crowded in the pub, and extremely loud, but Rik had managed to find a space in which to dance with her to *Something*, a personal favourite of both, it transpired. It felt as if they were alone, and he was so close to her, she could feel his ribs expand and contract. Rik smelt vaguely of the sea. Isabella knew exactly what George Harrison meant when he wrote that song.

After the dance, he had disappeared back into the crowd, and then had left with Rupert and Penelope for the manor. She hoped no one else had noticed them but should have known nothing would have escaped Hattie's searchlight. 'Maybe we have. Anyway, let's talk about that tomorrow as I really need to get to bed. Lunch is at three o'clock, so let's expect them at two, shall we?'

'So, just to confirm, we've got Tom and Karen, Joe, Nell and Rik. It'll be an odd number with Neil, but Gemma does take over, so it's nice for him to fly solo. With Rita, Libby, Luca and us, that makes eleven.'

'Nell and Karen are bringing puddings. I told Joe we'll make a traditional roast as it's his and Luca's favourite. Come over at midday as I need a lie in.'

Nathan's clothes were strewn across the bedroom floor. He sat up in bed, phone on his lap, wondering if he should send his text to Rita. She was probably asleep by now as it had gone one o'clock. Adrenalin was still pumping through his veins after the evening's events. It was the wildest night The Alderman had ever seen, and probably the most profitable, as Nancy had doubled the usual fee.

The band unanimously agreed to pay Rita as she had been without doubt the star of the show and was now a member of Hartburn, thanks to him. Jodie insisted she take the seventy quid as she'd worked hard for it. Rita had been genuinely shocked, and said it had been a privilege to sing, and to thank everyone for letting her do it.

Nathan was in trouble. The more he saw of Rita, the deeper he was sinking despite doing his utmost to stay afloat. He hadn't 'discovered' her. How could he? But he felt a certain pride at having invited her to audition. Who knew Rita had a voice like that? Her outfit, too, was a total knock-out. He felt genuinely sorry for Claudia as next to Rita, she was a park player. The *Judas* song - well, Nathan had to laugh at that as fair play to her for the dig which he deserved. Luca was right to have insisted he sort it out with her before the gig. Claudia didn't buy his line about being too busy for a relationship, but with a queue of understudies waiting in the wings for her, he was already history.

Luca's face when Rita walked onto the stage was a picture. He looked like he might laugh and cry at the same time, silly git. His cousin had worked next to her for two bloody years! How could he not know Rita had the voice of an angel? The phone burned in his hand. *Maybe I'll send it anyway as she's bound to have her phone switched off. It's only to say congratulations. She can't think I'm hassling her as I'm the one who got her there after all. I'll give it a few days before I ask her out officially. If I don't do it soon, everyone will be after her.*

Nathan pressed the 'send' button, switched off the lights via a remote button on the bedside unit, and within thirty seconds, his snores filled the apartment.

Luca was wide awake. He tried to focus on the night sounds, but Rita's image stubbornly refused to fade; sitting on the stool, legs just about reaching the bar, tiny feet in those sandals, that gorgeous outfit, guitar resting lightly across her body, eyes twinkling like the night sky. But all of that faded into insignificance when she began to sing. Rita's voice gave him goose-bumps. That was one well-kept secret. Maybe he'd pluck up the courage to ask her about the song? He could scarcely wait to see her tomorrow at Isabella's lunch, to sit next to her, to see her lovely face again.

A long-forgotten pain in his heart had joined forces with the holler in his head, finally waking him up to the fact that he, Luca Santini, was in love with Rita Redwing.

Chapter 23

Isabella had bathed, dressed and breakfasted by nine o'clock. She had slept soundly for the most part until she was awakened by her own cry out to something out of reach, a silhouette, fading from view. This strange, unnerving sensation followed Isabella throughout the morning as she carried out the tasks of laying the table, preparing vegetables and tiding up the cottage. The Sunday morning sky, a thick sheet of fossilised grey, cast a gloom over Blackstock and beyond which increased her uneasiness. There was no doubt snow was on its way. Isabella concluded that a good dose of uplifting music to shift this mood was a wise move, as by mid-morning, Dean Martin had worked his magic.

She decided to call Tom. Whitecross may have been a mere twenty miles east, but it was easy to get stuck in a sudden snow dump. Apparently, the snow was forecast for the evening, which meant that he and Karen still very much wanted to join Isabella but planned to make tracks at around five o'clock. Isabella smiled. It seemed that everyone was coming, despite the weather.

In the quiet hour before Hattie arrived, Isabella found what she'd been looking for: a CD, tucked between the pages of the hypnotherapy book, which held the recording of a past-life regression she underwent many years ago. At that time, she and Hattie had attended a talk by a clinical hypnotherapist about the discovery of life between lives. Hundreds of patient sessions had been compiled and collated over decades, revealing startling similarities. Patterns emerged, describing how, after death, each soul reconnects with its 'cluster group' to review the past life, and to help discover their purpose in the next life. Isabella had been so interested by the talk she booked a session to find out more.

The fire's warmth enveloped her as a reposeful voice came through the speakers. She was back in the quiet room which had overlooked the sea, lying comfortably on a couch, her consciousness hovering in the hinterland between the past and the present. The conversation ignited the memory of the visit.

'Recall the face of your wife from your previous life. Who is this person in this life?'

Isabella clicked off the stereo. Now she was sure.

Hattie put her empty mug back on the coaster and leaned back into the armchair. 'How about that? The mystery of the face is finally revealed.' A massive grin revealed two slightly overlapping but endearing front teeth Hattie had no wish to straighten. She studied the face of her dearest friend, witnessing a spectrum of emotions, from shock to release to concern, flash across Isabella's face as she described the recording. No wonder, as it was a brave soul who came literally face-to-face with their unfinished business. Poor Bella. There was nowhere to run. 'How do you feel?'

'Actually, it's a relief. If I don't think about what might be, the situation will resolve itself, won't it? When I first saw Rik at the funeral, my heart recognised him, but my head had forgotten which isn't surprising, as it was so long ago. At some level, he knew it too, I am sure of it.'

Rik knew alright. His reaction to Isabella at the church and later at the pub, confirmed it. 'Will you talk to him about it? I'm sure Rik won't be surprised or dismissive. After all, he has been amongst various civilisations and peoples whose beliefs often encompass reincarnation in one form or another. Oh, I meant to show you something.' Hattie dashed off to the kitchen, returning in a flash with a magazine in her hand. 'I knew I'd heard of the name *Rik Faulkner* before. He writes articles for various magazines, this one included. Have a look.'

Isabella glanced at the cover, *The Environmentalist*, scanning the article's title, *Islanders Get Creative*. It made sense. Joe had mentioned Rik's Cambridge credentials, how he'd been a map maker, now living somewhere remote, so there was plenty to write about. 'Thanks, Hattie. There's a website. Shall we have a quick look?'

Isabella and Hattie sat at the table waiting expectantly for the website to open. Two seconds later, there he was, a small picture of a woollen-clad Rik Faulkner, editor of *Stories from the Small Isles*. Isabella laughed as Hattie read the description:

'Coille. Our tiny island floats contentedly between Skye and Mull on the west side of the Atlantic Ocean. She may be the most petite and inaccessible of the Small Isles but oh! what treasure to be discovered: ancient woodland and pine forest; rugged moorland; rich fertile soil; spectacular beaches; abundant flora and fauna; standing

stones; faeries. Her environmental credentials, in part due to the Gulf Stream's temperate effects, enable forty-two humans (soon to be forty-three) to inhabit various crofts and parcels of land. We cultivate and sell our flourishing sustainable vegetable crop to neighbouring islanders and export our art and wool crafts…'

'Don't think I'll be going there any time soon. Trust Rik to live on the most out-of-the-way island. I love the photo of him and the beautiful dog, though. A sheep dog, I think. This certainly fits the profile of educated-loner-adventurer-environmentalist type, doesn't it, Hat? And possible heartbreaker. We don't know about Rik's romantic history, but he must have one, mustn't he?'

Hattie sensed Isabella's relief at the island's geographical location. Her friend would inevitably use its inaccessibility as an excuse not to go if the opportunity arose, but this wasn't the time to challenge her. 'I'll leave that bit of digging to you, my dear Bella. Now, shall we get these spuds in the oven?'

Chapter 24

Isabella was in her element. So far, the afternoon had passed off tremendously well. Blackstock Manor's tender grass-fed beef and Hattie's splendid cashew and chestnut mushroom loaf, served with honey-roasted carrots, parsnips, cauliflower cheese, dark leaf greens, huge Yorkshire puddings doused in a delicious gravy, were greeted with cheers. The desserts were equally heralded, as was the cheeseboard, which was slowly being nibbled away as the wintry afternoon wore on.

Isabella was pleased that Neil had decided to join them. He may have married the most beautiful of the Burnett daughters, but Gemma was the most challenging, and had led poor old Neil a merry dance. But here he was, looking so relaxed, chipping into the chatter which was a nice change. Talk was mainly about the success of the St Valentine's gig, how Joe's knees were killing him, and how many throats were still sore from the racket they made.

'I can't believe you know every word to *American Pie*, Karen. What a song for an encore.' Tom's face was suffused with love for his new partner whose crimson colouring could not be passed off as a hot flush.

'It's such a relief to know I'm not the only lyric nerd. Rita knows what I mean. It's something that starts at a young age, doesn't it?'

The colour of Rita's cheeks reflected her unease as the centre of everyone's attention, but she hid it well. 'It was so generous of the band to play it, Karen. But as the chords are easy, and the musicians so good, I knew they'd indulge me. So many people sang along.'

'But you weren't the only star of the show, Reet. Apparently, there were quite a few women asking about your jumpsuit. Your ma's going to be busy.'

There were nods at Libby's assessment. It was another piece of good news. This was the first time Nell had been around a dinner table with Rita. She was generally a happy bystander, but her motherly instincts were strong, and she was curious to know more about this young woman with big talent. 'Where does your mum make these fine clothes? She must need quite a bit of equipment.'

'Oh, no, Nell. Quite the opposite in fact. She has an ancient Singer machine and does much of it by hand. Her bedroom isn't big enough for more, but even if it were, I'm not sure she'd be into new gadgets. And of course, we can't make too much noise in the flat because of the other tenants, so Mum does her sewing during the day.'

Rita's humility had touched the group. It was Joe now, who was curious as to what she thought about her new status in the deli. 'It's great to do what you love and get paid for it. With a bit of luck, Luca might even pay you a bit more.'

They laughed, as Luca and Isabella were known for their generosity.

'It was really embarrassing as I was given seventy pounds last night. Jodie said I was now a full member of the band, and this was my share. I'm going to put it towards a new mattress for the sofa bed.'

'You don't have your own bedroom, Rita?' Karen was the mother of a daughter whose welfare continued to torment her, although she was finally learning to ease off. The thought of this lovely young woman living without comfort hit her square in the heart.

'It's fine, honestly, Karen. I'm always the last to bed, so it's easier to use the living room. The Redwings are snug as bugs in Larkspur House, aren't we Lib?'

'Yeah, the flats are great. In fact, compared to what we've lived in before, I'd say they are a luxury. Although I can't wait to move into Spinner's Cottage, Isabella, thanks to your generosity. And you too, Hattie, for offering to train me as assistant manager. You may not know this Karen, but Isabella and Hattie have been our sponsors since we came to Blackstock. It's part of the agreement to attend certain classes and courses when you move into Larkspur House. To have such people looking out for us is amazing. I can't imagine ever leaving such a loving community.'

Karen smiled in relief. 'It's so interesting how things work out. At the same time as Hannah left for university, Ellie, my best friend, unexpectedly moved away. When she suggested I take over her meditation group, I was stunned, and not a little nervous, but it has turned out to be the best thing I've ever done. The group has become a close community, a family you could say.'

'And now you have the lovely Tom, too. The group sounds interesting, Karen. Have you room for one more?

Hold on to your hat, Hattie, but I'm thinking of exploring life outside of Blackstock, and just might make it to Whitecross.'

Karen blushed to the roots of her fair hair, flattered to be asked. 'We'd be delighted to welcome you, Isabella, although you don't exactly look as if you need another group.'

Everyone laughed. Tom knew what his sister-in-law was getting at. He was thrilled to see Isabella and Karen making a connection. Perhaps they would become friends? 'It'll do you good to go to someone else's group for a change, Bella. I can vouch for the cakes (laughs). We visited Karen's friends a few weeks ago at their gorgeous Welsh retreat. Can you believe Hamish Bell was there, apparently a close friend of Ellie's? It turns out that her husband, George Wood, built my house.'

Karen blushed at Tom's enthusiasm for her best friends. 'How about your family, Libby, are you close?'

Libby fiddled with the hem of her blouse. Karen's question deepened the colour in her already hot cheeks from hearing Hamish Bell's name. Talk about six flippin' degrees of separation. Like Rita, she wasn't used to the spotlight. Keeping her head down had become a necessary habit, but life in Blackstock was gradually rebuilding her confidence and challenging her previous experience that not everyone was out to get something. Here it was safe to speak out, and Libby liked Karen. There was something comforting about her.

'I've got two brothers somewhere, that's if they're not dead by now. Last I heard, one was dealing drugs. The other one tried to get me to see him a while back, but I said I didn't want anything to do with him. Callum taught me to drive. I've been a mini cab driver amongst other things in my short life, even though sometimes it feels like I've lived forever. I've also been a thief, but Hattie knows all about that. She said I'd be able to spot the shoplifters before they get in the door.'

There was much laughter at this confession although Libby pulled no punches. Reflecting on this exchange, Neil thought about his daughter, and how little hardship Juliet had endured and yet was still unhappy. Maybe she had yet to find her purpose in life? As if reading his mind, Hattie's question took Neil by surprise.

'What about you, Neil. Now your children are off hand, how will you spend your quieter years?' There was more merriment, as it was obvious who cracked the whip in that family.

'As it happens, I do a little bit of sketching here and there. Nothing much, just the odd thing that catches my eye. I used to love art at school. I had a great teacher who encouraged me to take it further. My dad said there wasn't much of a living to be had in it, so that was that.'

Rik sat motionless while quietly observing the group. It often happened that when sitting around a fire, or breaking bread in community, wishes and dreams rose to the surface to be shared and encouraged. He had witnessed such happenings on many occasions throughout his travels.

'There are several gifted artists on the island willing to share their talents, Neil. Why don't you come and visit us sometime? I'm sure we can find a few jobs for you to do in exchange?'

Neil's embarrassed reaction confirmed it. Maybe he would go. Why not? He could feel the influence of

Isabella's guests sinking into him: the ambiance, the fact that people were listening to each other; the kindness. He had managed to get a full sentence out without having his words snatched away. It would have been easy to sit at home after last night's party, but he was so glad to be here. The memory of his art teacher's voice, like a ghost from a distant past, floated through his mind: *you must take every opportunity to express your gifts and talents boys, otherwise they shrivel and die, which is the greatest tragedy.*

Isabella looked at her brother-in-law. It was startling to think that after being in each other's lives for so long, she didn't know him at all. If only Gemma could see her husband in this light. She wondered how many couples truly encouraged each other's independence. Hattie and Rik were magicians, dream-makers whose wands revealed a person's true nature to themselves. They asked the type of questions whose answers usually got lost in the static. Neil caught her attention and winked. This was turning into a most interesting afternoon.

Luca had been quietly absorbing the conversation. He was seated opposite Rita, surreptitiously watching her throughout the afternoon: the way she cut her food into tiny pieces; how she waited until everyone else finished speaking until she spoke; the hint of a dimple on her left cheek; the soft contour of her top lip. A couple of glasses of Isabella's excellent Shiraz had loosened him up. They were here together, without Nathan.

'How about you, Rita. Are the Redwings taking flight any time soon?'

Rik's enquiry straightened certain spines around the

table. Luca was on high alert. Rita blushed at the unexpected nature of Rik's question, but such was the warmth and friendliness of the guests, she decided to speak out. 'I read about The Sunrise Trust's house in Blackstock five years ago. Even though there was a long waiting list, somehow, I knew Larkspur was going to become our home and we'd finally be safe, so I wrote to them explaining our circumstances. It *is* home for me and Finn, but I think my mother still loves Finn's dad. He's due for parole so I expect she'll hear from him sometime soon. Until it happens, I try not to think about it.'

Luca's heart slowed almost to a stop. Nathan had said Rita didn't know who her father was but said nothing about the family leaving. 'Couldn't you adopt Finn? Stop him going back to…'

'I don't think that's possible, Luca. Alison is Finn's mother, and she is now doing well. No court in the land would allow it.'

Isabella added her weight to Hattie's on the subject which promptly brought it to a close. She sensed her beloved nephew's growing anxiety as it was shared by the group, but it would be a shame to spoil a blissful afternoon with speculation. Isabella suggested they have coffee and brandy by the fire, as time was getting on, and Tom wanted to get Karen home before the snow fell.

Chapter 25

As the afternoon shadows closed in, the guests relocated to the living room where they spread out comfortably around the fire on sofas, chairs and on the rug. Rik sat naturally upright in the centre of the room, a modern-day chieftain in his fleece-lined check shirt, tartan waistcoat and thick woollen socks. He seemed happy to answer questions about island life: yes, the weather could be rough; yes, there was a lot of work to do in and for the community; no, he never got bored or lonely even though he had no television. 'I've learnt many skills, such as lambing, sailing, coppicing and dry-stone walling. I mostly work on the woodland and grow vegetables in polytunnels which are sold to other islanders.'

'We read one of your articles in *The Environmentalist*, about island life, Rik. You have a captivatingly poetic style. No wonder people are flocking to the islands.'

Rik coloured at Hattie's review. 'Thank you. I write a few articles and have been asked to write a book about my travels. It is possible to live an affordable, sustainable life if you can adjust to the climate and have few wants. Interestingly, the number of women crofters has doubled in the last five years and so has the demand for woodland crofts. The movement towards this way of life has already begun.'

'Do you ever get lonely, Rik?' Nell was as keen as the rest of the group to find out if he had a partner, but so far, he hadn't mentioned it, and the others were too polite to ask.

'I live with a very demanding but most affectionate lady called Lyla.'

Eighteen eyeballs rolled towards Isabella whose face matched the colour of the Shiraz.

Rik's eyes glistened in amusement. 'She's a working dog, my constant companion who keeps me nimble. No one who reads is ever lonely, and there is a small community centre, and a pub. There are regular inter-island ceilidhs as most people play the fiddle, squeeze box or Celtic whistle.'

'What does that sound like?' As Rik produced a small whistle from the inside of his waistcoat, Joe smiled. My little brother carries the world in those pockets, he concluded, feeling proud that Rik had so many talents and looked so at home in the group.

'I made this one from a piece of maple. Shall I play a little for you?'

A universal 'yes please' echoed around the fire-lit room. Rik made a few whistles to warm-up, after which he played a tune that was familiar and timeless, almost a lament, but far too beautiful to be melancholic. It suited the mood of this very special afternoon. After much clapping, Rik said he'd play one more before the weather set in. Just a few seconds in, Rita recognised the tune, *Mary of Dungloe*, and sang along in that heavenly voice so recently revealed. She was joined by Karen who, thanks to a couple of very nice glasses of Isabella's fine wine and years of unconsciously imbibing her daughter's eclectic musical tastes, felt comfortable enough to risk her voice in public.

Isabella and Hattie stole a glance at each other in acknowledgement. Everyone, including themselves, were changed by the weekend. Nell and Joe had tears streaming down their faces while Neil and Tom looked on affectionately, perhaps a little envious of Joe's ability to openly express himself.

Luca's lenses had zoomed in on Rita. He had sufficiently recovered from the shocking news of Trevor Jenkins' parole to have been drawn back to the sound of Rita, the songbird. He could scarcely wait until tomorrow morning at eight o'clock, when they'd sit together over milky coffee and toast and plan their day. Maybe then she'd tell him about her family? She may even have taken on board his suggestions to adopt her brother. Isabella often said how every cloud had a silver lining which may have been a cliché, but right now Luca was willing to go along with it.

Such were the magical stories of life on the isle, Nell announced that she, Joe and the girls would be spending this year's holiday with Rik, if he didn't mind. Hattie threatened to sell her Norfolk cottage and buy a croft, but no one took it seriously, although knowing Hattie, wild horses wouldn't stop her visiting. Libby and Rita were happy to be invited as it made them feel ever more part of the family.

As Tom and Karen were waved off, the rest of the group cleared up in no time at all. One by one, the friends and relations bade fond farewells, sorry to be leaving the intimacy of Isabella's snug cottage, but the journey was for them at least a short one. Neil gave his sister-in-law such a hug, Isabella's alarm bells started ringing. 'Is everything okay at home, Neil?'

'Not really, Bella. It's been such a great afternoon, so friendly. All we seem to do is argue. I think it'll ease off now Juliet has gone to her aunt. I don't know how Gemma will be without her. They're as thick as thieves. Thanks for asking, sweetheart, and thanks for a lovely meal. Rik's an interesting bloke. He's given me something to think about.' He kissed her affectionately before she waved him off, not a little sadly, as soft, fat snowflakes bounced off the shoulders of his woollen overcoat.

Rik was the last to leave, not yet having got to his boots out in the utility room. He turned to face Isabella. 'Would it be inconvenient if I stayed a little longer? Rupert and Penelope aren't expecting me for supper as I told them I'd be well-fed.'

Isabella laughed at this, as she was known for her sumptuous table, and was pleased he felt able to ask. She had already planned to offer him a glass of something warming before he went on the hike back to the manor. 'Of course not. I was just about to have a brandy, or in fact, I have a very nice whisky, if you'd like to join me?'

Rik nodded in the affirmative and took himself back into the living room. After restocking the stove, he moved towards the oak-lined walls to study Isabella's extensive book collection. A series of *Everyman* classics sat next to a row of art books: Titian, The Dutch School and Anthony Gormley. His attention spiked at a few surprising titles: *Seven Years in Tibet*; *The Ring of Bright Water*; *Philosophy for*

Polar Explorers; biographies of Gertrude Bell, Janet Frame Shephard, Franklin, St Exupéry.

Her film collection too, was impressive: Truffaut, Bergman, Fellini. He had forgotten how much he loved *The 400 Blows* and had been haunted ever since by the final image of the lost boy looking directly into the camera. He knew what that felt like, the remembrance of which sent a shiver through his body. Isabella, meanwhile, had silently returned with a tray on which sat a full bottle of *Talisker* with two cut-glass tumblers and was met with a raised eyebrow and a smile. She was the most interesting woman he'd met in a long, long time.

They sat opposite each other, separated by the fire. Isabella felt her stomach churn as Rik watched her take a sip of whisky. She wasn't usually given to nerves, but Isabella could not recall a time when she'd been alone with a man who excited her this much. How to react? *Just be yourself.* This thing has its own energy, of that she was certain, so best to wait and see. 'So, Rik, is your visit turning out as you expected?'

Rik studied Isabella's features, taking in the glow on her cheeks, her fine, coffee-coloured eyes, her full red lips. How to answer such a question? How could he know his brother's family would beguile him with their open, loving ways? Could he have predicted that this small English town would feel so familiar? Why did he feel so protective of Libby and Rita, strangers from different shores? How did he know he would meet a woman he felt sure he had known before and who would break his heart when he left?

'The short answer is no, but as I am no stranger to

154

hospitable hearths in inhospitable lands, I am heartened by the welcome I've had. It was unexpected.' His long fingers wrapped themselves gracefully around the tumbler as he slowly swirled the golden liquid, lost in his thoughts for a moment. When he looked up, Isabella's eyes were resting on his. 'And you, Isabella, has anything unexpected happened this weekend?' The question was deliberately loaded, but Rik was intrigued to hear her reply. It wasn't just his arrival that was jogging this community about, that was clear. Observing the family over dinner, it appeared there had been much change of late, and Isabella was at the core of it.

'Yes, it has. Rita's singing has stunned us all. She has worked beside Luca and me all this time and we didn't know she could sing so beautifully. There's going to be an almighty row between Luca and his cousin over her.' A pause. 'And now, Rik, you are here.' Isabella, true to her nature, fired the arrow right back. This was what he wanted to hear, she was sure of it, as sure as she had been about anything in her life before. Isabella wanted to tell him about the book and the regression but chose to bide her time. If she was wrong, it was best not to unlock that secret.

The lean, inscrutable man got to his feet, gently replaced his glass and moved towards her. He reached for her hand as if to steady her as she rose. They were so close to each other that Isabella caught her breath, the crackle and sizzle of burning logs the only other sound in the universe. Rik took her face so gently in his hands, and kissed her eyes, cheeks, brow and finally, her waiting lips. Smiling now, Isabella took Rik's hand and led him to her bedroom.

Chapter 26

The steady, peaceful waxing and waning of Rik's breath comforted Isabella as she lay her enclosed in his long, sinewy arms under the heavy duvet. For centuries, poets, songwriters and storytellers have described love as stars colliding, a force of nature, love unsought, eternal, animal passion. And yet for Isabella, all of it and none of it applied. There were no words to describe how she felt. Whatever was going on, she was so happy it was happening to her.

Rik stirred and looked surprised to see a lover in his arms. He smiled sleepily, kissed Isabella's mouth and raised himself up. While he was in the bathroom, Isabella got out of bed and wrapped a silk dressing-gown around her. The soft fabric amplified her voluptuous body which had itself been properly awakened by Rik's loving hands. She went downstairs to put another couple of logs into the stove, to lock the utility door, and to make tea. She didn't hear Rik enter the kitchen through the noise of boiling water, especially as he moved so quietly. He slid his arms around her waist, pulling her to him, took a deep breath of her scent and whispered, 'Take a look out of the window.'

Isabella pulled up the blind to reveal through the darkness

a thick blanket of snow which had covered the garden and the landscape beyond in just a few hours. She could not have wished for better weather to complete this blissful time with Rik. Intuitively, she knew there were not going to be many days like these. She turned to face him. 'Will you stay with me? Tell Rupert to expect you tomorrow?'

Rik laughed. 'You mean, you're not releasing me back into the wild just yet? I was led to believe you were a hard woman.'

They laughed together as they knew he would stay.

The couple spent a luxurious evening by the fire, listening to Celtic folk music and ate a supper of olive bread, cheese and cold beef. Rik finished the chocolate nut torte while Isabella made a pot of jasmine tea.

'You have made a beautiful home, Isabella. The Scots call it *cosagach*, or *coorie*, depending on who in the tourist board is writing the copy. Lately it appears to have been hijacked by the fickle UK trendsetters. I can see why your family love to be here with you.'

'Thank you. My home is important to me, perhaps too important and not such a good thing. Although now you've seen my guilty secrets, you may not be so impressed by my pretence of a simple lifestyle.'

'No, I think a copper bath and sumptuous bedroom would definitely keep me at home.' They laughed as they navigated their way through each other's sense of humour.

'Why don't I run you a bath, Rik, and then you'll know what the fuss is about? And before you ask, I will decline any offer to get in with you as I fear we'll never get out again.'

Rik confessed later that night, once again wrapped up together, that the experience of his body soaking in warm, scented water while his woman washed his hair was so moving, he'd never forget it. Isabella wasn't quite sure what alarmed her more: that he had called her 'his woman', or that he may never repeat the experience. She concluded that in her current state of physical, sexual and emotional exposure, every word carried tremendous weight. Enjoy the moment, Hattie would say, so she snuggled up as close as possible to 'her man' and fell asleep.

Chapter 27

Rita tramped her way through inches of boot-crunching snow to get to her destination. It had taken her twice as long, and many of the Blackstock shops weren't yet open, if they opened at all. Luca had sent a text telling her not to rush in, but they both knew nothing would stop her getting to the deli. Faulkner's Bakery was already open for business. Isabella's hospitality hadn't kept Joe to his bed this morning. Rita stamped her wellingtons free of snow before the wind blew her tinkling into the shop.

'Rita, 'meter-maid' made it.'

Rita laughed, delighted that Luca had come back to himself from wherever he had been. This time she didn't blush. The colour in her cheeks mirrored the fresh wintry air.

'Morning, Luca. School's closed today even though the main road has been gritted.' Luca reminded her this was her first year in Blackstock snow, and the council only gritted the main roads, leaving the side roads and tracks to their own devices. He had put a few croissants into the oven as he'd guarantee to see at least half a dozen of the regulars, despite the lack of grit. Without asking, Luca brought coffee and two warm *pain au chocolate* to the table.

The deli was able to function for a few days without delivery as their cheeses and meats had a long shelf-life, and the vegetables for the soup were still fresh. With their home-baked pastries and Joe's bread just a stone's throw away, Luca was confident they were able to supply his customers' needs. They'd see how the week panned out. At least if it was quiet, he and Rita could get on with reorganising the stock and researching the café project. She'd come up with some fabulous ideas since he'd given her the iPad which confirmed he'd been on the right track.

Rita sat herself at the table, rubbing life back into her small hands. 'Wasn't it lovely at Isabella's yesterday? She's the perfect host, bringing together so many friendly people. Our little flat felt quite cold after so much warmth and hospitality.'

Luca was noticing just how upbeat and complimentary Rita was, and so polite. It was genuine. He wondered if Alison had instilled such manners in her daughter. If so, it went a long way with people. 'Yeah, Bella is amazing in so many ways. I am lucky to have her. Did I tell you she has signed the flat over to me? I haven't mentioned it to anyone, so…'

'That's marvellous, Luca, a place of your own! Of course, I won't say anything, not even to Libby. That means you'll be able to save a little more for the café project.'

Rita was astute in business and money, that was clear. It was probably having so little that made her careful, although with her mother's talent she wouldn't need to buy anything off the shelf, not like aunt Gemma, or Juliet, or Nathan, come to think of it. This snow would keep his cousin away. Luca felt like singing. 'I forgot to mention we are closing early today. Rupert and Penelope have invited the traders up to the manor for a snowman-building competition, followed by warm cider, hot chocolate and crumpets. Are you up for that? Loads of us are going. Chloe and Cherry are still here as they couldn't get to the station, and so is Syd. Why don't you ask Finn, and your ma, of course?'

Rita was thrilled. Finn was at home from school and would simply love the adventure, and perhaps her mother might venture out to join them. She'd call the flat after coffee to find out. 'That's a brilliant idea. Talking of ideas, I have another with regards the shop. Why don't you have a grand opening when the building work is done? Invite a few special guests, Lord and Lady Huntley perhaps, and get an article in the local paper?'

Was there no end to Rita's talents? Luca saw the scene open before him: a warm summer's evening, twenty guests, champagne. 'Rita, you are a star! I will call Ben today to arrange a site meeting as we are pretty much ready with the plan, aren't we? Then I'll do my figures. If it's feasible, we'll have a goal. Did you know Rupert's son Gus has just qualified as a chef? When I mentioned my idea at the pub, his face lit up. You never know, he may fancy dipping a toe in Bonetti's new venture. Between us and the manor we can supply fresh, organic produce.' Luca danced around the shop, punching the air like *Rocky Balboa* after his victory boxing match.

Rita laughed out loud. She had never seen him so chilled out, and he said 'we' twice.

The doorbell tinkled. It was after nine o'clock. Luca laughed as Jenny Cox tumbled into the shop.

'Yoo hoo! Hello Luca. What a morning out there. Are you going up to the manor later?'

'Yes, Jenny, with Rita and Kit. We're looking forward to taking Terry on. If I remember rightly, he won the competition last time, didn't he?'

'He did, but you're in with a chance this time as Terry's in bed. Done his back in. Your party Saturday night did it. He danced so much the poor soul couldn't walk this morning. We've had to raid the pharmacy for painkillers. It was a fabulous night. Oh, there you are, Rita. It's you I've come to see. No offence Luca.'

Rita and Luca exchanged bemused glances. Jenny Cox was the sort of person who was as inoffensive as an afternoon tea with the W.I.

'Morning Jenny. Nice to see you. How may I help?'

'I know it's short notice Rita, but we're having a do for my brother Gerry's sixtieth birthday this Sunday, and we wondered if you'd come and sing a few songs for him? We'd pay the going rate, of course, we don't expect any favours. They'll be just a small gathering, say thirty or so, at his house near Hertford.'

Rita stood immobile, twisting the strap on her apron, unsure as to whether she heard correctly. Luca's spotlight was shining right on her, reducing her skin colour to a blanched white. 'Umm, may I call you later as I just need to check a few things? What sort of music does your brother like?'

'He'd love that *Moon River* song, and anything by The Carpenters, you know, easy listening. It's at three o'clock, just for a couple of hours, with breaks, of course, but you'd know all about that. Don't worry if you're too busy. Best get back. See you at the manor. Byyyeee.'

Luca led Rita gently back to the chair. He too, was astonished, but she looked as if she was about to faint. Rita truly had no idea how talented she was, and he suspected these offers were about to become a regular occurrence. Assuming she was free on Sunday afternoon, and without a car, the only way to get to Hertford and back at that time was by taxi which would cost and arm and a leg. 'I'll take you. That is, if you'd like me to, if you want the gig. The band are meeting at The Alderman at eleven that morning, which gives us plenty of time to get to Hertford and set up.'

Rita's eyes widened, her colour returning. 'You would? That's so generous of you, Luca. But what do I do? I've never sang on my own in public before. Maybe you could sing with me? I know lots of songs.'

Luca scanned Rita's earnest face, the shade of which had gone from white to vermillion in a blink. She had guts, that's for sure. It took five seconds for him to make up his mind. Things were moving fast, but he was in control, he felt good, and so happy for Rita. There was no way he was going to let her down. 'Okay, let's do it. If you don't have to rush off after the snowman competition, how about coming up to the flat. I'll show you my guitars…'

Despite her inner turmoil, Rita shrieked with laughter. 'That's a come on if ever I heard one.'

It was Luca's turn to blush. 'No, I didn't mean it like that…'

Her beaming smile said it all.

Chapter 28

Isabella's phone had hiccups. For over an hour, it seemed that every trader, friend or family member was trying to get in touch with her: did she want to join the snowman competition; has she got enough wood for the fire; how was the Sunday roast? You name it, she was asked it.

After crying off with a cold, in desperation she switched the phone to silent and looked over at Rik who chuckled quietly over his poached eggs. They decided to spend the day together with the proviso he'd make her a bean stew for dinner, an island delicacy apparently, to which Isabella contentedly acquiesced. Not counting the family, she could not remember the last man to make her dinner.

Blackstock would be deserted by now. An invitation to the manor was not to be sniffed at. The last competition had been great fun, but even if Rik hadn't been here, Isabella would have declined, such was the ache in her back. She must get it sorted out soon. Perhaps she'd join Rik for a walk as it was a fabulous landscape, especially with the branches drooping under the weight of fresh snow, and the fields, untouched by human or dog prints. There may even be deer about.

The sullen skies had been usurped by a magnificently

gleaming sun under which the snow glinted, and blackbirds hopped hopefully. Isabella rightly sensed Rik's need for air, so she suggested they venture out. The cottages bordered on the densely wooded part of the Blackstock estate into which public access was permitted via a footpath. The competition would be at the other end of the estate, so there was little chance of running into anyone.

Rik smiled at Isabella's intuition. It was a little disorienting to be locked away in this bubble, but he didn't want to break the spell Isabella had him under, or at least, he helped to weave. They were no longer strangers. He was sure to get to London tomorrow, but even those plans could be shelved. No business was so urgent that a phone call couldn't resolve it. Isabella and he had melded into something greater than the sum of their individual parts so very quickly, and before too long, he'd be back on the island. They had to make the most of their time together.

An hour later, Rik was in the garden building Isabella her own, bespoke snowwoman. She watched him from the kitchen window as he gathered up mounds of snow, moulding it into the iconic shape but with the addition of a waistline. Isabella's straw hat topped out the ceremony. Every now and again, he turned to look for her, to smile, to wave. Isabella could easily imagine how Rik had been as a boy: eyes shining, bursting with vitality, at home in the outdoors. She took a couple of photos of the snow-bound companions which would later be added to her precious collection of printed, mounted and framed photographs.

Rik sat with Isabella, once again by the fire, nursing steaming mugs of hot chocolate and munching toasted muffins, their own version of a Blackstock Manor treat. Isabella's feet rested on Rik's out-stretched legs while his left hand gently stroked her toes, as if they sat together like this every day. He talked about Alejandro, his partner of five years whom he met in Chile during the final assignment for the institute. They agreed to settle down somewhere off the beaten track and as Rik harboured a desire to live on one of the Scottish islands, Alejandro agreed to give it a try.

'She loved the wildness of Coille and to begin with it went well. We set up the croft, she learned to spin wool, and taught Spanish to the islanders. But she missed Santiago, her work as translator, her family. Alejandro couldn't settle there, it was too open, too few people.'

'How did you feel when she left?'

'Empty, for a long while. She had to go home; it was just a question of when. She loved me but her heart was somewhere else. After eighteen months it became obvious. We decided it best she leave as why waste any more of our lives?'

Since then he'd lived alone. They had both been alone. When Isabella asked him about children, Rik's eyes became grave. 'I'm certain that was another reason why she left. I had testicular cancer as a child which left me infertile. I never had much of a sex drive, which was probably due to the treatment, but I did okay. Alejandro said it didn't matter, that it was me she loved, not me as a father. I thought we might adopt one day although we never discussed it in any detail. I heard a few years later that she'd had a daughter.'

Isabella explored each crag and fissure of Rik's face

expecting to find sorrow, but there was none. 'That must have been difficult.'

'I was happy for her. She wanted to be a mother, and I couldn't give her that naturally. It took a while to get used to her absence. A little of my heart left with her.'

She understood how Joe might think his brother was cold. There was a continent between how he appeared from how he felt. He carried his pain on the inside.

'And you, Isabella, why do you not have children?'

'I assumed I would. I thought that someday I'd meet the father of my children. Like you, my former lover had a child with someone else. But the years went by, the business got busier. There is still a sadness, a mourning which I am learning to acknowledge, with Hattie's help. I've found other ways to be fulfilled: my godchildren, my family and friends, the community. I've never really considered life beyond that.'

They were quiet for a moment, each lost in the memories of past loves. After making a fresh pot of tea, it seemed as if there was more to say. Isabella asked him about his relationship with Joe. Rik confessed to his surprise at his brother's hostility, although he felt the visit had already done much to recover their friendship. Nell was serious about coming to the island and Joe was already being pressed by his daughters for dates.

Isabella talked of her family, and her recent scaling down of work. They were open about everything, including their finances as Rik expressed shock at the amount of his inheritance. He made a modest living from various enterprises and still had quite a bit left from his father's endowment. 'This big injection of cash will make a difference. Hearing you talk about The Sunrise Trust has inspired me to perhaps set up a centre for those looking to try island life, or perhaps offer new experiences to refuge families. There are plenty of ruined barns crying out to be converted. What do you think, Isabella?'

Isabella was flattered he had asked her opinion. She hadn't realised how wonderful it was to share such dilemmas with him, and what it must be like to have a partner to discuss things with, every day, over dinner or a cup of tea. Statistics proved that those living in harmony with a partner lived longer, which was hardly surprising.

'That's a fantastic idea, Rik. I'd like to help Libby and Rita as much as they will allow but they are fiercely independent and proud women. I was thinking of offering Rita's family my other cottage, Needlepoint, but I have held back as I don't want to influence her decision with regards Trevor Jenkins. While the family live at Larkspur House, he is prohibited access. If she lives in the cottage, Trevor could potentially move in. Is that selfish? Am I interfering?'

'The Redwings have a secure place to live for the moment. My guess is Alison Redwing will do what she wants, regardless of her address. As Rita so wisely said, why worry until there is something to worry about?'

Late afternoon crept in, soft and comforting under the fire's homely glow. Isabella told him of Hattie's innovative programmes, of the success of Off Centre, and how she had introduced Isabella to several weird and wonderful esoteric practices. It seemed as if the moment to talk to Rik about the regression was upon them. Isabella took a deep breath. 'Would you mind if I played a recording of a past-life regression I received some years ago? I'd like to know your thoughts about it.'

Rik smiled, and Isabella got up to organise the disc. He listened attentively without speaking until the recording finished and then looked at Isabella. 'I've met many different peoples and encountered various customs over the years, so reincarnation isn't unfamiliar. You and Hattie know this, I assume, from your exposure to various practices. But what is the significance of the information to you? Why do you need to know whose face it is in this lifetime?'

'I wanted to find out if there were patterns of behaviour my soul had carried from previous lives into this one. If we are here to learn and to grow as humans, the information revealed through deep hypnosis can be useful. Who wants to go through life repeating the same mistakes, or missing opportunities because they fear the unknown? The paradox is, we don't know what the patterns are, as we come into this world with a sort of amnesia, a clean slate as it were. There are signs and clues, if we wake up and take notice.

'When I first saw you, I knew yours was the face from that life, albeit a different gender. Let's say it is true, and I treated you so badly back then, now we have met again, I have the chance to put it right, to finish our business, as they say.'

Isabella was flushed with the effort of trying to explain in a way Rik would understand. To say it out loud didn't sound so bad, and she showed him the book that had started the entire journey, which, in her view, had culminated in their meeting. How could they otherwise explain this familiarity between them? In any event, they were here, right now, and what would become of this reunion?

Isabella continued. 'The regression uncovered a few lives in which I had no children. A pattern. Perhaps my time spent with my nieces and nephews, and the subsequent work at the Sunrise Trust has given me what I lacked by not being a mother. It has filled the void. You too, have no children. Maybe this is part of our agreement, to meet at this specific time in our lives, under these circumstances, older, wiser, with the financial and energetic means to help others. To encourage each other to take a different road.'

Rik had remained silent for some time now, a characteristic that no longer troubled her. 'There is no doubt in our mutual feeling, Isabella. When I saw you on Friday, I felt everything drop away, leaving me feeling exposed, vulnerable. In fact, you may have noticed how startled I was, although I hope it went unnoticed. It's an interesting philosophy, and I'm happy to believe it. But what we must talk about, Isabella, is what happens to us now?'

His directness threw her. Rik's intuitive assessment of that first encounter surprised her. In a few days he would be gone, and what then? He'd never consider relocating to Blackstock and neither was she about to ask him as that was not their destiny. What was the alternative? 'What are you asking, Rik?'

'For you to come to Coille, or at least to visit, to see what you make of us. My croft isn't as elegant as this, but I have a kitchen, two bedrooms, and the loo is inside.' They laughed in a way that confirmed this conversation was the right thing to have.

'If it were Hattie sitting here, she'd pack her bags in five minutes flat. But I'm not sure. I need to be here without you to know how my heart feels.'

Rik moved towards Isabella and wrapped her up, aching to feel her heart close to his. This was not a decision to be made in the heat of sexual passion. Life on the island did not suit everyone, but numbers were increasing as people searched for more meaningful lives. This new information only confirmed that there were knots to tie with Isabella, a karmic cycle to complete. Either way, he hadn't bargained for such a feeling of loss.

It felt as if he'd been waiting for Isabella his entire life. Rik had loved Alejandro, but that experience could not be compared to this. 'May I stay another night? I must go to London for a couple of days, and then I have a speaking engagement in Cambridge, at the Polar Institute. After that, there is a dinner at Clare College, a gathering of the alumni.'

Before a stunned Isabella could reply, Rik continued, suddenly emboldened by this rush of feeling. 'Would you meet me there on Friday? You can help me pick out a black dinner suit and come to the lecture as my special guest. My friends have invited me to stay overnight. We'll leave after breakfast. Joe and Nell are organising a farewell lunch on Sunday which I'd like to attend.'

Isabella was once again taken aback by his declaration, and at this invitation. It seemed his feelings mirrored her own. To meet his colleagues, to hear him speak, to enter his world was daunting, to say the least, and yet, the excitement of a glimpse into Rik's life was too big a temptation to pass up, not to mention the delight of spending another few nights lying in his comforting arms. Even if she felt out of her depth, Isabella wouldn't have to say much, she was a good listener and would be so happy to accompany Rik.

'I'd love to come. It sounds so interesting, and I've been planning to go to The Fitzwilliam Museum for ages - that is, if we have time for that, too? I must check with Luca as it's one of my working days, but I'm sure I can swap it. After all, we must make the most of our remaining days together.'

Chapter 29

Joe sat by the fire, lost in a world of his own. Dora was curled up in her basket, keeping watch. The troupe were up at the manor, which was thrilling for Nell as the huge snow drifts meant Chloe and Cherry were stranded at home until the roads were cleared. Her daughters had been moved by their uncle's generous gifts and his willingness to sit with them, trawling through the photograph albums to catch up with their shared history. They decided to put together a photo book for him. Joe was overjoyed to see his girls so enamoured of Rik and in no rush to return to London.

The bakery had sold out of loaves by eleven that morning. By midday, Blackstock was a ghost town, its traders having bunked off to have fun elsewhere. Joe waved his treasured trio farewell, armed as they were with the requisite paraphernalia to dress the snowman. Once they'd gone, he brought his mother's box of letters down to the living room, made himself a large mug of tea, and sighed a long, deep sigh.

If Joe had to describe his mother, the first word that sprung to mind was meticulous. Long before her sight was failing; Marion Faulkner had kept her affairs tidy. Her documents, bills and statements had been neatly filed in alphabetical order and were kept up to date. Rik's cards and letters received the same treatment and were dated chronologically over a thirty-year period until Christmas last.

Joe untied the blue ribbon from the first batch of cards which were from Rik's years working for the Institute. The first was from Greenland: *Mum, I've been lent a copy of Icelandic poet, Jonas Hallgrimsson. I'll track down a book and send it to you. In the meantime, here are two poems for you,* 'I Send Greetings' *and* 'The Solitary.' From Alice Springs: *Mum, I've just been to see some fabulous artwork at the Albert Namatjira Gallery. Glad to read you are feeling better.* From New Zealand: *Mum, try and get a copy of Janet Frame's* 'Rain on the Roof.' *It's fabulous. So good to hear Cherry is doing well. You and Dad must be so proud.'* From Santiago: *Mum, if you want to know what Chile looks like, here is Pablo Neruda's 'Ode to tomatoes…'* and on it went.

In one of his letters, Rik had mentioned Alejandro, and how she was almost ready to join him in Coille. Then a few years later, she must have left the island, *'Yes, Mum, I am very sad, but Alejandro says she must follow her heart and who am I to stop her?'* Rik had signed off every card and letter, *'love to Joe and Nell'* and later *'love to Joe, Nell and the girls'*.

Joe tore another tissue from the box to wipe his sodden face. How had he become so estranged from his brother? Rik and Marion had enjoyed a lasting, loving friendship, one which was sustained regularly through their correspondence. If it weren't for Walter's old-fashioned attitude, Marion may herself have travelled. Instead, she had lived her life vicariously through her youngest son who acted as a comrade, a travelling companion who brought the wonders of the world to her via the pages of his letters.

Although Joe couldn't see what his mother had written, reading between the lines it was clear Rik had managed to keep her worries about him to a minimum. He'd been in Coille alone, without his love and no children of his own, and in not one letter did he complain, or look for pity. Joe realised it was he who had been selfish. He felt ashamed to recall his anger and jealousy at his mother's absence as she cared for her sick son. In Joe's sixteen-year-old opinion, his mother seemed to be unnecessarily fussing at Rik's bedside, every minute of the day. For Rik to discover at such a young age he may never father his own children, let alone survive cancer, must have influenced his choice of career. Why would he stay in England? Rik's desire to explore the great unknown had dominated his young life. After those long, agonising months of treatment and subsequent imprisonment in his sick bed, it must have driven him to plan a life of excitement, of new horizons if he lived. What if he was worried that one day, the cancer came back?

Nell tapped lightly on the living room door carrying a cup of tea. She looked invigorated, rosy-cheeked from the capers in the snow. Dora's intense relief at her mummy's return alerted Nell as just one look at her wet-faced husband with the letters on his lap told her all she needed to know. She held him tight, rocking him, so that he could finally cry for his brother, for his loss of their familial past.

Joe finally came back to himself, blew his nose, and looked at Nell's fresh face. 'Seeing Rik with Chloe and

Cherry this last week broke my heart. For so long I've denied them a relationship with their uncle, saying he was remote, an ice man, putting him down, and there he was, writing heart-felt letters to our mother, sharing stories, poetry, reading about us, and he couldn't have children of his own.'

'My love, Rik's made a good life for himself. He shared that with us yesterday at Isabella's. He must have known even as a teenager he was never cut out for a conventional life. I wouldn't feel too sorry for him, love. Rik seems to be doing okay.'

'I have denied myself a brother. From what I've read this morning he never shut the door on me. Envy is a terrible, destructive thing, Nell. I clung to Mum's apron strings, afraid to be away from her right to the end. I took over the business, had the family, the grandchildren as a way of getting her to notice me.'

Nell's eyes flashed. 'Don't you talk that way, Joe Faulkner. Your mother loved you in your own right, as much as she did Rik. She told me so many times how lucky she was to have you before and after Walter died.'

'Did she, Nell? I was never cut out for the great outdoors, was I? Rik had enough courage for both of us. I hope he can forgive me.'

'Darling Joe, I don't think Rik knows how to hold a grudge. At first glance I thought he was stand-offish, but that's just his manner. You forget how unusual you are, showing your emotions like you do. The fact that your brother keeps his tucked away doesn't mean he is unfeeling. Rik Faulkner is one of the warmest men I've ever met, apart from you, baker boy.'

Joe pulled his wife close, wrapping his arms tightly around her warm, comforting body. His tremulous sigh marked a turning point. As if by osmosis, the letters were helping him unwrap the enigma that was his little brother. 'You don't think it's too late, Nell?'

Nell laughed as she took the tearstained face of her husband in her hands. 'You silly bugger. It's never too late for anything.'

Chapter 30

Rita left her outdoor gear in the shop and followed Luca through a locked door and up a dark, narrow staircase which led into his flat. Immediately her sight was blinded by white: ceilings, walls, shelves, coffee table. Everything shone, even the wooden floor was highly polished, and she'd never seen anywhere so clean and stylish. Luca motioned her to the sofa while he made a pot of tea. They'd had a couple of glasses of warm cider at the manor which had made Rita slightly tipsy, so a good strong cup of builder's tea would put her right.

It seemed as if the entire Blackstock retailers' association, past and present, plus a few energetic locals had turned out for the competition. Rita had never seen so many different types of snowman and woman, from long, scarecrow types to huge doughnut-shaped figures wearing all manner of costumes. The winner, and the funniest by far was Pavel and Jana Doubek's reclining snowwoman wearing sunglasses, sunhat, bikini and sipping a martini. Rupert Huntley presented the trophy which was quickly followed by an almighty snowball fight. Kit, Finn and Luca were in league against anyone that came within range, while Rita and Libby almost wet themselves with laughter.

In a rare quiet moment, Rita told Libby about Jenny's party invitation along with the unbelievable news that not only had Luca offered to accompany her on the songs, but they were to rehearse in his flat later. Libby was elated. At last, the international man of mystery was about to reveal his intentions to her dear, darling best friend. She had watched how he had watched Rita at the gig as well as during Isabella's lunch. It confirmed her prediction that Luca was in love.

The shit was truly going to hit the fan once Nathan found out. *I hope Rita won't be there as it ain't gonna be pretty.* Plus, there was the business with not-so-clever-Trevor to come. Despite knowing their life in Blackstock might soon end, Rita found the strength to simply enjoy these moments as if all was well. That was one of the many things Libby loved about her.

Luca put his mug into the sink. It wasn't that long ago since Greta had been in his flat, but that memory belonged to another life. Rita was here, admiring his Fender guitar as naturally as if she was part of the furniture. Luca was amazed how quickly she had got into his system and he hadn't even told her how he felt. It had to be done soon, but something held him back. Maybe it was the potential reappearance of Finn's dad, and a terrible sinking feeling that Rita might leave? What if she fell in love with him? Would Rita stay behind if her family went away? Looking at her now, she didn't seem too bothered by it.

To hear Rita's laugh while they frantically built the snowman had lit him up. She looked heart-breakingly beautiful with curls escaping from her woolly hat, and her eyes as bright as summer. He loved the way she was with Finn, helping him scoop up piles of fine, white snow and their sibling hands patting the sides of his snowman with pride. When they were in the manor's grand hallway warming up with drinks, Rita kept a firm reign on her brother as some other children were bombing around wildly and she didn't want him to be a nuisance, even though Rupert and Penelope didn't seem to mind in the slightest.

He roused himself from the reverie as he went over to join her on the sofa. 'So, Rita, now you've caught your breath, have you decided to accept Jenny's invitation?'

'I talked it over with my mum before we came out, and she said I must do it. It will be good for my confidence. And she's making me a new dress to show off in. So, it looks like I - we are doing it.'

Luca was overjoyed by this new version of Rita. 'Right then, we'd better talk about a play list. We know what type of music Gregg likes, and Hartburn have obviously got a back catalogue, but I was wondering if you had some songs in mind. After all, you are the main attraction.'

Rita's cheeks flushed violently. She loved it when he made fun of her, like friends do. She pulled his iPad and a folder out of her satchel in readiness for their discussion. Over the years, Rita had collected hundreds of songs which spanned many different genres as she dreamed that one day, she'd be sitting with a fellow musician doing exactly what she and Luca were now doing. 'Jenny mentioned The Carpenters, so I thought we might sing, *I Won't Last A Day Without You*. Do you know it?' Rita called up the song on *YouTube*.

After the first few bars, Luca nodded. 'It's lovely. We don't want to be too gloomy, but not too cheesy as certain songs are so well known. Although I must confess that *Please Mr Postman* is my all-time favourite song' at which Rita giggled, slowly getting to know his humour.

Luca, meanwhile, had budged up next to her to look at the lyrics as the song played. He felt the warmth from Rita's body sink into his own. Had they ever been this close before? After a few seconds they were singing together, the words gathering meaning as the tune ended. Was this another song that Rita had chosen as a message for him? He decided to believe it was true and allowed himself to be touched. After all, that was what music was for, wasn't it? 'Yes, I like it. We'll play this on guitar in a minute. What else had you in mind?'

The couple spent the rest of the afternoon considering a range of songs upon which they mostly agreed but were happy to relinquish their view for the other. There was a good mix of ballads and crowd pleasers. When Rita played the first verse and chorus of Tracy Chapman's *Fast Car*, Luca was delighted in her rendition. He felt excitement rise into his chest, so happy to be part of this duo. There were so many songs he would never have considered, particularly Eric Clapton's acoustic version of *Layla* which he got through quite well. Gregg's guests were in for a treat.

It was well past six o'clock when Rita packed up her satchel. They agreed to have a guitar session on Friday evening to put the finishing touches to the performance. That gave them time to do their own run through. As Luca watched Rita gather together her notebook and pencils, a sudden pain of separation flashed in his chest. He didn't want her to go. 'Umm, Rita, I don't suppose you'd like to stay for dinner? I've got fresh ravioli and can whip up a sauce.'

Their eyes met as the room fell away behind them, the gentle hum escaping from the fridge and a distant yapping the backbeat to Luca's thumping heart.

Rita's face crumpled. 'I'm so sorry, Luca. My mum's expecting me for tea, and I promised Finn I'd help with his homework. Can we make it another time?'

'Sure, of course we can. I meant to ask you this before, but what with the fun and games this afternoon I almost forgot. Most of the traders are closing early again tomorrow as the weather is keeping people away, so I reckoned we'd do the same. I've got to go into Marsham if the road's clear, and thought you might come with me? From there, we can go on to St Alban's, do a little recce of the cafes and restaurants to see what sorts of interiors they've got. Perhaps we'll have dinner at Piccante?'

Dinner. At Piccante? How Rita stopped herself from jumping in the air, she would never know. 'Yes, please, I mean, thank you, yes, I'd love to come with you. After all, it's in work time, isn't it? Not that it matters…'

As Rita mumbled and stumbled over her words, Luca felt another chunk of arctic ice slip from the glacier of his heart and his face broke into the world's biggest grin.

Chapter 31

Alison Redwing sat on the edge of her bed. A single, thin white page of child-like scrawl hung loosely in her trembling hand. It was only eleven o'clock and she really needed a drink. Rita made sure there was no booze in the flat and checked her mother's bedroom regularly as that was their agreement. Alison accepted it as she was determined to get herself well, and Blackstock had proved to be a good move.

For two years, Alison Agnes Redwing had been an alcohol-free zone. *So why am I in such a bloody state? I don't have to let him back into our lives. The court gave me custody, I have my kids, a job, a secure home.* This was entirely true, but it didn't account for an inexplicable longing to see him again. Alison had found it hard to sustain friendships as she trusted very few people, and even those had let her down, big time. Trevor Jenkins was the only man she had ever loved, whatever that meant.

Things had been good for the first few years. He'd broken off contact with the old crowd, had stopped stealing and got a regular job at Carter's Warehouse, even working extra shifts for the baby. On Sundays they took Finn to the park, like every other normal family. They didn't consider their drinking to be excessive as at least they could wait until lunchtime, unlike many of Trevor's friends, but he was weak and had got into the wrong crowd. To be sent down for aggravated robbery and he swore he was only the driver, well, that just about summed him up.

Alison was only just forty, young enough to have a different life. She had felt so much better this last year and needed to take fewer tablets. She and the kids had put on a little weight, and for the first time in her life, had saved some money, honestly earned from sewing. And what a good night they had on Saturday! To see her daughter on that stage almost broke her up. Rita had been right there throughout. She didn't deserve her. Rita was so good with Finn and was always encouraging her mother's endeavours. But as much as Rita could hate anyone, she had no time for Trevor Jenkins. Alison was sure he had never laid a finger on her beautiful daughter, but she was too scared to talk about it. She would be shocked to know what Rita carried in her satchel.

There was Hattie Summerfield – she was steadfast, a strong, loving mother-figure who had introduced Alison to other women who, like her, were learning to overcome their difficulties, to own their lives, to take responsibility for themselves. To know you weren't alone was such a relief. Much of what Hattie said went over her head, but a few things stuck. She did not have to be a victim in this life just because her early circumstances were difficult. Often it was those who experienced the worst time growing up who made the biggest transformations as they were better equipped to overcome physical and emotional hardship.

Isabella had also been there throughout, quietly looking after them, taking Rita on in the café as she did. And there was Luca, looking out for her boy. But here it was, a letter, offering her and Finn a new start in Aberdeen where Trevor had himself found a sponsor, Father Alistair. He'd been promised a flat, and a job working as a labourer for Bell's Construction. All he was asking was she think about it, to consider their son who he hadn't seen in over two years, and who he would very much like to see again, and to please write back care of Father Alistair.

Alison folded the letter and put it back into the envelope. The inner voice had finally spun itself to a stop. She had time to decide, and yet, the decision was already made. The hardest part was how to tell her children.

Chapter 32

Westleigh Electrical had taken a couple of days off. The new job had been delayed, so Neil took the opportunity to catch up with paperwork and get a few quotes out. Gemma was due back from Milan anytime soon if the runways were clear. She wasn't happy to catch a train and taxi home, but Neil wasn't prepared to risk getting stuck. They managed another blazing row when all he did was to call her to check on her flight.

Gemma had been furious with him because he hadn't paid the credit card bills which meant she couldn't fuel her shopping addiction while in Milan. He had hoped to slow down a little, to pass more of the work onto Nathan and perhaps take on an apprentice, if only Gemma would reign in her spending. God knew how much she might have spent last week on Juliet, who was as reckless as her mother when it came to clothes. And she'd have bought her precious son a few 'bits and bobs', as she called them. As if he didn't know how much an *LBM 1911* sweater cost. Did she think he was stupid?

Over the last few days, Neil had unexpectedly found a little free time during which he reflected seriously on his marriage. This was no doubt prompted by the meal at Isabella's cottage. He was over the moon to see Tom and Karen so loved up, especially as he and the boys had been through such a lot. Joe and Nell still looked as happily married as ever, *and* they worked in the shop together. Watching them dance the night away at the pub had him and Ben in fits. He wished he had Joe's flamboyance. Even Luca couldn't hide his light for little Rita who was a cracking young woman, both she and Libby. Christ, they'd been through it, and look at them now!

Neil felt ashamed at his own children's ignorance although it wasn't their fault they'd been spoilt. They were adults now, though, and must learn to stand on their own two feet, like he and his brother had. What surprised him the most was to watch Isabella and Rik together. No one deserved happiness more than her. His electrician's radar had picked up the sparks flying across the table that afternoon.

Rik's invitation to visit the island had wrong-footed him but the more he thought about it, the more the idea was taking root. There was no way Gemma would be interested, but there was no reason why he couldn't go alone. After all, they hardly spent any time together these days. When Isabella asked him not to mention Rik to her sister, Neil didn't need to ask why. Gemma had such a trap on her, and Isabella was a private person. He understood completely.

It was amazing how quiet the house had been. Even Nathan commented on it one evening over dinner. It had been great to be at home with his son, just the two of them, eating the odd take away and watching the television. Last night had been particularly good fun, drinking beer and crossing cultural divides.

'Dad, who's Smashie and Nicey?'

Neil laughed. 'Why do you want to know?'

'Someone made a comment about the gig. '*keep raiding the back catalogue - loved the Smashie and Nicey*'.

'Have you never seen *The Fast Show*? Paul Whitehouse and Harry Enfield were DJs, whose characters were based on Tony Blackburn and Alan Freeman, if I remember rightly. The Bachman Turner Overdrive song you play, *You Ain't Seen Nothin' Yet* was their theme tune. Tell you what, Nate, why don't we watch the DVD tonight over a Thai curry?'

Father and son sat and cracked up the entire evening watching comedy DVDs, which was the closest they had been since Neil had watched his son play football ten years ago. Nathan was good company and so relaxed, not worrying how his hair looked or fussing with his clothes. He was up to something, though, as during their last week rewiring the barber's shop, it seemed as if Nathan was dashing off to the deli every other hour.

After the St Valentine's Day gig, Neil realised it wasn't the coffee he was after. The band's website had been inundated with comments about the new singer, and what a great night it had been. When Neil returned from Isabella's lunch, Nathan was annoyed he hadn't gone after all. He didn't know Rita was going to be there and tried unsuccessfully to hide his disappointment. Neil may have been somewhat older, but he recognised a love-sick look when he saw one. Poor bugger. It was rough having the boot on the other foot for a change.

The front door banged loudly, yanking Neil back to the present with a jolt. He jumped off the sofa and headed for the hallway to greet his wife. She was earlier than expected, not that there was anything to hide, but he should have shaved. Gemma hated his stubble, even after one night. 'Hello Gem. Welcome home.'

'Bloody cab driver wouldn't drop me outside, so I had to pull this bloody case up the street.' She tore off her long cashmere coat and scarf, dumping them on the newel post. Gemma swore as she struggled to pull of her boots and pushed Neil's helping arm away. 'I'm sweating. Where's Nathan?'

She gets one toe in the door and she's off, thought Neil. He left her huge suitcase in the hallway and called up to his son. There was no answer, so he followed Gemma into the kitchen, watching her as she looked around, no doubt, doing an inspection. 'He must have his ear plugs in. I'll go and get him.'

'No, leave him for a minute.' Gemma squared up to her husband with hands on her hips, ready for combat. 'What I'm dying to know Neil, is why you didn't pay the credit card bills? Have you any idea how shaming it was to stand by the cashier in Prada and have my cards refused? Juliet almost ran out of the shop. We felt like criminals.'

Neil looked at his wife's beautiful face and wondered how it could look so ugly. She used to say he was the downtown boy married to the uptown girl, and he let her believe she was right even though she too came from a similar London background. He was proud to be working-class, whatever that meant these days, and he had done very well for himself.

Gemma, on the other hand had spent her very short working life as a holiday rep before having the children, after which she messed about in her friend's clothes shop for one day a week. He wondered what was so 'uptown' about that? 'If you remember, we had a serious talk about your spending. You promised to cut back, and you'd think about working an extra day. That was six months ago, and I've just about had it.'

Gemma ignored her husband's comment and pushed passed him to walk upstairs, attempting to lug the case behind her. He took it from her and followed. A massive row was on the horizon and he was in the mood for it. They stood facing each other in the middle of their enormous bedroom. He watched Gemma's semi-permanent eyebrow slowly arc in disgust as she studied their king-sized mahogany bed, taking in the dishevelled duvet and pillows. Her ocular beam swivelled around the room, documenting every single piece of evidence to prove he was incapable of keeping one room tidy in her absence, not even managing to shave.

Neil was beyond caring. 'Look, Gem, can't we work this out, together? Look at these wardrobes, stuffed full of clothes you've hardly touched. I can't carry on working at this rate of six bloody days a week to support your habit.'

Gemma's eyes narrowed. 'So, my daughter is now in exile, my son can't afford his own house, and you want me to sit at home and do exactly what, Neil? Next, you'll be forcing me to cancel my spa breaks, health club membership and the hairdresser.'

The volume of her voice had crept up. It was a defensive mechanism that switched on when she was on the ropes.

'You agreed that taking Juliet to work with her aunt

was the only way of keeping her from those junkies. As for Nathan, have you any idea how much money he has frittered away on his cars, his music kit, watches, trips abroad, skiing and what-not over the years? He has almost nothing left of your dad's legacy. I was at Isabella's on Sunday, amongst young people who have come from the worst circumstances imaginable, and they are making a good go of it.'

'Don't you dare compare my children to that Sunrise lot! I know all about Rita Redwing. Juliet was in tears, saying she'd been betrayed by the band. Out of the country just one week and she swans in, like Barbra-effing-Streisand. We've seen the comments on the website. And I'll bet Luca was at the meal, crowing over the flat …'

As the row grew in decibels, Nathan heard his name in the shouting. Not that this was unusual as they always argued about him and Juliet, and he had learned to turn a deaf ear. This time he'd caught a whiff of something else, about Rita, and a flat. He quietly pushed open his door.

'… about Luca's new job title, and how Isabella has signed the flat over to him. Did you know that? Our son is living at home while his cousin has his own, fully paid up flat. The next thing will be the shop, just you wait and see. Oh, and I hear Claudia is out of the picture. Doesn't Nathan know Ronnie Huxtable is *minted*. He'd have paid for a wedding and probably even a house for his precious daughter to live in. And I suppose Tom was there with his new partner? Boy has *she* landed on her feet.'

'You are unbelievable. Karen is a senior manager with her own house and money. If you'd bothered to invite them over, you'd find out that she is the last person to take anything from anyone. As for Luca, he's worked like a dog in that shop, he hardly ever takes a holiday and has paid his rent for years. How much rent does Nathan pay us? What type of car does he drive, Gem?'

Gemma couldn't answer. She sank heavily into the chair beside the bed, her kohl-lined eyes brimming with frustrated tears. He felt for her, but she had pushed him too far over the line and neither one knew if they'd come back from it this time around. For some reason unknown to him, Gemma painted herself as the hard-done-by middle sister, the one who had been ripped away from her London school and friends, who sat and watched her siblings do well, while she groped around, not knowing where her strengths lay. If only she would lose that big fat chip on her shoulder.

Gemma hadn't always been so demanding. The first time he saw her was burned into his memory. A bunch of rowdy thirteen-year-olds returning to school after the long, hot summer holidays; kids hustling and bustling, swapping stories about growth spurts, acquisitions, adventures, and there she was. The entire class stared at the striking new student with her long raven tresses, defiant eyes and a skirt that Neil felt sure to be at least two inches shorter than permitted, and certain to get her sent to the headmaster before the day was out.

By the end of that first week, Gemma had sussed out who the 'in group' was and had mustered up her own flock of sheep. She'd made a play for his older brother Ben but had been unceremoniously batted off as he already had a serious girlfriend. Gemma had no eyes for Neil, but like the rest of the love-struck boys, he lived in hope. He used to love Mrs Matthieu's French class as Gemma's accent was gorgeous, and occasionally, she would entertain them by speaking in Italian.

Fast forward to Ayia Napa, seven years later. He and his mates were there to celebrate their twenty-first birthdays. As the group fell into yet another bar, there she was once again, Gemma Burnett, this time sitting in a row on the floor, her orange neck scarf tied around her head, banshee-style, moving side to side to *Oops Upside Your Head,* those same feline eyes, that same cockiness. He had loved her back then, and there was no way he was letting her out of his sight this time around.

Gemma had remembered him alright, Ben's little brother, the one that was so good at art, and who now lived in his own terraced house with his own electrical business and was on the up. He was flattered she knew anything at all about him. After four years of serious partying, Gemma's contract was about to end, which was timely as she was ready to come home. He gave her the huge white wedding she wanted, they moved to a bigger house after Nathan arrived, and then came Juliet.

Those early years were wonderful. Gemma loved being a mother, forgetting her own needs to take care of her babies. She had so much love for them, but for him? Neil had always felt more for her, but he had brushed that aside as there were compensations. Being part of her large family where his children had lots of cousins holidaying together, growing up together, that had been fabulous, but as time went on, as the children needed her less, Gemma needed him less. His role was simply as provider for her increasingly materialistic needs.

Neil couldn't remember the last time they'd been intimate. Maybe Gemma had met someone at the health club as she was there so often? In many ways he wished she was having an affair. He really felt like being let off the hook. Maybe Gemma's stubbornness came from her will to do the opposite? 'Contrary', that's what Maria Burnett called her daughter. Neil was worn out trying to work out the *modus operandi* of his complicated wife.

Neil gathered together a few things for a night in the spare room. For the first time in his adult life, he craved peace, space, to be alone. Gemma's silent, accusatory eyes follow him around the room. The worst was almost over. 'By the way, Joe's brother has invited me to Scotland. I've decided to take a week off this summer and join him. It looks as if there will be a crowd of us.' He left his wife sitting stupefied in the chair as he quietly closed the door behind him.

Chapter 33

Nathan was frantically pacing the floor, no longer listening to his parent's fight. He'd become immune to his mother's constant wailing and his father's unsuccessful attempts to pacify her. Just once he wished his dad would stand up to her, whatever the consequences. He was sick and tired of his mother's interference, and knew it was time to strike out on his own. Over the takeaway the other night, his father had alluded to it, saying that houses regularly came up for auction, and he and Ben were happy to help with the renovation. He liked the idea very much. Nathan couldn't remember the last time he and his dad laughed together as there was always so much strain in the house.

Until just a few moments ago, Nathan had been ecstatic. The feedback for the gig was still coming in. It was like nothing they'd ever seen. '*Who's that girl? Lovin' the new sound; Hartburn rocks the house!*' and on it went. Everyone knew Juliet wasn't up to it, but it was difficult in a family band, and she'd had so many singing lessons, bless her. If only she'd have let Jodie or Rosa in, rather than insisting she sing this or that song, many of them too poppy or too wishy washy. But that was in the past as Juliet would never come back to the band even if they begged her, of that he was certain.

Hartburn *were* a great band, he'd always known it. Rita had proved it. Somehow, in just one night, she'd brought the sparkle back. Perhaps once they were together, he could persuade her to record a few songs. Rita was embarrassed to say she'd written several songs when they met for the drink last week. Maybe, with her voice and his backing, they could sell the music on the internet. They didn't even need to find an agent these days.

If he was clever about it, if he just held back, Nathan could see a time in the not-too-distant future when he and Rita broke from the band to set up as a duo. He might even be able to give up the tools and concentrate on music. When his mother mentioned Luca taking over the shop, he didn't recall anything being said about Isabella giving it away.

The fact that lucky bastard Luca now owned his own flat wouldn't make a blind bit of difference in the long run. If he got his head down, paid off his debts, sold a few things, maybe even the car, it wouldn't be long before he had a deposit for his own gaff. Nathan didn't need any of them. All he needed was Rita.

Chapter 34

Isabella sat in Hattie's cluttered kitchen drinking a cup of nettle tea, watching shards of freezing, grey rain hit Blackstock's pavements. She had swapped her Friday for Wednesday, giving Rita a well-earned day off. That young woman had a lot of energy, but with so much going on, Isabella was determined to keep watch over her.

Luca's offer to take Rita to Gregg's party had pleased her immensely. They were soon going to 'make sweet music together' metaphorically and physically, although she was certain the budding friendship had yet to blossom into that realm. There was still the business of Alison's potential departure and Nathan's intentions but so far, Luca hadn't voiced too much concern about any of that. Isabella was still holding back before offering Needlepoint Cottage to Alison, but it wouldn't be long now. Rik was right. The Redwing's future was their business.

The airy, brightly painted room felt cosy, despite piles of brochures, sample boxes, health products and crockery littering the sides. Not one scrap of empty worktop or tabletop could be seen. Hattie picked up a pile of letters and dumped them on top of another pile to make room for her vegetable chilli. It had been over forty-eight hours since

Isabella had disappeared into the great unknown with the explorer, and Hattie was keen to find out over supper what discoveries had been made. 'So, Rik is now in London and you are meeting him in Cambridge, Friday lunchtime for…'

Isabella folded and unfolded her napkin, a nervous habit she'd recently become aware of. 'He is giving a talk entitled 'Outposts' at the Polar Institute after which there will be a reunion supper at his former college. Rupert and Penelope will be there. We'll stay overnight with Simon and Catherine Dunwoody. Simon is a Cambridge fellow.'

'Well, get you, Miss rubbing-noses-with-the-intellectuals Burnett. That sounds so fab. It also sounds serious. Are you serious about Rik?'

Isabella looked at her dearest friend. There wasn't much they didn't know about each other and now wasn't the time to start keeping secrets. 'I told him about the regression, about our loose ends and the rest of it, and he didn't blink. Rik asked me straight out what that means for us, what will we do about it now that we know. I can't tell you how much that man shakes me up. To look at him, you'd think he was quite unemotional, but I can tell you Ms Summerfield, without telling you, he is passionate.'

Hattie laughed. She didn't need details as it was as plain as day her friend had lost her heart to this man. Quite how this film was going to end could not yet be predicted, but she knew Isabella well enough to know that it didn't matter, so she let the scene unfold. 'I assume he has asked you to go to Coille?'

Isabella recalled their last evening together. Rik produced an iPod out of his long, mystifying pockets. She lay against him on the sofa, carried away to dark Persian skies on the soundwaves of an enchanting flute music called *Ney*. In Turkestan, Rik had been received with such hospitality from a village of proud but impoverished people, it was profoundly humbling. He and a friend made a pilgrimage to the Hafez tomb in Shiraz. The poetry had bewitched him, *'I caught the happy virus last night. When I was out singing beneath the stars. It is remarkably contagious – so kiss me'*.

That afternoon, those mystical, melodic motions filled the nooks and crannies of Isabella's fire-lit room and had soaked into the seams of her heart. Rik talked of extraordinary nights under the bejewelled Syrian desert sky as a guest of the Bedouin and tried to describe to her the sound camels make when asleep. He had packed so many captivating stories into his trunk of memories, she wanted to spend the rest of her life hearing about them. Overcome with desire, he had drawn her onto the rug, and when she confessed to a bad back, it had them roaring with laughter, and him reaching for cushions.

Hattie watched her friend. Isabella was lost in a memory that had the power to make her body language change in front of her. She had never seen Isabella like this, not even when she and Daniel Overton first got together. Hattie was simultaneously happy and fearful for her friend but felt sure Isabella was sufficiently mature to deal with the uncertain future. Rik's mirror would reflect Isabella's fear of the unknown and it may well dig her out of her self-imposed cocoon. It wasn't for her to spell it out.

Isabella sensed Hattie's gaze and brought herself back from the bliss of just two days before. 'Can you see me living without my armchairs and bathtub?' They smiled as they knew she could if she chose to. 'Seriously, I cannot imagine myself living on the island with Rick working all day. How can I shear sheep with my bad back?'

Hattie nearly choked on a forkful of rice. 'Don't write it off, Bella. You said he was to inherit quite a sum, and perhaps set up a venture, a bit like Off Centre but by the sea. Wouldn't you love to be a part of that? I'd jump at it.'

'You are fearless, dear Hattie. Why don't you offer Rik your expertise? Wouldn't it be great to give our Sunrise families a place to go, to learn new skills, to do 'Women in Wellies' courses, to be truly out of their usual environment? Now that we're talking about it, maybe I *could* see us running a few courses out there. Perhaps I'll suggest it to Rik as he asked me for advice. But right now, I want you to give it to me straight. Tell me what you really think.'

The friends looked at each other. 'Are you sure?'

Isabella nodded. She needed to hear Hattie's interpretation of this massive event as she felt sure none of it was a coincidence.

'Okay Bella, you asked for it. You have taken steps to change your life already, which is to be commended. You've said you'll travel, but we both know it won't be far as you don't like to be away from home for too long. Nothing wrong with that. So why, after fifty plus years, now you have finally resolved the mystery of the face, the one you couldn't name ten years ago, why has it happened now? My guess is that Rik is the only person who will be able to prize you away from Weavers, from Blackstock and everything you cling so tightly to.

'Rik has come into your life to lead you into the water, to swim in the loch, to climb the Scottish hills and mountains, to get you to feel the Atlantic wind in your hair. To put it crudely, to open your legs and move. Maybe your back pain is an expression of your fear to get going, keeping you in Blackstock? It's time to let go of the material things along with your emotional support of others. Your family can survive without you, my darling.

'With Rik, you'll find out what it means to be alive, rather than slowly shutting yourself down in the safety of your armchair and bathroom. He cannot pretend, Bella, and you of all people deserve to love intensely for however long it lasts. It's time to rescue the snow globe from the river.'

Silence filled the space between the ancient friends. It was brutal but it was true. No one knew Isabella better than Hattie Summerfield. Isabella wiped her streaming eyes. 'Phew, Hattie. That was some resumé. I thought it was me who fired the arrows.'

'Darling, you know I say this because I love you. Once the doors to the heart are open, why would you want to close them? When the time comes, you'll know what to do.'

Hattie smiled. She could have written this script herself after all. It was fantastic to see Isabella enlivened. There was, however, one other piece of important news to share. 'Alison has been to see me. You can guess why.'

Isabella's stomach did a summersault. She'd become so fond of the Redwings, more so than any other family that had stayed in Larkspur House. Hattie felt the same way about Libby. 'Trevor has finally been given parole, hasn't he? When will Alison go?'

'She has asked me to accompany her to Aberdeen, which I am delighted to do. I have friends nearby, so I can make myself scarce. Trevor has a sponsor, Bella, a certain Father Alistair who will be present. There is a flat and a job in the offing. It will be tempting.'

'Do you think Alison will go back to him? She's done so well here, especially with these requests for her dress-making skills. And Finn has settled in school, he has friends now.'

Hattie studied the lines of concern across Isabella's friend's brow. She was a little more optimistic. For two years, Alison and Libby had attended the women's development group during which they had released several deep-seated fears about their identity and were coming to terms with much that life had served up. Libby had seen her anger replaced by empowerment, and Alison too, was undergoing important transformation. Both women were beginning to adjust to the knowledge that the fate of their lives was in their own hands. They had free will.

Without breaking confidentiality, Hattie replied that she was upbeat, and best to get the meeting over and done with. She had booked an overnight sleeper for travel next Monday. 'All that's left is for Alison to tell Rita and Finn. I believe she will do that after Rita's concert on Sunday afternoon.'

'Alison is a good mother. Let's hope it ends well, Hattie. We can do no more than that.'

Chapter 35

Libby walked a tightrope between elation and despair. Watching Rita's metamorphosis was truly inspiring and yet, a creeping sense of inevitability followed Libby like the shadow of a malevolent spirit. In the women's class, she had got to know Alison independently of her friend. She was shocked to learn of the traumas Alison had experienced but rejoiced to see her recognise this new-found strength, to acknowledge herself as a talented working mother as well as a woman who no longer lived in fear.

The group were aware of the letter and the power this man still appeared to have over her. No one advised Alison as it was her decision alone to make, but everyone felt her distress, especially Libby. She did not want to lose what she considered to be her real family. When Isabella offered her the Spinner's Cottage tenancy, Libby genuinely thought Rita would jump at the chance to live there with her. The two bedrooms were a good size and the house was warm and cosy. There was no way Isabella would let it be otherwise. In fact, she had updated it recently, and Mrs Abbott had kept both house and garden in immaculate condition.

Rita had been so upset to miss the dog walking in favour of the little concert. Libby didn't mind in the least as it was much more important Rita sing her heart out. That was her therapy. She would have Luca to take care of her now as he must declare his love soon, and that pleased Libby no end, but this business between Alison and Trevor kept her awake at night. He had some hold on her, and she doubted that their long separation had done much to diminish it. Libby had no choice but to watch and wait, however distressing it was.

St Valentine's day came and very nearly went. Rita spent most of the afternoon rehearsing her list of songs while the gentle purr of the Singer next door offered a comforting presence. The afternoon light was fading but the lamps cast a homely glow around the room, and it was warm. Luca and Isabella insisted she had a half day. It seemed as if they were taking extra care of her.

True to his word, Luca had driven her to St Albans where they spent the snowy afternoon nosing in cafes and various restaurants, explaining how they were looking for inspiration for the new venture. Several managers were only too willing to allow Luca to take photos as he had such a disarming way of saying how he admired their interior and how they made great use of space and so on. They were even offered free coffee, which they declined gratefully, but said they would come back when they had more time.

Rita wasn't sure what part of that day she enjoyed the most: being a passenger in Luca's car listening to The Red Hot Chilli Peppers; discussing ideas and plans for the deli; feeling his hand on her back as they meandered through busy streets; sitting opposite him in Piccante's vibrant restaurant as they mulled over the menu. Her choice of beetroot tortellini was scrumptious as was Luca's lobster tagliatelle as he insisted that she try a morsel. He persuaded her to have a dessert, or at least to share his, and so they took turns scooping the orange sorbet. Luca had laughed as she squinted at the tangy flavour. They talked about the upcoming gig, how she felt about it, was she nervous? She asked him about his Italian family, what he loved about music, what his favourite food was.

When Luca finally broached the question of her family life, Rita talked openly about the circumstances in which her mother finally freed herself from 'that man'. Alison was pregnant at sixteen, an accident, the consequences of which forced her mother to leave the family home to live in one hostel after another.

'We had several good years living back with my gran. She said I was musical and that it was a gift I should nurture. After my gran passed away, Trevor came on the scene. Initially, Finn was a distraction, but it wasn't long before his true nature reappeared, and his awful behaviour pulled the family downhill. The constant racket he and his cronies made finally drove the council to evict us. After that, my mum's drinking got worse the more we moved around. He got into a dodgy crowd, ending up incarcerated at Her Majesty's pleasure.'

As they made to leave the restaurant, Rita thanked him, not just for that day, but for everything he'd done for her and her family. She was so grateful to have such a good friend. That may have been the reason he replied how he was looking forward to their plans. *Their plans.* As

Luca dropped her home that night, there was an awkward moment. She got out of the car, and he had driven away with a wave. No kiss, no touch, just a smile. If that was all she was to share with Luca Santini, it was enough.

As Rita got ready for bed, her phone beeped. Luca. Maybe he had something to tell her even though they'd only been apart for a few hours? Her heart drummed as she rummaged in the bottom of her satchel, desperate to see what the message said.

Happy Valentine's Day Rita. Hope it was a good one.

Check out the Hartburn website x

Her disappointment at receiving Nathan's text was out of proportion to the event itself as she hoped he'd turned his attentions elsewhere. He'd sent her a couple of texts after the gig, one of which she replied to, the other, too personal for comfort, she had deleted. It was easier to say the old phone didn't work too well, or that there was no signal should Nathan ask why she didn't reply. Pulling out the iPad, Rita typed in the website address. There were so many messages congratulating her and the band, how they'd loved hearing this or that song. Bookings were coming through thick and fast. It was astonishing.

Did Luca know and hadn't wanted to tell her? It was unlikely as they had been together almost every day since the gig. Maybe he hadn't checked the website as he was busy with the project? Rita suddenly realised the enormity of the undertaking. Now that she was a member of Hartburn, what was going to happen if her mother decided to move back in with Trevor? There had been no news that she was aware of, but her gut told her it was coming.

Her mother had been edgy, and had smoked a couple of cigarettes, the first time in over two years. At least she hadn't started drinking again. Rita could easily share that lovely cottage with Libby and live in Blackstock indefinitely, oh, but her brother. Tears welled up as she thought about Finn. He'd settled in so well. The terrible eczema that had driven him to distraction had all but gone, and with the remedies from Hattie's health shop friends and the change in diet, Finn's skin was as soft as any other healthy eight-year-olds'. He'd won a poetry competition that term, as well as being voted the most helpful child in year three by his school chums. There was also the football, cricket, the cycling club, and his friendship with Ben and Luca. Finn hadn't asked after his father in a long, long while.

Luca's suggestion to adopt Finn hadn't been too far off the mark as she'd thought about it many times. No one wanted Trevor in Blackstock. Alison would have to go to him, but what if she could persuade her mother to leave Finn behind? That, as far as Rita was concerned, was the best solution.

Chapter 36

Isabella set off for Cambridge just after ten o'clock when the worst of the traffic had passed. As usual, she avoided the dual carriageway on which Amanda had been killed. The thought of it still made her blood run cold, and the effects of the accident continued to impact the entire family dynamic, drawing her ever closer into the fold. Isabella was the axis around which the familial relationships rotated. It fulfilled her desire to be at the centre of a structure bigger than herself and one which gave her purpose. Whether through family ties, the Blackstock community or The Sunrise Trust, Isabella recognised her need to be needed.

Isabella's unconscious outward image of a confident woman of substance, however, masked a profound insecurity when it came to life outside the realms of Blackstock. The closer she got to Cambridge, the more her stomach knotted. What could she contribute to an academic gathering? Isabella hadn't travelled far; she hadn't gone into higher education; she had little interest in politics. Hattie said that life was the only teacher, but Isabella didn't possess Hattie's confidence or opinion. However anxious she felt it was too late to back out now.

The plan was to meet Rik at the Dunwoody's house after

which they'd have lunch. It was a gorgeous late winter's day; cold, crisp and framed within a cobalt-coloured sky. There remained just enough countryside to give the impression you weren't yet drowning under a concrete sea. As Isabella approached the ancient city, snowdrops lined several verges along the residential streets while the appearance of purple crocus further raised her spirits.

It was astonishing how nervous she felt at seeing Rik again, more so in an unfamiliar environment. Isabella had reflected on Hattie's summary It was so easy to become fixed, to say 'no' to invitations, for one's world to shrink. 'To love intensely': she was already lost to such emotion, but could that be enough to unchain herself, to untie her self-imposed bindings? If there was one thing she knew for certain about Rik, his world would never contract.

Isabella knocked on the smart charcoal painted door of number ten, Goldfinch Road. The classic Regency period town house had gorgeous views over Midsummer Common which outwardly gave the appearance of wealth and prestige. Before Isabella had time to gather herself, a tall, striking woman swiftly opened the door, thrusting a woollen-clad arm towards her guest. 'Isabella, hello. I'm Catherine Dunwoody.'

Her contagious smile immediately infected Isabella. It was going to be alright. She followed her host into an unexpectedly large, high-ceilinged hallway edged in a beautifully ornate white cornice which contrasted against *Rectory Red* walls and dark pine exposed floorboards. A huge vase of Stargazer lilies sat atop a much-used antique mahogany table. Evidence of children was everywhere:

hockey sticks and cricket balls resting behind the door; various-sized coats hanging on the old hat and coat stand; a trail of dark scuffs up the hallway stairs. Underneath the floral scent, Isabella detected the unmistakable smell of dog.

'May I take your coat? It's stupendously cold out there. Rik and Simon are in the garden shed. It's a common disease which seems to affect the male of the species. How was your drive?'

It was hard not to smile. 'Fine, thank you. The snow seems to have been washed away for the time being.'

'It's a blessing, alright. You can imagine what the streets have been like here, Isabella. Cambridge is in danger of becoming obese, outgrowing itself at an alarming rate. We've lived here forever and remember a time when Sundays were actually quiet.'

Small talk over, Isabella followed her gangly host into the kitchen, not quite the *Homes and Gardens* affair she was expecting, but was relieved, nevertheless. An elderly, lumpy Golden Labrador heaved itself out of a hairy basket and lumbered towards Isabella who was delighted to find a four-legged ally. She and Libby agreed that dog-lovers were nice people, although she'd been proved wrong on occasion. Isabella bent over to stroke the weary dog whose tail almost mustered a wag. 'What's his name?'

'This is Rodney. He's fourteen, a grand old age for a Lab. We put it down to a raw meat diet, cod liver oil and lots of cuddles from Daddy. He can't get around like he used to, but we do just fine, don't we Rodders?'

The dog was clearly adored the mistress of the house as he trundled behind her to a sideboard in which certain delicacies were stored and was duly rewarded for his effort.

'May I offer you tea, or would you prefer coffee? It's a little early for anything stronger, although I won't tell.'

Catherine winked, and her deep hearty chuckle caught Isabella by surprise. She was about to ask for tea when a salmon-faced Simon Dunwoody bounded in through the door, followed more sedately by Rik. Before Isabella had the chance to say hello, Simon grabbed her hand and shook it vigorously, saying how splendid it was to meet her, and how Rik had told him almost nothing about her to which the foursome laughed. Rik sprang to his own defence, saying they would find out everything they needed to know that weekend.

Simon led them into the drawing room. Rick caught Isabella's eye and smiled as they sank into a huge floral sofa in which gravity pulled the body downward and the knees travelled alarmingly in the opposite direction. Isabella moved a couple of cushions into her lower back hoping the action went unnoticed.

Catherine had fetched in a tray containing a quartet of miss-matched mugs, a cracked teapot, milk jug and a rather rosy fruit cake, setting it before them on a low, walnut table. A generous fire burned in the grate of a grand fireplace above which hung an exquisite study of a model's head. It had to be a John William Waterhouse.

'You like the painting, Isabella?'

Isabella blushed. She was being observed, but it didn't feel uncomfortable. 'Very much, Simon. If I'm not mistaken, it's a Waterhouse.'

'Yes, a family heirloom. He's a great, great something or other. What kind of art do you like?'

Isabella was on safe ground and breathed out.

'I was born in Italy so it would be rude to ignore the heavyweights, although I often wonder what Michelangelo would think of his *Creation of Adam* being used as a mouse mat.' They laughed, Simon's pitch an octave deeper than his wife's. Isabella reckoned he was a baritone. 'I am drawn to portraits. I once saw a painting by Ingres, 'the Princesse de Broglie', and was mesmerised by her fine blue satin dress. And there's a haunting self-portrait in the Louvre, a Delacroix, I think. His eyes followed me around the gallery. The painting I've seen more than any other, though, is at Kenwood House…'

'Don't tell me, *The Guitar Player*.'

'You know the Vermeer, Catherine?'

'Isabella, I *love* the Vermeer, especially its florid history. How marvellous to have that in common. And Rik, of course.'

Rik had not yet had the opportunity of formally greeting Isabella, but he watched this initial exchange with fascination. Simon and Catherine were his oldest friends and had brought their sons to visit him on the island. Simon kept him up to date with Cambridge life and expressed his delight when Rik finally agreed to attend the Cambridge reunion and to speak at the evening's event. He had persuaded Rik to write a book based on the 'Outposts' talk, the wheels of which were already in motion.

Rik sensed his life was about to take an unprecedented turn. His friends would be as delighted by Isabella as he was – in fact, she had already disarmed them which somehow filled him with joy. Rik could scarcely believe how turbulent his emotions had been since leaving Blackstock just a few days ago. It was deeply unsettling.

Isabella looked stunning: her fresh translucent skin, her dark eyes reflecting the brilliant winter light. He had to get her out of here, take hold of her, bury his head in her hair, her neck, her breasts.

Thankfully, Catherine was aware of the schedule, and subtly drew the conversation to a close. 'Don't get Simon started on art, Isabella, or you'll be here all day. He says that scientists need to reconnect with art as we are in danger of becoming too specialist. Be prepared for a grilling.'

Rik got up, quickly followed by Simon who was a little embarrassed by his wife's gentle admonition. He had instantly taken to Rik's friend, (although he suspected she was his lover from what Rik alluded to in his own sparse way). She was neither intimidated or overawed by his status, or his interrogation, as Catherine called it. 'I await with pleasure our next conversation, Isabella, if not tonight, then over brunch tomorrow.'

With coats buttoned, scarves wound securely, and instructions as to which tailor would best suit Rik's temporary needs, the couple set off at a brisk pace, laughing at the adventure. As they passed a quiet, uninhabited lane, Rik pulled Isabella into it, tightened his arms about her and kissed her full on the lips. The couple remained like this for what may have been a few seconds or aeons before reluctantly drawing apart. Rik grabbed Isabella's gloved hand and they set off at a pace towards the ancient city centre.

Chapter 37

The afternoon passed in a flash. Thankfully for the most part the lovers were indoors and the adrenalin that pumped forcefully through their bodies kept the cold firmly out. The tailor's appointment was a remarkably swift affair with the appropriate suit and shoes to be collected later. Rik had arranged lunch in a small French café in one of the many warrens of backstreet Cambridge. They chose the same from the menu fixe: French onion soup, cassoulet and the lightest crème brûlée that made Isabella's taste buds zing.

If she had any suspicions that Rik was ignorant of good wine, they disappeared under the haze of an excellent Provence Bandol followed by a glass of *Courvoisier*. By the time they'd finished the tour around Clare College, Isabella's experience of the history and the architectural grandeur misted into a contentment she rarely felt. Thankfully there was time for a rest, shower and change before the evening's events. As the weak winter sun retired for the night over the majestic Cambridge spires, Rik and Isabella made their way back to Goldfinch Road.

After an hour of hushed, ardent lovemaking, this time it was Rik who washed Isabella's hair as she soaked luxuriously in the guest bathtub. He soaped her entire body so gently, she felt as if she was in convalescence, recovering from a mysterious bout of loss that had just been found. As he took his turn to bathe, she dried her hair, applied a minimum of make-up, and stepped into her evening dress of a navy silk, overlaid with chiffon and drawn in at the waist. Isabella pinned her hair to reveal a gorgeous aquamarine and white gold choker with matching earrings. Even Gemma would approve of her tonight.

Rik stood at the bathroom doorway, a thick peach towel wrapped around his slim waist, admiring her. How this had come to pass, he neither knew nor cared. He was overjoyed that Isabella wanted to share what was for him the honour to be invited to speak before his peers and venerated elders. He longed for her to see the world as he saw it, to experience his experiences, to see what made him what he was. It was a shocking realisation.

Isabella's beauty emanated from the inside, spilling outwards, drawing him closer. The strength of his desire was disturbing, never having been driven by sexual appetite, even when he was with Alejandro. With Isabella, however, he felt unleashed. He longed to hold her but didn't want to spoil her hair or dress. Isabella had no such qualms as she walked into his arms once again.

It was midnight and the city sounds were muffled by the greenery surrounding the house. Entwined under the thick eiderdown, Isabella felt she had travelled to another world: rarefied, privileged, safe. Rik's talk was outstanding. He was welcomed on to the stage with a roar of applause. Many of the guests hadn't seen each other in years, which became apparent during and after dinner, as good-humoured anecdotes flew about with wild abandon and greeted with raucous laughter. Isabella had never enjoyed so much attention, much of it spectacularly unsubtle as she was fêted and flirted with throughout the evening.

When she could get Isabella's ear, Penelope Huntley whispered how divine she looked and was the envy of many of the women, as Rik was apparently something of a catch. Rik's friends remarked that he was a sly devil, tucking away such a gem in his long, *Narnia-esque* pockets. They reminded Isabella of adolescent schoolboys on a weekend pass. She smiled to herself, thinking how glad she was to have had the courage to accept Rik's invitation.

Before the grandfather clock in the hall struck one, Rik had fallen into a deep sleep. His breathing, a soft rise and fall, lulled her as she curled into his back. It was like lying in a boat, being rocked by gentle waves lapping the shore. *In a few days he will be gone.* A sudden tightness clasped at her throat, choking her. Isabella quietly wept for the loss they were about to experience, although how she could feel so bereft having known him for such a short time, was hard to comprehend. *But you've always known him. You are old souls, travelling through time, your energies waxing and waning, moving in and moving out. Now that you have found each other, you can no longer remain separate.*

With these words soothing her troubled mind, Isabella drifted into a deep, sweet slumber.

Brunch was a noisy, ebullient affair as the word had got around Rik was still in town and Catherine found herself catering for twelve hungry post-party guests. Isabella

216

brushed aside her hosts' feeble attempts at refusal and took the task on willingly. Bowls of fresh mango, kiwi and yoghurt followed by smoked salmon and eggs benedict, crispy bacon, waffles and maple syrup were received with cheers. The Dunwoodys were generous hosts but Catherine's talents did not extend to cooking.

As the gathering settled down to coffee and pastries, talk turned to Rik's imminent return to Coille. Twelve pairs of bespectacled eyes rested on this prepossessing, darkly attractive woman who had caught the ice man's imagination. It was Penelope who asked the question on everyone's mind. 'Do you intend to join Rik as a castaway, Isabella?'

The table fell silent. Rik and Isabella's eyes anchored. Isabella knew she was being scrutinised, however kind everyone was. She was an outsider, a novelty perhaps, but she was surprisingly undisturbed by this. An energy, or force had taken over, and the band of tension which had encircled her torso suddenly released itself.

'You know Rik much better than I, so forgive me, as my impressions of him are still embryonic. What I sense is that after a career in which Rik has exposed Mother Nature's most intimate secrets to the human footprint, he has come to feel ashamed of his part in that. To draw a line, a boundary, is to separate, to fragment humanity, rather than to join it.

'Rik's atonement if you will, is to live and work with the elements, much like the writer Nan Shephard had done. They understand like few of us perhaps ever will, that Mother Nature's mystery isn't to be solved, or plotted, or conquered, or mapped. To stand barefoot by the sea, or on top of a mountain - it is the act itself that unlocks the mystery.'

Such was the charged atmosphere and the suspension of breath, only the tick-tock of the grandfather clock could be heard. Isabella finished her summation of this stranger whose present contemplation of her was acute. 'I'm not sure I can answer your question, Penelope. Rik's world may be intoxicating, and I may yet find the courage to meet him on his shores for a short while, but I fear our parting will contain all of the sorrow and little sweetness to make it bearable.'

No one spoke for what seemed like an eternity, each brilliant mind assimilating Isabella's words. Heads nodded and eyes were moist. Isabella had somehow captured the spirit of this man they had known for almost thirty years but realised how little they knew him. Rik was shocked at how deeply Isabella understood him, and how she stirred his quiet soul.

Simon Dunwoody was spellbound. 'I beg your pardon Isabella, but what college did you say you attended?'

'I couldn't go to college, Simon as I suffer with an 'auto-didactic' disease.'

'Oh, I *am* sorry.'

A heartbeat. Rik roared with laughter, quickly joined by Simon and his friends who had by now, tuned in to Isabella's wavelength.

'It's a terrible word, isn't it? *Self-taught* is much more appropriate, and to be admired, don't you think?' said Professor Dalton. Rik's aged mentor had been quietly observing his protégé and this extraordinary woman who between them, had unsettled the group. Rik had been by no means the best scholar, but he possessed an unusually perceptive and sensitive mind which set him apart from the more academic under graduates.

'I think what Isabella is hinting at is that intelligence is not the same as intellect. No formal learning is required to live in harmony with nature as many tribes and First Nation people have done so for centuries. Indeed, one could question man's contribution to our present perilous condition since the advent of education and so-called progress.'

Professor Dalton's observations led the conversation into the much more familiar realms of academia which ignited an intense debate. Rik, meanwhile, continued to regard Isabella. He marvelled at her quick mind and articulate manner which was without irony. She was transparent: a pearl.

After another hour of erudite banter, Catherine invited the men to clear the table while the women sat in the drawing room with a fresh pot of tea.

'Isabella, how can I thank you for your fascinating conversation, the delectable breakfast and for bringing your fabulous basket of delicious breads and pastries? This weekend will be remembered for a long time.'

'I agree entirely. And how wonderful to see you in a different light, Isabella. I fear you've broken a few hearts, Rupert's especially. But I must confess I wouldn't trade places with you, as fabulous as Rik is. I feel quite upset to think he is about to leave us until who knows when. I can't imagine what that is like for you.'

Isabella was touched by this genuine concern. 'I never expected to feel this way, Penelope. Life before Rik is a blur.'

The professor's wife, her wise eyes sparkling like crown jewels, had been listening intently to these young women. Jocelyn Dalton was also quite taken with Rik's companion who had handled the men very well. 'You know my dear, Joseph and I are still intimate after more than sixty years of marriage and we have spent many long periods apart. You may find a way to maintain a long, loving relationship even from a distance.'

'Thank you, Jocelyn. That's comforting to know, but let's not get too sad. I've had a terrific time meeting Rik's friends as I feel I know him a little better as a result. And thank you Catherine, for your hospitality. If you are in the area, please drop in for tea.'

Chapter 38

Hartburn's line-up sat around the long pine table at the back of The Alderman Pub, tucking into bacon butties, scones and mugs of hot, builder's tea, courtesy of Nancy Beck's hospitality. This had become a ritual throughout the band's history, and the landlady was only too happy to take care of her number one live attraction which just so happened to include her precious children. There was a tremendous buzz as by now, tickets for all the forthcoming performances had sold out.

Nathan's mood had somewhat improved after his mother's awful homecoming, but still an edgy, impatient sensation pulsed throughout his nervous system. His parents had called a truce, although the jury was out as to their future, even he realised that. Nathan was, however, proud of his dad for not caving into his mother's moods and demands and he'd even slept in the spare room which was a first. The news of Luca's recent property acquisition had also been pushed to the back of his mind. He had a plan in place, one which did not include his smug cousin.

There was something different about Luca this morning, however. He couldn't quite work it out to begin with. Ah, yes, he was puffed-up, laughing and joking more than usual.

Rosa and Rita were at it too, playing happy families. *Don't you worry mate, I'll have the last laugh.*

Nathan was the self-appointed chairperson though you wouldn't say it was a formal meeting. Jodie co-ordinated dates, availability and bookings and her notebook was at the ready. They discussed the invitations that had come in, but at this stage, had no idea if Rita was available. Nathan banged the table to call attention to proceedings. 'Okay, let's get cracking.' He looked over at Rita, wondering if Luca had given her the heads up on how the sessions worked, but she just smiled right back. That was encouraging. Rita hadn't responded to his text on St Valentine's day, so he had no idea what she'd been thinking. 'Rita, just interrupt me if you want to know anything, okay? Can we have a show of hands who's up for next Saturday's gig at The Brewery? Oh, all of us…well, that's good then. It starts at eight, so arrive by six-thirty latest. Suggestions for a playlist?'

It didn't take long for the band to fire off their ideas. The list of songs grew like a virus, as Jodie struggled to write them down, some of which they hadn't played for a while. It was obvious they had taken note of the feedback. 'This is impressive - a nice mix. I guess you could call it 'the Redwing effect,' eh?'

All heads turned towards the small, glowing face.

'I'll go along with that. Rita's been a real shot in the arm.' Louis Lockhart, usually a quiet voice, burned bright red as he realised his drug reference may have upset Nathan. Everyone knew Juliet had taken cocaine which was the main reason she was out of the band, although they let her think it was her decision to quit. They held to a strict 'no drugs' agreement with no exceptions.

Nathan didn't react as his mind was on other things. He seized his chance to big Rita up. 'So, Rita, what do you make of the list? We value your ideas.'

Rita was silent. She was weighing up how much input to make. After all, as the new addition, the last thing she wanted was to appear a know-it-all.

'C'mon Rita, you're among friends. We loved your suggestions last week, and so did the crowd.' Ethan Lockhart, the older and more confident of the brothers, had no problem speaking out. He was happy to let Nathan act as spokesperson, but occasionally had to exert his knowledge over his cocky cousin when it got out of hand. It was generally known that Nathan was the weakest musical link, much like his sister, but he worked incredibly hard to keep up. Playing with gifted musicians had upped Nate's game and Ethan appreciated it even though his cousin was sometimes a peacock.

Rita pulled the iPad out of her satchel. She coughed awkwardly but sensing that everyone was on her side she began to run through her ideas. 'Thanks, Ethan. It was great to spend time with your dad and Karen, by the way.'

Nathan's ears pricked up. 'When was that?'

He'd forgotten the lunch, or if he was honest, he'd buried the knowledge as was his tendency, rather than facing up to why it upset him. His dad said it was the reason he blew up so quickly and it wasn't healthy. It was far better to talk about things. Nathan wasn't in the habit of confiding in anyone.

'You were invited to Isabella's lunch last Sunday, Nate. Your dad said you were busy.' Luca wasn't in the mood for one of Nathan's strops. Best to nip it in the bud.

Rita sensed tension brewing between the cousins. She had no idea if the other band members were used to it although she suspected it was not unusual even if they didn't like it. Rita's strategy was to either bolt at the first sign of a quarrel, or try to smooth things over, depending on the circumstances, as she disliked conflict of any kind. She coughed. 'These tablets are brilliant, aren't they? A friend lent me this one, so I've made a list of a few songs.'

There were embarrassed looks around the table as the group knew Rita lived over at Larkspur House, which generally meant hardship of some kind. Louis told the others that Rita had refused his offer to join Hartburn's *What's App* group as she didn't think it was possible with her old mobile phone. They agreed not to draw attention to her lack of finances.

'I was thinking how great it would be to showcase each of your talents. It doesn't always have to focus around the main singer, and everyone sings so well, not that I'm an expert or anything…' Rita tailed off, feeling self-conscious as she reached for her glass of water.

Jodie and Rosa exchanged a glance and smiled. At last they had a sensible ally who could get the lads to shut up and listen. She and Rosa had despaired many times, listening to total crap from Juliet or Nathan who were brought up to believe that those who speak loudest know the most. They relied on Ethan to shut them up. 'Go on Rita. What you've said so far has been so interesting. Sometimes it takes fresh eyes to shake things up.'

The murmur of agreement spurred Rita to continue.

'Thanks, Jodie. I'm glad you don't mind. You see, I've watched you perform for almost two years, and the songs which get the biggest reaction are the least played. Look, I've made a list.'

Rita passed around a list of songs called 'Big Hitters', popular songs the band had forgotten about. Attached to the list was another sheet of paper, with the title 'Suggestions' along with their main musical parts. 'So, for example, rather than playing a Blues Brothers number, how about *Dead Ringer* with Jodie and Ethan singing lead, which by the way would be brilliant with Louis on the trumpet and Seth on sax.'

Rita called up the tune in case they needed a reminder. Jodie and Ethan looked at each other and within seconds, everyone was laughing loudly as they pictured the scene. Neither of them had played or sang up front before, but it was such a rocky, fun number, and it was such a brilliant idea, they were up for it. Now the band were pitching in suggestions for arrangements and who would play what. The floodgates had well and truly opened with new possibilities pouring in.

Luca didn't think it was possible to feel any more for Rita. During their meal at Piccante, he had listened to Rita's history with a heavy heart. He felt ashamed. Two years he'd spent working with her and not once had he asked Rita how she had ended up in Blackstock. He remembered seeing a duvet and pillow in the living room during the only time he'd been in the Redwing flat, but in his embarrassment, Luca had filed away the memory of it.

Over the years, he'd met several Larkspur House women and their kids who were mentored by Isabella and Hattie, so he wasn't totally in the dark about the Redwing's circumstances. Rita may have been physically small, but Luca was amazed by an inner strength he'd scarcely seen before. He made a promise to himself that he was never again going to neglect this lovely young woman, whatever relationship they had.

Despite this self-declaration, however, and his attempts to remain on a friendly but business-like footing, Luca's self-imposed barriers had lifted these last couple of weeks and love rushed headlong through his veins. He prayed that no one else noticed it but didn't think he could hide it much longer. Their afternoon in St Albans and subsequent meal was fantastic. Rita was chock full of enthusiasm and ideas and had caught the attention of the café owners who were drawn to her polite, attentive manner, which had them eating out of her hand.

She'd been so grateful when he paid the restaurant bill. He had to force her to put her little 'Scottie Dog' purse away. And then, when they were in his flat rehearsing, the Carpenters song had lifted him in an unimaginable way. How Rita knew so much about music he just did not know. The sound of her sweet chirp brought him back to the very loud conversation '…so, how about Paul Simon's *Obvious Child*? It's not such an obvious song but have a listen.'

Luca watched each one of the faces around the table, their brains whirling as they visualised each part to be played.

'Nathan, you could take the main drum part, bolstered up with extra drums, percussion, trumpets, two acoustic guitars, perhaps Luca singing, and a big drum solo at the end. What do you think?'

'Rita, that's brilliant. I've got a steel drum, Louis' got a…'

226

'Djembe. You're right, Ethan. We've also got a couple of timpani' and they were off again.

Luca kept a close watch on the time which had once again slipped through their fingers, something that happened a lot when Rita was around. He softly nudged her as he nodded his head towards the great metal clock above the bar.

'I'm so sorry everyone, I've got to go. We've covered a lot, though and you'll come up with a playlist before next Saturday, won't you? Where is the gig, by the way?'

'It's in Letchworth, at The Brewery. You can come with Seth and me, or with Luca. Going anywhere nice today, Rita?'

'Umm, as a matter of fact Jodie, I've been asked to sing at a friend's birthday party, a small gathering.'

Nathan's ears were clanging. 'You're doing a solo? Today?'

Rita crimsoned. 'Erm, yes, well, it's not strictly a solo as Luca is helping me out. He's giving me a lift. In fact, we'd better get going. So lovely to see all of you, and thanks for listening to my ideas. Once you've decided on the final playlist, perhaps I could pop over to the pub, get a copy?'

'Sure, Rita. We'll get that arranged.' Jodie appreciated Rita's attempts to move the spotlight around, but she was by far the best singer and she wasn't going to let her off the hook. 'I think *you* should do another couple of solo numbers next week. Have you any ideas?'

The table was hushed as they waited expectantly to hear what Rita had to say.

'My secret's out. If it's okay with you, may I sing *Nothin' Compares to You'*, in the style of Sinead O'Connor? And if you'd like me to do a screamer (laughs), how about *River Deep, Mountain High*, and maybe Rosa can help me out with that, if you've got time to practise, Rosa, with your finals coming up?'

It was Rosa's turn to blush. None of them were going to be allowed to hide behind their instruments, however good they were at playing them. It was so good of Rita to acknowledge her studies. Rosa was finding it a struggle to get back home for the gigs, even though she was under no pressure from the band. It gave her a breather from the high-brow, intensive atmosphere at the music college.

She understood why her brother had backed away from their parents' pressure to go to university. If it hadn't been for the upset, he may have ended up like me, she thought. Rosa was grateful Rita had come along, and if, as she suspected, Rita and her brother got together, she for one would be chuffed to bits. 'Good luck today, Rita. I'm sure you'll be fantastic.'

Nathan, meanwhile, was silent. As the others followed noisily behind Luca and Rita, high fiving it, and elbowing each other boisterously as they left, Nathan absently said his goodbyes and took himself off to the men's room. He needed a moment alone.

Nathan wiped cold, dripping water from his face, and stared at his reflection. A deep furrow had insinuated itself like a metallic bridge between his dark eyes which wasn't a good look. His face had that classic square shape, the one the experts said was the most pleasing. Okay, his lips were a little thin, but he hadn't lost any hair, unlike Louis whose head was already sparse in places. Those long hours spent slogging away at the gym had produced just the right tone without being muscle-bound.

Luca may have been taller, but his cool manner kept people at a distance and Nathan got the attention. He was always first to buy everyone a drink and no one could beat him on his wardrobe. How his mother had managed to buy him the penny loafers without her credit card, Nathan would never know.

So why did Rita treat him as if he was invisible? Well, that wasn't strictly true as she had pointed him out as main billing in the Paul Simon song. Thinking about it, she talked to everyone equally and left no one out, but that was just it. Nathan was treated *the same as* and he wasn't used to it. Maybe he imagined she was singing that Alison Moyet song just for him last week. It had driven him mad, wormholing into his brain. Those lyrics about bodies twisting had stirred him up, thinking about the two of them under his duvet.

And now, Rita was duetting with Luca. How the hell had that happened? That slimy git must have slid in there somehow, probably while they were in the deli. It was almost too much to take; shop, flat, the family lunch, Rita. There was nothing else to it. He had to find out once and for all before he went mad and ask her out, this week.

Chapter 39

The roads were almost empty on the way to Hertford. Luca and Rita arrived in good time, and with little equipment to set up, were able to chat to the guests, to meet Gregg who by now was tremendously excited about the performance. Rita insisted she and Luca share the fee as not only was he singing, but he had given up his afternoon to drive her. Luca, however, was not giving way on this one.

He could not believe how calm Rita had been during the drive to the party. Butterflies were supposed to be a good sign, even a dry mouth which he'd experienced from time to time, but with Rita, she seemed to have evaporated, gone to some other place. One day she would tell him where that was, but for now, he was still at the starting post when it came to Rita's character.

She had blown them away with her suggestions this morning at the pub. It was so clever the way in which she included everyone. It was almost as if Rita didn't want the band to rely on her…of course, it was because she might have to go away! What an idiot he was. Instantly, his mood nose-dived. The days had gone by in such a dream, Luca had forgotten about Trevor. It could be any day now. Rita hadn't mentioned it once, and he hadn't thought to bring it up again.

Those six months spent with Greta had been the longest relationship he'd had. Luca's sixteen-year-old heart had taken forever to mend, and it angered him to recall how little his parents took it seriously. He'd scarcely forgiven them for their attitude and could barely think about Caitlin's mum and dad without boiling up. He and Caitlin never got the chance to be together. At least now he could say her name without that terrible pain in his chest.

What if Rita left? Was it worth taking the risk? Luca had made a promise to himself he was never again going to allow this to happen. That was what his mind urged, but his heart - an overwhelming YES surged through it. He *had* to tell her soon before he burst with it.

They could have been at The Albert Hall, for all the racket. Gregg was thrilled, especially with Rita's pitch perfect rendition of James Taylor's *Fire and Rain*. With his brotherly arm around Jenny, Gregg made an emotional speech about the importance of family, and how grateful they were to Rita and Luca for their fabulous performance. Just two guitars, a harmonica and no amp. It was amazing.

When they set off in the car, Rita opened Jenny's envelope to find two hundred and fifty pounds inside, with a card which expressed 'masses of thanks for your sensational performance.' It was another high point in a life of so many lows, but the trend was on the up. Rita knew all those years ago that Blackstock was the place in which her family would finally put down roots, and so far, she had been right. 'Luca, have you got to get back? I was wondering if I might treat you to dinner in town. We've got this extra money, and I hope you'll let me do this without an argument.'

Luca laughed in surprise. "Thank you, Rita, I'd like that very much.'

They settled opposite each other in the restaurant, scanning the menu. Luca had enjoyed the afternoon much more than he imagined. Seeing the guests dance together, to hear them sing along to songs he hadn't heard in a lifetime let alone sung in harmony, was great. Rita insisted he sing *Catch the Wind* so she could play harmonica which was genius as it suited his voice perfectly. She had captured the Donovan vibe so well, he had to seriously swallow his emotions during that song.

Rita Redwing could easily get signed up. There was such a lot of dross around and her voice was pure gold. And here she was, inviting him to dinner to spend her well-earned fee, money she needed. How could he refuse? His mind quietened. The time had almost come to share his past with her, whatever the consequences might be, but not today. Today was a celebration of the first of many such events.

The young couple had so much to share. As it was still early, there were only three other tables filled. The soft Oriental music and hushed atmosphere provided a perfect contrast to the thrilling session at Gregg's party. Luca ordered a glass of Prosecco for Rita and half a cider to keep her company, although she said she'd be happy to drink jasmine tea, but he insisted they celebrate.

Over dishes of satay, noodles and sweet mango rice, Rita talked about her previous boyfriend who she met when the family stayed in Nottingham. Alison had a connection there, so they were housed in a bedsit until the Sunrise Trust were ready to offer them a flat. Scott was a regular in the café, as it was next door to the library where he worked. 'I liked him. He was gentle, quiet, and he helped us so much. Scott's father arranged for my mum to see someone about her back pain. The doctor said it was her liver and had to stop drinking otherwise she would be seriously ill. I think it frightened her. That's when she cut right down.'

'What happened when you told Scott you were leaving?'

'He wanted to come with us, but I explained the circumstances, how strict the Sunrise Trust were, and that I'd contact him when we settled in. I never loved him, I just wanted to let him down gently as he was such a kind and generous man. Six months is the longest I've ever been with anyone. How about you, Luca?'

Luca looked at Rita's earnest, open face. It was impossible not to love her. Poor bloke. He hoped Scott had since recovered his wits. Rita was asking him about his past, but he didn't feel this was the right time and place for his story, not least as he didn't know what his own reaction might be once he started talking about it. 'There was someone once, but I'll tell you about her another day. Today we are celebrating the present. Here's to you, Rita. May you have many more wonderful moments.'

It was eight o'clock by the time Rita got back to Larkspur House. She was extremely tired, but so, so happy, and couldn't wait to share her joy with her mother. Luca had loved her new dress. He said she looked a little like Audrey

Hepburn, and she said she was surprised he knew who the great actress was, but he wasn't offended at all. As they parted, he kissed her on both cheeks, as naturally as he did with Isabella. 'Good night, *'lovely Rita, meter-maid'*, he said. *Lovely* – that was the first time he had ever said *lovely*, just like the song.

The flat was quiet. Rita saw her mother sitting by the window. The faint glow of the lamp created a halo around her strawberry blond hair. There was no television or radio on, just the distant sound of a Sunday evening programme floating in from the flat next door. Alison suddenly straightened up, releasing her unconscious grip from the gold chain around her neck. 'Hello Rita. How was your concert?'

Rita felt the timing of her heartbeat slow, the result of which almost made her faint. She quickly moved to the chair opposite her mother as she didn't want to reveal her sudden pallor. 'It was lovely, Mum. Jenny gave me two hundred and fifty pounds, so I treated Luca to dinner. He refused to take his share, saying it was my first real performance and I should treat you and Finn. You know Luca when he gets like that, so I said okay.'

'I'm so glad for you, love. Now, I want to talk to you about something, but I don't want to involve Finn. Do you understand? You're not to tell him what I am about to tell you.'

Rita nodded, scarcely breathing. Her mother passed her the letter. It was as Rita feared, worse in fact, as her name wasn't even mentioned. Did that bastard think she was going to let her brother live with him without her to watch over him? Rage rushed up from her gut, causing a heat to burn in her face which was even more shocking as it completely purged her of the joy of just a few moments before.

'Before you say anything, Rita love, I'm going to tell you what's been arranged. Hattie is coming with me. Tomorrow we'll take the overnight train to Aberdeen. She's got friends there. This Father Alistair will be there when I meet Trevor to talk about the future. Whatever you might think, I must go, love. Finn is his son and he has a right to know at least what's been going on. One day you will understand.'

'Trevor gave up those rights when he was slung in jail. That's what you said, Mum, when we came here. You *promised* us that was it, that we'd have a new start.' Rita was too angry to shout or cry. Even if she wanted to, she rarely raised her voice, and didn't want to wake her brother. But it seemed there was nothing to say as her mother's mind was made up.

Rita stood up slowly and walked out of the living room, closing the front door as quietly as possible. She climbed the fourteen steps to her best friend's flat and knocked lightly on the door. Libby led Rita into her kitchen, encircled the little body into her protective arms, and held her until the sobbing stopped.

Chapter 40

The sound of rain splashing petulantly against the windowpanes woke Isabella. It took her a moment to remember where she was and that there was a man in her bed, so unaccustomed was she to sharing it. A quick glance at the clock revealed the shockingly early time of five-thirty and yet Isabella was by now wide awake. The dream troubled her. Images of fishing boats being pushed and pulled against their ropes by the current, one of them breaking free, and crashing against murderous rocks; a solitary figure, standing on the shore, watching the waves. It made her tremble to recall it.

Without disturbing the sleeping figure of this man who had captured her heart and soul, Isabella crept downstairs to light the stove and to make a pot of tea. Rik's flight wasn't until midday, so there was time to say goodbye, although in some ways, she wished he had stayed with his Cambridge friends as that may have spared her this growing sense of despair.

Almost as soon as they returned from the wonderful visit to Cambridge, Rik took her to bed. Such was the fervour of their lovemaking, Isabella had clung to him and cried. She didn't want to feel this way. Rik had unlocked a door into the past which inevitably made the future uncertain. Her life was ordered, controlled. There were no gaps waiting to be filled. She knew exactly what her role was until he arrived.

Rik had got into the very core of her even though he scarcely spoke any words of love, of his feelings, or what was in his heart. He was not that kind of man. It was the absence of words that spoke to her. Listening to his talk at the Institute, of open spaces, where the sky meets the sea, of people who were untouched by the decay of what was known as *civilisation*, had moved her: it touched every person in the audience. Their collective breath had been suspended as Rik took his audience to places where few feet had touched the earth, and the only friends were mountains, or forests, or wild expanses of land and sea. How could a man like that live in a place like this?

Hattie said that Rik reminded her of 'The Prophet', Kahlil Gibran's mysterious visitor called *Al Mustapha* who captivates the Orphalese people with his tales of wisdom and insight before leaving their shores for home. Rik's departure would undoubtedly leave many people bereft although he would brush off such idolatry. Rik's humility humbled her, his simplicity refreshed her, his love had brought her to life. In a few hours' time, she would leave him at the airport to begin his journey home. They had shared so much during their last twenty-four hours together, shutting out the world to be present for each other. Their only break was Rik's farewell lunch to which she was invited but declined as the family, and the brothers, needed time alone.

When he returned to her later that afternoon, Rik described how Joe had broken down after showing him their mother's box of correspondence. He asked Rik to forgive him. 'How can I forgive my brother when he's done nothing wrong? It was me that went away. At least now we have put things right. I may have lost my mother, but I have gained a new family.' He was overjoyed with the photo album from his nieces. It fit snugly in his long pocket.

They laughed at that, as Isabella knew how much Cherry and Chloe must have loved getting to know their estranged uncle and were almost certainly making plans to visit him as soon as possible, but what about her? Rik had asked her to come to him: there was nothing in the world to stop her.

Chapter 41

Monday morning had never felt so sweet, despite the grizzly rain. Luca jumped out of bed at six o'clock, raring to go. He wanted to get as much organised as possible which would give him time to sit with Rita. Luca was pleased to hear how Rita had managed to hang on to a relationship despite her turbulent family life. He'd have been surprised if she had not. She told him how music saved her from going mad, as every song had a message for her, to keep believing in life and love, and that one day, her dream of finding a home would come true.

If Luca were a betting man, the odds against Rita having feelings for him were slim. They clicked in so many ways: their passion for music; family; hard work; getting along with people, not to mention their chemistry. He *YouTubed* the songs Rita talked about. Could it be she really was sending him a message? He was a crosshair from kissing her last night but bottled it in favour of a kiss on both cheeks. It was agony to be a quarter of a mile from her. He may as well have been in Australia.

Luca made a decision. If Rita were free tomorrow evening, he was going to ask her out, not on the pretext of work, but a date, pure and simple. He couldn't imagine any issues with them working together and seeing each other. Neither could he imagine a time when they'd argue, let alone publicly, so perhaps they might both stay in Hartburn after all. Decisions were taken collectively, and Nathan was the only one likely to raise an objection. If he was unhappy, perhaps he too might leave the band.

It was time to expose his heart to a new love. The past was over, and he had to move on. As Luca buttoned up his neatly ironed white shirt and reached into the drawer for a clean apron, an idea to get Rita a gift was forming in his mind. Nothing over the top as he didn't want to embarrass her, just a small gesture that expressed the depth of his feelings. He grabbed the keys to the shop along with his phone and made his way downstairs with steps as light as a feather.

The doorbell tinkled right on time. Rita, buttoned up and shaking her umbrella, almost stumbled into the shop such were the gusts of wind across the square. Rather than walking directly towards him, it seemed to Luca that Rita was taking an age to sort out her brolly, and she hadn't responded to his usual greeting. He turned to put the coffee on the table, during which time Rita had quickly removed her coat and tied her apron before she sat down opposite him.

Something was wrong. The temperature inside the shop plummeted. Luca had everything planned: his greeting, how they were going to laugh about yesterday, what the day had in store, but the look on Rita's face swept it away in an instant. Her blood-shot eyes weren't the worst of it: her face was a mask of such sorrow Luca felt an acute pain in his chest. There must have been an event of some magnitude happen last night, yet he was afraid to ask her what it was. He was mute.

Rita managed a weak smile as she sipped at her coffee. A moment later, she reached her small-boned hand across the table to rest on top of his. 'Please don't worry about me, Luca. I had a bad night, that's all. I might be coming down with a bug. I'll feel better once I've drunk this lovely coffee.'

The million questions that ran around his mind were rapidly side-lined as Luca readjusted his planned declaration and invitation. It was obvious that whatever had happened, Rita was not up to discussing it. The way she touched his hand confirmed it was nothing to do with him which was a major relief. As much as Luca wanted to help, they had a busy day ahead. 'Rita, do you want to go home?'

She shook her head.

'Then promise me you'll go up to the flat any time you feel you need a rest. I'll call Kit. He'll come in a bit earlier and stay late.'

'That's not necessary, Luca. Honestly, I feel better already. Shall start with the cold meats?'

By the end of the day, Rita had recovered her equilibrium. There was little time to think about her mother's decision and anyway, it would not have changed Alison's mind. Libby said the same thing. It had been on the cards for so long, the pretence that Trevor had disappeared into the ether was over. No matter which way they spun it, neither Libby nor Rita could change how Alison Redwing felt. Even though Rita had considered Libby's house-share offer, nothing and no one in the world was going to stop her abandoning her brother.

Jenny popped in to thank the duo once again for such a fabulous party. She wondered if it was okay to post their comments on the Hartburn website, or did she have one of her own? Rita asked her to hold off for a while, knowing it made little difference in the long run. At least the band had adopted her proposals to take turns to sing out front and she would at least have the opportunity for one more gig. They'd probably ask her to come back whenever she could, as Aberdeen wasn't the end of the world.

The thought of Blackstock, The Alderman, to return to the place that had become home was out of the question. There was Libby, Isabella, Hattie…and Luca. How could she ever see them again? A heart can take only so much breaking, she said to Libby, and out of necessity she had learned to shut it down.

As she buttoned up her coat, Rita's phone beeped.

Meet for a drink at pub tonight, seven o'clock? I've got good news. Nate.

She sighed deeply. What on earth could Nathan want? Luca heard her phone and the sigh. He was still concerned with Rita's state of mind, even though she had acted her way through it very well, chatting to the customers, stroking their dogs. He wasn't fooled.

'Is everything alright, Rita?'

'Erm, it's a text, from Nathan. He wants to meet me tonight for a drink.'

Luca's temperature spiked. 'What for?'

'He says he has good news. Do you know what that might be?'

No, he didn't, but he wouldn't put anything past his smooth-talking cousin. Luca's mood had slumped throughout the day which wasn't too surprising as he'd been on such a high that morning it was hard to sustain. He'd forgotten about Nathan. If his cousin had wanted to take Rita out, he'd have been in there by now, even though Luca was certain Rita wasn't interested. He walked that dangerous line between frustration and anger, desperate to ask Rita how she felt about him, but was unable to find the words, or the courage to ask her.

Thinking back over the time he'd known her Rita had always been consistent. She'd never been sick, moody or awkward. There was a steadiness to her that he'd only ever seen in Isabella. His gut told him there was nothing to worry about, but Luca did not handle tension well and any hint of uncertainty was destabilising. Most of all, he wanted to keep Rita from harm's way. 'I've got some stock to sort out in the café kitchen tonight, so if you need me, give me a shout.'

'Thank you, Luca. I will.'

Chapter 42

Joe sat drinking a cup of Isabella's lovely coffee in front of the stove. He was keen to find out how she'd got on at the airport. It was Nell who pointed out the growing intimacy between his brother and his best friend and little escaped her notice. Joe was undergoing his own painful transformation and was so much happier to have reconciled with Rik. It was interesting how perception can be skewed through the prism of time as Rik didn't know what a grudge was while Joe had conjured up all manner of unpleasant scenarios.

His mother had tried many times to share Rik's adventures with him, but he had petulantly rejected them. Joe cringed at the memory, but it was Nell that brought him back to the present. And now, what a turn up! Isabella and Rik: could life get any better?

'How did it go, Bella? Much traffic?'

'Not too bad, thankfully. The weather forecast is good for Rik's scheduled trip to Coille. He'll be back home tonight.'

Joe scanned the face of a woman he might easily have married. She looked a little strained. Would she be offended if he asked about the friendship? You could hardly call it a relationship in such a short space of time. Isabella was too sensible for that.

She beat him to it. 'Joe, I've got something to tell you. I hope it doesn't shock you, and please keep it under your hat for now. I love your brother and I am sure he feels the same way about me.'

Joe spluttered as his coffee travelled the wrong way down his tubes. Isabella laughed and offered him a tissue. His mind whirred as he wiped the mess from the front of his shirt.

'So sorry, Bella, silly me. That's better. Did I hear right? You and Rik? Well, I'll be damned.'

'You mean you didn't notice, Joe? I bet Nell did.'

Joe laughed. 'It was Nell that pointed it out to me. Love, eh? But now Rik has gone, what plans have you made?'

'Rik couldn't live here. Neither he nor I expect that. I will visit at Easter, if I can wait that long. He said he'll come back here, to Blackstock, to see us. After that, we'll have to see.'

Joe stood up and put his arms around Isabella, pulling her close. He couldn't help but see the irony of their situation: he had gained a brother and she had lost a lover. He was happy and she must have felt miserable, poor love. God knows he couldn't be apart from Nell. Joe released her from the embrace and was astonished to see she was crying. 'Oh, my dear Bella, you really do love him. I wish there was something I could do to ease your pain. Tell me how I can help you.'

Isabella blew her nose. 'Joe, your presence here this afternoon has helped. After all, I'll have to make do with Rik's brother and you can help me fill in the gaps.'

They laughed. 'It'll get better as time goes on, and I have to learn to write letters. The one thing we know about Rik is that he loves a letter.'

When Joe had gone, Isabella sat wearily in the armchair. She had planned to run a bath, but for now, she wanted to rest in the quietness of the warm room, listening to the sizzle of oak logs burning and relive the events of that morning. She had loved Joe for many years, and now she loved his brother. This 'love' clearly wasn't the same, as her feelings for Rik were completely different than for Joe. If only it hadn't become such an impoverished, misused word.

How Isabella had kept herself together for those last few hours, she would never know. The strain between them that morning was intense. It wasn't caused directly by Rik's imminent departure as the fact of it was there from the start. She loved him *because* he was different, unconventional, that he wouldn't be buying a two-up, two-down in Blackstock. They had sat across from each other over breakfast in painful silence.

Before she could break it to say something, anything to bridge the gap between them, he put down his knife and fork, pausing as if to gather himself before he spoke. 'Isabella, will you write to me? I'm in desperate need of a pen pal, now that my mother has relinquished her duties for higher tasks.'

It was exactly the right thing to say as their laughter instantly lightened her heavy heart. 'I assume that's agreed. I'm so much more comfortable with a pen and paper in front of me. Now I have met a new band of friends, perhaps you'll update me with their news.'

It wasn't a question. Isabella felt relieved to have something concrete to connect her with Rik. 'When is a good time to visit, apart from Easter? I assume there are busier months, like lambing, or other projects, and I don't want to get in the way.'

'Let's talk about that when you come over in April. I hope you'll like the island enough to want to return. You do realise, Isabella, this cannot be a one-way affair. I will come back to Blackstock, later in the year. How could I not?'

His gaze was so intense, she couldn't speak. Rik was so unpredictable. She hadn't even considered he'd come back to visit, assuming she'd have to travel to Coille to see him. Isabella jumped from her chair to get to his lap, kissing his face, his eyes, his hair in pure joy, in relief. As Jocelyn Dalton predicted, they *would* sustain a lasting love affair from a distance.

Rik laughed at Isabella's spontaneous reaction. He could already feel a difference in her. She was beginning to free herself, untying the knots that bound her to this place, to her people. Isabella would soon discover a different dimension to her life, to her relationships: her loved ones in turn were going to grow in her absence. Together they would be enhanced by new experiences and new landscapes. He and Isabella agreed that after the initial shock of parting, they were sure to rebalance themselves as they adjusted to this new life.

And yet, as each mile was eaten up in the approach to the airport, Isabella had felt a growing panic. She had finally found the love of her life and now she had to give him back to the wild arms of the Scottish Isles, to his home, his place in the world. Rik said he'd write to her as he found talking on the phone difficult. They had held hands as they walked into the terminal, their fingers entwined. She told him she couldn't wait until his flight was called, that it was better for her to leave. He said nothing, but simply held her so close she felt his heart beat before he kissed her goodbye.

Isabella did not remember getting back to her car. Tears had blinded her way, so it took a while to locate it. Safely inside, she wept until her tears dried out. It was a miracle she got home safely, but home was, nevertheless, waiting. The fire was still warm, so Isabella made herself a pot of tea and while it was brewing, went upstairs to change. Joe wasn't due until later, so there was plenty of time to recover herself

As she entered her bedroom, there on her pillow sat a small package, wrapped in brown parcel paper and tied with string, under which sat an envelope. She quickly undressed and pulled on her thick dressing gown, not wanting to waste a second before taking the precious items downstairs where she would open them.

Her hands trembled as she tore off the paper to reveal a wooden box, inside which sat an elliptical-shaped piece of cherry wood that had been painstakingly carved into a Celtic love knot. It left her in no doubt that Rik loved her, and they would always be tied to each other. It would pass, but right now she wanted to sit with the exquisite, feverish pain of loving, watching it move around her body, through her veins, arteries, to sink into her bones. There was nothing to be done, no tablet she could take, no book to read, or painting to gaze at.

Perhaps in a few days she *would* write it down, perhaps in a poem, and send it to him. That's what lovers over the ages have done, so why not her? Holding the love knot in one hand, Isabella read the exquisitely scribed parchment paper:

'*My darling Isabella,*

I will be on my way back and you will be sitting by the fire, surrounded by your books and your treasures, and now I know every detail of that setting, I can conjure the image up to comfort me. You said in Cambridge how our parting will leave you with little sweetness, and yet, there is sweetness in sorrow, in the same way there is joy in pain, and darkness in light. Without it, life is bland, dull, numb even.

When I think of you, Isabella, I think of reds, and golds, of fire and dark nights, of heat and passion. You are so alive, and you have ignited a passion in me. I carved you a love knot as it is said to transcend nations and boundaries. Did you know Celtic sailors used to present intertwined rope knots to their sweethearts when they reached home? I should have waited to do that, but I could not, although your home has become mine, as mine will become yours. The love knot's history is Italian, sixth century, I believe, although it probably has been around forever, like love itself.

I chose cherry wood as it is your wood. It is imbued with powers to help overcome obstacles and carries the pure energy of will and desire. The fruit is magically linked to sex and birth, life force and the attraction of renewal. A perfect match.

Please know my love, you are the piece of my heart that has been missing.

Until the next time, Rik

Isabella held the carving in her hand, her thumb running over the intricacies of the knot and felt comforted.

Chapter 43

Nathan sat waiting nervously at the table he had shared with Rita barely two weeks ago. He had taken particular care over his appearance, making sure not to splash on too much fragrance as it was easy to overdo it. The grey merino V-neck jumper, sky-blue cotton shirt, jeans and his new loafers were a good, casual choice. No need to be too formal but he wanted Rita to see he had made an effort. There was too much scruff these days.

He downed his beer way too quickly but still felt as if he was about to audition for a reality television show. Better stick to juice. As Nathan headed back to the bar, he spotted Rita enter the pub. He rushed over, saying how nice it was to see her again while leading her to the table. By the time he'd got back with two glasses of apple juice, Nathan was dismayed to see she was wearing the same jumper and jeans she wore the last time. Shocked at his shallow appraisal of the young woman he was supposed to be mad about, Nathan pushed the judgement aside as he sat down opposite her.

'How are you, Nathan? Have you had a good day?'

It was such a formal question he wasn't quite sure what to say. She looked tired and her eyes were puffy. 'I'm fine.

We started a new job today, over by the leisure centre. How was your party yesterday?'

'Oh, yes, the party. It went very well, thanks.'

That was it? Nothing about the songs she sang, the people she sang for. At least he didn't have to listen to how great Luca was. He'd had a gut full of hearing about the wonderful world of Luca Santini.

'Sorry, Nathan, I'm not quite myself. You said you have news?'

That was it, Rita was coming down with the flu, or a cold, nothing more. What was wrong with him? He was so uptight. Of course, she's going to be shattered, working at the shop all week and singing on the weekend. Nathan shook himself up and reminded himself why he had asked her here. 'Look, Rita. I was wondering if I could take you out on a proper date? I can't stop thinking about you. We've got great chemistry, in the band, singing together…'

Nathan stopped mid-flow. Rita's expression was truly alarming. Surely, he hadn't got it that wrong? Whatever target he was aiming at his throw seemed to be way off. She said nothing in reply. 'You don't feel anything for me.'

Rita's eyes brimmed over. She had just about recovered from her mother's news and now she had stupidly given the impression she was interested in Nathan. 'I'm so sorry Nat…'

'There's someone else, isn't there?'

Rita's silence confirmed his suspicions: Luca. He'd bet a million quid she'd fallen for his cousin. Nathan's embarrassment was cringeworthy. *I bet he knows Rita is here. He's probably laughing right now.* 'Does Luca feel the same way about you?'

No answer.

'Ha - he doesn't know! Why doesn't that surprise me? Shall I tell you something about your precious Luca? He only took you on because he felt sorry for your brother. Why do you think he takes so much interest in him, with the football, the cycling and everything? It's called guilt, Rita. I bet he hasn't told you about Caitlin, how he got her pregnant when they were at school, and how her family took her away? He never saw her again after that. He doesn't even know if she had the baby.'

Rita was crying now. Nathan's face had transformed into such ugliness, it reminded her of Trevor after he'd had a drink. She was frightened and made to stand up. Nathan grabbed her hand to keep her seated. His eyes were slits. 'It's not you he wants, Rita - it's Finn.'

Nathan stood up slowly, put his jacket on and left the pub. He was blinded by fury, fuelled by an escalation of disappointments, of his own lack of progress, of injustice, and now the humiliation of knowing that the woman he wanted had thrown herself at someone who didn't give a toss about her.

Nathan banged furiously on the back door of Luca's flat with no response. Seeing the lights on in the café kitchen, he let himself in to find his cousin sitting at the table with his laptop. Nathan immediately saw the disappointment on Luca's face, no doubt thinking it was Rita, come to tell him all about the encounter. He spat out his disgust.

'Sorry to disappoint you, cuz, it's just little ol' me.'

'What the …'

Nathan spotted the mood board hanging by the door.

'You could fall in a pile of shit and still come up smelling of roses. I know about Bella giving you the flat and your slick new plans for a restaurant. Why do you get all the luck?'

A tendon in Luca's jaw pulsed, his musculature contracting in prehistoric readiness of imminent attack. 'I have no idea what you're on about. Where's Rita?'

'I left your ladylove in the pub crying. She knows you're only interested in her little brother because of what happened with you and Caitlin.'

In an instant, Luca sprang at Nathan. His instincts took full control as he made a grab for his cousin to shut his ugly mouth. Nathan aimed a wild punch that landed on his right cheek, after which Luca locked Nathan's arms into his body to prevent any further attack. The cousins struggled as Nathan tried and failed to break free of Luca's iron grip. Betty's furious howling rattled through the plaster as the two men fought, one to restrain, the other to lash out.

Suddenly, an almighty screech filled the entire kitchen which stopped the battle in its tracks. In the silence that followed, the cousins looked up to see Rita standing in the doorway, her right hand raised up in the air like the Statue of Liberty, holding what could only be a rape alarm. Her sorrowful expression made the earth weep.

'I'm leaving Blackstock. My family is moving to Aberdeen.' In the next second, she was gone.

Before the combatants had a chance to unlock themselves, Nathan's new loafers slipped on the tiled floor and the cousins tumbled to the ground. The sound of the crack was sickening.

Chapter 44

'Don't move, Nathan. The ambulance is on its way.' Isabella had managed to work out what caused the fight even though her nephews were tight-lipped. Thankfully Luca called her first as if Gemma had been here, God only knows what would have happened. She placed a rolled-up towel under Nathan's head, and covered him with a blanket.

'Aaaahhhhh - my arm! I think it's broken.'

'Of course, it's broken. Try not to move. Your dad and the paramedic will be here any minute.'

Luca sat at the table with a bag of ice on his cheek. He felt a swelling but was sure it was nothing serious. Years of boxing had taught him what to be worried about. He looked down at his cousin's-stricken face. Luca was concerned that Nathan had broken both bones as his arm was grotesquely twisted. He'd need an operation and was probably also concussed as he'd blacked out earlier. Stupid bugger.

The door clattered open as a breathless Neil flew into the kitchen. Isabella had explained to him over the phone what she knew of the incident, leaving the rest for her brother-in-law to work out for himself. Hot on his heels was the paramedic who soon confirmed that the lower arm bones were fractured, and the ambulance was due in less than ten minutes. It was a necessary precaution as Nathan had passed out, probably due to hitting his head.

'So, he'll need surgery, a plaster cast and all that?'

''Fraid so, Mr Westleigh. At least six weeks, and then the pins will be removed if it goes well. I don't like the look of it. The sooner we get him x-rayed, the better.'

Neil and Isabella shared a look. No more band for a while.

By nine-thirty the café kitchen was restored to order. Neil followed the ambulance, having arranged to meet a hysterical Gemma there. Isabella made a strong pot of tea. Aunt and nephew sat opposite each other in the calm after the storm.

'Do you want to tell me what happened?'

'It's funny as I don't feel angry now. It seems so stupid, grown men fighting, but I guess things build up, don't they? You know what he's like. Nathan asked Rita for a drink, saying he had good news. He'd got it into his head she was interested in him, and as nice as Rita is, she was never going to say no. He's been acting strange, coming into the shop every day, hinting that they could do good things together.

'Anyway, she must have put his hat on straight as he came barging in here, fuming, saying he'd told Rita the truth about Caitlin and the baby, and how I was only interested in her because of Finn. But now Rita's going. The family are leaving Blackstock.'

Isabella studied Luca's distressed face. The bruise was going to be impressive, but she had seen worse. After the terrible incident with Caitlin and the family, Luca had taken up boxing to deal with his anger, the results of which were frequent cuts and bruises. He felt as if his life had been hijacked by two sets of extremely selfish parents who had no idea what it was like to see the girl he loved disappear. No one predicted the depression that followed. Weeks of lying in bed, listless, refusing to study, refusing to eat.

It was Ben Westleigh who suggested to get him out 'on the tools.' Luca was a strong lad, quick-witted, and he liked the outdoors. Ben and Neil were doing well and needed an apprentice. Whether it was a deliberate snub to his parents' aspirations for university, or simply following his own lead, Isabella never knew what Luca's motivation was. Ben's mentoring however paid off, even though Luca never completed the brick-laying apprenticeship. By that time, the opportunity to work in the deli had come up, and Luca never looked back. Isabella put her arms around her distressed nephew.

'What shall I do, Bella? I love her, and once she's gone, I'm terrified that the awful depression will come back. I don't even know how Rita feels about me.'

Isabella looked at him, wiping his eyes gently so as not to hurt his swollen cheek. 'My darling, don't be afraid. It will all work out. But now I must go and see her. You know Alison went to Aberdeen, with Hattie? No? Oh well, I imagine that's why Rita was in a state. If it's okay with you, I'm going to suggest she take the rest of the week off as when Alison returns, there will be a lot to talk about. I could also do with being busy.'

Luca's neurons were frantically making connections, releasing mini a-ha moments for him to assimilate. That was why Rita had been so upset! Her mother had gone to see Trevor. What will Rita think of me now? He had to tell her it wasn't about Finn at all. Then he remembered that Rik had gone. Isabella must be struggling as it was obvious, she and Rik were sharing something important. 'Bella, I'm so sorry, wrapped up in my own world. How are you? It must be so strange without Rik.'

Isabella took her nephew's hand. She felt so much love for this boy, and so much admiration for his strength and his sensitivity. 'Looks like you and me are suffering from a bout of love-sickness.'

They laughed, knowing it was true. 'Don't leave it too long to tell her.' Isabella kissed her nephew and walked the quarter of a mile to Larkspur House.

Chapter 45

Alison walked through the front door to find her daughter on the sofa with her guitar on her lap. Her initial reaction was worry: it was Wednesday so why wasn't Rita at the deli? Was she sick? She laid down her holdall, hung up her coat and went towards the sofa.

Rita looked up. 'Hello Mum. Nice to have you home safe. Before you ask, I'm not sick, Finn is okay and I'm taking a couple of days off as Isabella and Luca have things to sort out in the shop. Would you like a cup of tea?'

'Yes please, love. Shall we have a sandwich for lunch? I've got a lot to tell you, so best we eat something first.'

Rita, for the first time ever, had been in the flat alone. On Monday night, after Isabella had been over to see if she was alright, Rita updated a flabbergasted Libby about the evening, and the accident. So, Luca *was* hiding something. She wasn't surprised. In a way Libby was pleased he'd had it rough and had experienced the pain of losing someone. It gave Luca a depth she hadn't appreciated. Nathan would bounce back. He had no deep affection for Rita, more like an infatuation. It was just a question of saving face. Give it a week and Nathan would be back with Claudia. At least he'd be out of the band for a while.

All of that, however, paled into comparison when Rita told her they were leaving. Although Alison was still away, Rita had taken this as a definite sign her mother was preparing to go. Libby wasn't so sure unless she had missed something, but no one knew for certain until Alison and Hattie returned. Libby insisted she look after Finn to give Rita the chance to rest until Alison came back.

It had been a quiet, calm time during which Rita had almost recovered her wits. Her anger quickly morphed into resignation. Now her mother was back, they'd make plans. She was used to leaving, but at least she'd be with her darling Finn. Rita hadn't been shocked to see Luca and Nathan fighting. At least it would clear the air of the tension that had been building. Even though she didn't like conflict, Rita accepted that strong emotions needed releasing from time to time.

She certainly wouldn't miss being in the middle of the cousins' energy field as much as she felt for Luca. The heartbreak of leaving was mitigated by her ability to 'shut up shop', as Libby described it, to batten down the pain, to smother it. Rita realised she'd been a fool to fall in love with Luca, but at least she hadn't made a bigger idiot of herself by declaring it. Rita didn't even know if Luca reciprocated as he'd said nothing, although her insides told her different.

It was much easier to get out now, to move on, to start again. Maybe it will be better next time? Maybe Trevor, like the Redwings, had turned a corner? Why not? Everyone had the potential to change. Hattie had said that many times. Even though Rita was soon to leave Blackstock, she would love Luca until the end of her life.

Alison cleared away the plates and mugs and sat herself next to her daughter. 'I'll tell you the ins and outs of the journey and about Hattie's friends later, but I'm sure you've waited long enough to know what's happening. I went to see him, Trevor, and we were left alone to talk. He was that pleased to see me, Rita, it did shake me up.

'He's done well, if you can do well in prison, but he's to be released early on account of his good behaviour, and the support of Father Alistair. He'll have to wear a tag and report in regularly, but it looks as if he's turned a corner. Like me. Like us, Rita.'

Alison took her daughter's tiny hand, concerned now to reassure her tearful child. 'I'm not going back. I am happy for Trevor, but there was nothing there. I felt empty. In fact, I felt sorry for him, and that's no reason to give up everything we've got here, in Blackstock.'

Alison held Rita close and let her cry her heart out. It was true, she felt nothing for Trevor, and couldn't wait to be out of that depressing place. He looked as if the stuffing had come out. She was shocked when he cried and said how he never stopped loving her, and thinking about her, and how he'd properly take care of her now, and his son. Alison had said almost nothing. She didn't want him to know she'd moved on, how she'd become a different person who didn't *need* taking care of by anyone.

Hattie said she had a *career* and was an independent woman with her own means. How could he understand that? Alison agreed that under the right circumstances, if Finn wanted it, Trevor would be permitted supervised access to their son. Father Alistair offered to co-ordinate it. She wished Trevor luck and left the prison without a backward glance.

When she met Hattie later that day, Alison was euphoric. A huge dark cloud had lifted, and the sun filled her heart. They celebrated her freedom, dear old Hattie and her wacky friends, with a nice meal and elderflower wine. Hattie said she'd help her set up her own proper sewing room outside the flat. It was a legitimate business which she could leave at the end of a working day. The journey homeward seemed to take forever as Alison just wanted to get back to Blackstock, to her children.

Alison tenderly wiped her daughter's beautiful, tear-stained face. She hoped it wasn't too late to be the mother Rita and Finn needed, rather than the other way around. Through her talks with Hattie and the group, she began to see how she had unwittingly stolen her daughter's childhood. She was the parent and it was her job to raise her children safely. Rita knew this and was sacrificing her own life to make sure Finn didn't suffer the same fate. Alison was certain that Trevor would fade into the background. He'd never been that bothered about Finn and he had two other kids that she knew about whom he'd hardly ever seen. This really was the end to the old life.

Chapter 46

Just as the Redwings were finishing their tea, they were startled by a knock on the door. It wasn't Libby, as you could hear her stomping down the stairs all the way from Marsham. Alison opened the door to Isabella and Hattie who came bearing gifts of chocolate, fizzy Raspberry and a book, *The Little Prince*, for Finn. Two minutes later, a breathless Libby arrived with a tray of glasses and a face full of expectation. 'Have I missed anything?'

'How could we possibly start our celebration without you, dear Libby.' Hattie expertly popped the bottle of fizz while Isabella opened the box of chocolate truffles and passed them around.

'What's the party for Mum? Have I won another school prize?'

Everyone laughed at the chocolate powder smear across Finn's cheek. Libby wiped his face.

'Not quite, young man, but there is always another term. No, Isabella has something to share, an offer you may not be able to refuse. As we now know, the Redwings will not be flying away from Blackstock any time soon, so this is timely.'

'Thanks, Hattie. Well, cheers! Here's to nest building.

Talking of which, Libby is to move into Spinners Cottage very soon, and hopefully with her new hairy partner…'

'You've given away my secret, Isabella. I was going to tell you about me and Hamish getting wed.'

Laughter rang around the room. 'I don't think the cottage is big enough for him, a dog *and* Rita. Best settle for a small four-pawed companion. Anyway, what I was going to say was that my other cottage, Needlepoint, is almost ready for letting and I'd like to offer it to you, Alison, and Finn. The previous tenants left an outdoor garden room that Ben has smartened up, so you'll have a place to make your marvellous creations, and, of course, Finn will have his own garden. The rent will be the same as it is here. You've done the hardest part, Alison. Now it's time to call Blackstock home.'

There was a stunned silence. It was too much kindness for Alison to take in. She put her arms around Isabella to hide her tears.

Hattie turned to Rita and Libby. 'The success of the Sunrise Trust is partly due to the continuation of the mentorship tradition. Who better than former tenants like yourselves to help the incomers? As you are staying in Blackstock, Isabella and I would like to invite you to join us in that role.'

'You mean, to do what you do, in the groups and suchlike?'

'Yes, Libby, with a bit of help, of course. When you think back to your arrival at Larkspur House, you were met by warm, supportive people who had been through similar circumstances. That's how it works best. Anyway, have a think about it.'

'No need, Hattie. It's a privilege to be asked, isn't it, Reet? That's what community is about.'

Rita nodded as she looked at her mother's damp face. Somehow, Alison had left her shadow behind in Aberdeen. It was amazing. They smiled at each other, knowing the past was over and good things, it seemed, were coming their way.

'We have another invitation. Rik, Hattie and I have discussed a joint project. From next year, we plan to offer courses and programmes to the Sunrise Trust families in Coille and wondered if you'd like to join us. Once a year, you'll come with us to the island and assist with the visits. You'll be paid, of course, including travel expenses.'

'Count me in, Isabella. It sounds fantastic, doesn't it, Reet, working holidays in Scotland? Will I be allowed to bring my dog?'

Everyone laughed. Rita was struggling to digest the waterfall of fabulous news, feeling ever so light-headed, but in a good way.

'There is one last thing.' Isabella passed Rita and Libby an envelope each. 'This is a gift from Rik. He was so moved to meet you and wanted to help you in some way but asked me to do this on his behalf to save his embarrassment. He told me our work with the Sunrise Trust has been instrumental in this gesture.'

Libby and Rita looked bewildered. The envelopes contained cheques for five thousand pounds each, such a huge sum. They could scarcely believe it of a stranger.

Isabella smiled. Rik had doubled the amount they agreed upon. He was indeed a generous man. 'His suggestion was perhaps to spend some of the money on a car to share, as it means you'll have the freedom to get around, but of course, the decision is yours.'

'I just cannot believe it, can you Reet? This means we can get to the rescue centre, and into town. What a lovely thing for Rik to do for us! We'll write straight away, to say thanks, won't we Reet?'

Rita's heart was so full to bursting, she remained mute. Her mother and brother were going to live next door to her and Libby, in their own little house, with their own garden. And Rik's cheque was so overwhelming. *There are people on this earth who truly are good*. It was too much to bear. It was left to Libby to thank everyone.

'Hattie and Isabella, on behalf of the Redwings and myself, we thank you. We hope you don't regret having this motley crew for neighbours, but I promise to get a dog that doesn't bark.'

Chapter 47

R ita pulled on her coat and boots and closed the door quietly. How she stopped herself from running to the deli, she would never know. The night was coal black, and the interminable wicked cold that had soaked into the country's bones was about to warm up. February had been the worst and best month of Rita's entire life, and today brought news she'd only dreamt of. Now she'd be able to tell Luca she could be a proper member of the band and help him with the shop and the new café. And the car, oh, the freedom of it! Not to mention the trips to the island, and to be asked to mentor the new folks. There was so much to say, she only hoped it wouldn't all come tumbling out in one go.

Rita stood by the pond, catching her breath, listening to the noises of the night. How she loved this town, its people and its warmth. Earlier that evening, Isabella had told her that Luca was at home and wanted to see her, no matter how late. *He probably wants to explain what happened before I go back to work tomorrow*, she thought, although the ball of tension in her belly had other ideas.

Over the last couple of days, Rita had reflected on her friendship with Luca. Did it really matter if he was fond of her brother? She was flattered that he and Ben took an interest in Finn as there was safety in numbers. If Rita hoped for something else, it was *her* imagination running wild, not anything Luca had promised. Nathan had mentioned a girlfriend and a baby. She really wanted to know what he meant, or if he was being spiteful. What if Luca's heart had been broken? It would explain so much.

Rita arrived at the door, racked with nerves. She rung the bell with one hand, her fingers crossed behind her back with the other. When he opened the door, Luca looked so relieved to see her, Rita stopped holding her breath as her mouth transformed its shape into a massive grin.

'Rita! I'm so glad you came over. Come on up.'

She followed him up the stairs, watching his tall, athletic body move easily. He took her coat, scarf and hat and hung them by the door as she pulled off her boots.

'Cup of tea, Rita, or a glass of white wine?'

'The wine sounds perfect, thank you. It's been such a day. I've got so much to tell you… Oh, your poor face! Does it hurt?'

Luca smiled to himself as he took a bottle of Frascati from the fridge and poured two glasses. He had sat there the entire evening, praying Rita might get in touch, and now she was here with things to say, he felt his stomach tie itself in knots. Her face was all concern, which was so touching.

'I've had worse. It's good to see you Rita. You've been missed at the shop. So many people were asking after you, even mardy Marvin, so that's a real complement.'

'Really? That's so nice. I've missed it, but Isabella insisted I take time out, and she was right. The last few weeks have been such a rollercoaster I hardly knew where I was.'

Luca forensically studied every millimetre of Rita's face. Her cheeks were pink from the cold, her eyes perfectly clear.

'And how are you now?' It was a critical moment. Her reaction determined his next move.

A beat.

'I am almost better.'

Her smile dismantled his heart.

The last two days had been agony without her, but Luca was warned by Isabella to leave her be. The family were about to undergo their biggest challenge, and Rita needed time to deal with it without worrying about the fight. Luca had called Nathan to test the waters of their relationship, to apologise for what he called a 'misunderstanding'. After all, why wouldn't he set his sights on Rita, it was just the way he went about it.

Nathan had sounded embarrassed, and he clearly didn't want to discuss it. There was no post-mortem, no recriminations, just the usual banter about the lengths Nathan went to for time off work. The entire family made a fuss about the unfortunate accident and were gutted he was out of the band but, if he managed to bang a tambourine, things weren't that bad.

Nathan was clearly enjoying the attention. When Luca and Isabella drove to Marsham to see him, Luca had to stifle a laugh to see an ecstatic Claudia Huxtable waiting on his good hand and feet as if it were her sole mission in life. Nathan and Gemma decided that while he was incapacitated, they were going to sell their unwanted gear on *eBay*. Nathan announced he was offloading his Beamer as what was the point of the car sitting there losing money while he was in plaster and Claudia had volunteered to drive him around. His mum and dad said they'd help him with a deposit on a house if he could raise some cash of his own.

Gemma was proud to declare to her older sister that as the house was too big, she and Neil were selling up, not only to release equity, but they wanted a new project, to renovate a smaller property *together*. Isabella watched her sister as she made her speech. Gemma looked different. Lighter, less tense perhaps? Isabella would never know about the long, terrifying night when Gemma finally realised she had pushed Neil too far. He'd never slept apart from her, and there he was, making plans of his own. She couldn't bear it.

Gemma had lain adrift in the huge marital bed, her mind in turmoil, envisaging countless nightmarish scenarios, most of which resulted in her living in a tiny house with little money and faced with the prospect of finding a full-time job. Was she really that unhappy? There was no denying how generous and hard-working Neil was, and she was certain he still loved her. He'd been so cold to her at the hospital, telling her to stop over-reacting at Nathan's accident, to grow up. When he left her there to drive home alone, Gemma was stunned.

Much later that night, she crept across the landing, quietly sliding into the bed where Neil lay with his back to the door. He turned to find her sobbing, saying how sorry she was for treating him badly, that she promised to change if he gave her another chance and life was going to be different, better. Neil held his wife as close to him as they had ever been. They talked long into the night about their estrangement. Gemma confessed to feeling bitter and angry after Amanda's death, somehow taking it out on those she loved, especially him.

She sorrowfully acknowledged her part in Juliet's behaviour and confessed to her fear of Nathan leaving home. Talk of a fresh start, to help the children in the right way excited the couple. They agreed to renew their vows, which, after thirty years of marriage, was timely. They made passionate, desperate love which kindled in Neil a hope that perhaps things might be different

As Isabella and Luca drove back to Blackstock that night, they laughed at the turn of events. The Westleigh family was much more entertaining than any television drama. Nathan's ability to bounce back was spectacular, while Gemma actually had her arm around a grinning Neil's waist, as if to stop him escaping. Isabella sighed. 'A renewal of vows, eh? You know how my sister loves a party. I'll bet you a bottle of brandy she ends up singing *West End Girls* to Neil on the karaoke.'

Luca laughed. That was something he'd love to see. He was pleased for his aunt, but especially Nathan, as he seemed to have extinguished whatever fire was burning in him, for the moment, at least.

Right now, though, Rita was here, and he was finally able to talk to her, to explain what happened to him, and here he was, tongue-tied. She looked like her old self: her quiet manner, her way of gazing directly at him. Rita said she was *almost better*…that could only mean one thing.

'You're not leaving?'

'No.'

Before she said another word, Luca sprang up and lifted Rita into his strong arms. Relief spread through him like a torrent, even more so as he feared she'd come to say goodbye. He held her tiny frame as if his life depended on it, and then suddenly aware he may have been crushing her, Luca gently put Rita back down, delighting in her howls of laughter. They had caught each other out. The moment came as Luca took Rita's face so softly in his hands and kissed her.

Chapter 48

There was so much to tell each other it didn't matter how late it was as this was the right time to talk about Caitlin. 'We started going out together when we were thirteen. Well, I say 'going out', but what I mean is that was when the hormones kicked in. I'd known her forever. The Ryans lived just a few houses away, and both sets of parents went to church every week. They made us go to Sunday school until we rebelled, probably about the time when it was impossible to kiss each other without thinking it was sinful.

'We used to cycle for miles over the forest and Caitlin would read me poetry, her long legs dangling from the nearest tree while I'd unpack our picnic. She was always climbing or running, trying to outdo her brothers. She was wild, free. I loved that about her.

'I knew the family were leaving England at some point as her dad worked for an international aggregates company which was expanding into America. He applied to work in Chicago as he had family there. They were supposed to go after Caitlin's GCSEs. She didn't want to go. I didn't want her to go, so we talked about ways of her staying behind. She might be allowed to live with my family to begin with, we'd find jobs, get a flat, that sort of thing. On St Valentine's

Day, a day I'll never forget, Caitlin said she'd worked out a way for us to stay together. She said she was pregnant.'

Rita took Luca's hand. It was agonizing to see him so exposed, so vulnerable. Her eyes remained fixed on his bewildered face as he gulped a mouthful of wine before continuing.

'We were fifteen, well, I was just sixteen, but still kids really. My first reaction must have shocked her because Caitlin ran out of the café so fast, I had a hell of a job catching up with her. When I got her to calm down, I said we needed to discuss what to do as it was such a life-changing thing. She asked me if I was happy about the baby, and when I didn't answer immediately, she went mental, shouting at me, saying I didn't care about her, I didn't love her. After that, she refused to see me.

'Anyway, it all came out. Our parents had a meeting, like we were a project. It was disgusting. I told them I'd stand by her and my gran, bless her, offered to help us. Caitlin's mother said no, they weren't happy about leaving their daughter behind.

'When I finally got to see her, everything had changed. It was devastating. She looked at me as if I had deserted her. I knew in that moment that whatever was going on between us was over. Caitlin never took her GCSEs as the family moved that Easter. My mum received a letter from Mrs Ryan. Caitlin had suffered a miscarriage. It was just after they arrived, sometime in April.'

'So, Nathan was wrong. There was no baby and the family were leaving anyway?'

'I've never discussed it with him, Rita. As far as I know, neither have my parents or Isabella, so he had no idea what happened to Caitlin after she left. He filled in the gaps and came to his own conclusion. You see, later that year, my grandfather died, and not long after that, Amanda was killed. The whole family was in meltdown, and my situation seemed so trivial compared to that.'

'It wasn't trivial, Luca. You've been through so much loss, more than most people in a lifetime.'

Rita held Luca's head to her chest. Every tear he cried released years of anguish, bringing him closer to unburdening the pain and darkness in his heart. If nothing else, Rita understood what suffering looked and felt like. That was why Luca could only allow so much of himself out, even when playing in the band.

Luca wiped his face. 'Maybe Nathan is right and in some strange way, what happened back then has influenced me. I've always felt connected to Finn and wanted to help him. I went through a tough time, but Isabella and Ben rescued me.'

Luca's radiant eyes settled on Rita. 'My feelings for you crept up on me and it got to the point where I could no longer hold them back. It has nothing to do with Finn. You see Rita, Nathan did me a favour. His interest in you, and his spitefulness helped me to realise that I had to let go of my old fears and allow my love for you to surface.'

He took a long breath. It was almost over. 'Rita, do you feel the same way about me?'

Rita's eyes shone. 'When Finn and I sat in the café with our hot chocolate that rainy day, something happened to me. It was instant. Don't ask me how. Hattie probably knows the answer. I never analysed this feeling in my heart. I simply accepted it without any expectation. When you spoke to Finn about the cycling jerseys, you were so attentive, so kind. And after a while, the Redwings were doing so well, with my mum's recovery, Finn's school and the shop. I really thought this was it and we'd stay here, especially after Isabella gave you the business. That was when you started to notice me.'

Shame burned on Luca's face. It was true. He hadn't seen her until then. 'I'm so sorry Rita.'

'Please don't be sorry. It was a miracle. When the audition came up, that was my chance as I hoped you'd realise those songs were messages to tell you how I felt. Ask Libby. I've driven her mad talking about you, wondering about you, but I could never tell you, especially with my circumstances of moving away so often.'

Luca grinned at Rita's ingenuity. 'I worked that out on Sunday night, after our meal. I sat in bed and *YouTubed* every song.' He was quiet for a moment. A flicker of concern crossed his face. 'Won't you get sick of seeing me every day?'

'I have loved you every day for so long now it's become a habit I have no wish to break. Now I know how fantastic your kisses are, my worry is how to stop the customers catching us out.'

They laughed as he kissed her again, finally and reluctantly releasing her from his embrace. 'It's getting late. I'd better walk you home. Do you think your new landlady will let me stay in the cottage when you move in?'

'I hadn't thought about that. I can't imagine Libby saying no.'

'Well, one day you might want to move in with me.'

Rita hid her shock well. 'But then I *would* get mightily sick of seeing you!'

Chapter 49

Every member of Hartburn was pumped up for the gig. With just half an hour until curtain up, the playlist was the most anticipated ever and the instruments were tuned to within an inch of their lives. You could feel the energy fizzing, both backstage as well as in the audience which was packed to the gunwales. Ethan's suggestion of dedicating the gig to Nathan, was universally agreed.

No one remembered ever feeling this stoked before, but they were professional enough to know how to ride the waves. Luca had the added excitement of hearing his sweetheart sing her solos. Rita looked fabulous in a slender aubergine scoop-neck dress and her hair pinned back in a low bun. She had bashfully agreed to spend that night at his flat. He had no idea how he was going to focus on playing rather than on what lie ahead.

Before the band were announced, Luca led Rita to a quiet corner and placed a small package in her hands. It was a necklace: a tiny bird perched on a branch, flecks of ruby on its wings and encircled in shimmering white gold. Tears filled Rita's eyes as Luca fastened this acknowledgment of his love tenderly around her slender, pale neck. 'There you are, Rita Redwing. Now you look perfect.'

Epilogue

The ferryboat bobbed gently, its small band of passengers gathering up luggage and parcels in readiness to disembark. Isabella remained seated on the bench looking towards the shore, her unfastened hair whipped up by a warm wind as the boat chugged in slow motion, ever closer to the jetty. A tall man in a navy sailor's coat, his hands tucked into the pockets, stood quietly by the water's edge, waiting.

Acknowledgments

Thank you, John, for your confidence, encouragement and unstinting good humour. Thanks also to Susie Keen and Angela Rigby who urged me to give Isabella and Luca their day in the sun. Much gratitude to Gaynor Callaghan, for your invaluable feedback. To Jane Gregory, your tremendous zest, expertise and encouragement knows no bounds. Thank you, Linda Storey, for producing such a wonderful book and cover. To Suzanne Clarke and Maggie Burgess, cherished friends and biggest fans, how could I do this without you? Lastly, thank you, dear reader, for giving me a reason for writing.

About the author

Deborah Rowland taught The Alexander Technique and Meditation for many years and has written several health and well-being books. Deborah's novel, *The Smallest of Dreams*, is part of a series entitled *The Hertfordshire Chronicles*. She lives in Shropshire with her husband.

For more information, please visit
deborahrowlandauthor.com

Other books by the author

Deborah Rowland, *The Roundhouse*, 2020

Deborah Rowland, *Take the Long Way Home,* 2018

Deborah Coote, *The Art of Meeting Yourself: Learning to Live Mindfully in a Busy World (includes meditation CD),* 2015

Deborah Coote, *Ingredients of a Happy Life: Tea, Cake, Meditation (includes meditation CD),* 2012